"Miss Wells, I can't say I ... **to find you here** ... **ell.**

I need to speak ... t the equation-filled s ... his mouth quirked i ... e. Do you ever take time of ... that fancy math?"

"Do you ever take time off from being a cowboy?"

The smile on his lips straightened into a firm white line, and he swung down off his horse. "I own five thousand head of cattle in the Teton Valley. I'm a rancher. That's a mite different than being the hired help we call cowboys."

"Indeed." She nodded curtly and drew in a long, deep breath. With Samantha sitting beside her, she couldn't exactly persuade him to let his sister graduate, but she still needed to ask about donating money to the academy. If only she could be polite long enough to make her request.

It was going to be very, very hard.

Books by Naomi Rawlings

Love Inspired Historical

Sanctuary for a Lady
The Wyoming Heir

NAOMI RAWLINGS

A mother of two young boys, Naomi Rawlings spends her days picking up, cleaning, playing and, of course, writing. Her husband pastors a small church in Michigan's rugged Upper Peninsula, where her family shares its ten wooded acres with black bears, wolves, coyotes, deer and bald eagles. Naomi and her family live only three miles from Lake Superior, and while the scenery is beautiful, the area averages two hundred inches of snow per winter. Naomi writes bold, dramatic stories containing passionate words and powerful journeys. If you enjoyed the novel, she would love to hear from you. You can write Naomi at P.O. Box 134, Ontonagon, MI 49953, or contact her via her website and blog, at www.naomirawlings.com.

The Wyoming Heir

NAOMI RAWLINGS

HARLEQUIN® LOVE INSPIRED® HISTORICAL

If you purchased this book without a cover you should be aware that this book is stolen property. It was reported as "unsold and destroyed" to the publisher, and neither the author nor the publisher has received any payment for this "stripped book."

Recycling programs
for this product may
not exist in your area.

 LOVE INSPIRED BOOKS

ISBN-13: 978-0-373-82997-2

THE WYOMING HEIR

Copyright © 2014 by Naomi Mason

All rights reserved. Except for use in any review, the reproduction or utilization of this work in whole or in part in any form by any electronic, mechanical or other means, now known or hereafter invented, including xerography, photocopying and recording, or in any information storage or retrieval system, is forbidden without the written permission of the editorial office, Love Inspired Books, 233 Broadway, New York, NY 10279 U.S.A.

This is a work of fiction. Names, characters, places and incidents are either the product of the author's imagination or are used fictitiously, and any resemblance to actual persons, living or dead, business establishments, events or locales is entirely coincidental.

This edition published by arrangement with Love Inspired Books.

® and TM are trademarks of Love Inspired Books, used under license. Trademarks indicated with ® are registered in the United States Patent and Trademark Office, the Canadian Trade Marks Office and in other countries.

www.Harlequin.com

Printed in U.S.A.

What doth the Lord thy God require of thee,
but to fear the Lord thy God, to walk in all his ways,
and to love him, and to serve the Lord thy God
with all thy heart and with all thy soul, to keep
the commandments of the Lord, and his statutes,
which I command thee this day for thy good?
—*Deuteronomy* 10:12–13

To Nathanael and Jeremiah, my amazing little boys. May you "grow in grace, and in the knowledge of our Lord and Savior Jesus Christ" (2 *Peter* 3:18).

Acknowledgments

No book could ever make its way from my head to the story in front of you without help from some amazing people. First and foremost, I'd like to thank my husband, Brian. What would I do without someone to cook dinner and watch the kids and love and encourage me through each and every book I write? Second, I'd like to thank my critique partner, Melissa Jagears, for trudging through all the hills and valleys of this story with me. My writing would suffer greatly without your keen eye and brilliant mind. I also want to thank my agent, Natasha Kern, for teaching me about writing and putting up with me even when I'm not that pleasant to put up with (which happens more often than it probably should). And my editor, Elizabeth Mazer, for her helpful suggestions and enthusiasm about my stories. Beyond this, numerous others have given support in one way or another— Sally Chambers, Glenn Haggerty, Roseanna White, and Laurie Alice Eakes, to name a few. Thank you all for your time and effort and helping me to write the best books I possibly can.

Prologue

Teton Valley, Wyoming
October 1893

"Hello, Ma." Luke Hayes removed his Stetson and stepped over the threshold to his mother's room. His boots echoed against the sturdy pine floorboards as he moved to where Ma sat at her vanity. A faint, sour scent wound around him, tickling his nose and turning his mouth bitter. The vase of purple coneflowers on the dresser nearly masked it, as did the rose water Ma dabbed at her throat. But the subtle smell of sickness clung to the shadows and haunted the corners, a constant reminder of the enemy that would steal her life.

"You've come to say goodbye," she whispered, her voice tired though she'd barely spoken.

Luke hooked a thumb through a belt loop. "It's time. Can't linger if I want to be back before the snow comes."

She turned to him, and the dreary, lifeless blue of her eyes hit him like a punch to the throat.

"You should be in bed."

"I thought I'd go riding…could ride down the trail with you a ways. To the end of the property at least."

Just like we used to, his throat ached to speak. How many times had they gone riding together? Felt the wind in their faces and the sun on their backs as they galloped through the shadows of the mountains?

Before. Not anymore. Never again.

But a person couldn't convince Ma of that. Luke ran his gaze over her gaunt frame. She'd dragged herself from bed and pulled on some clothes, her shirtwaist and split skirt hanging on her emaciated figure as though more skeleton than flesh. "No more riding. Pa told you as much over a month ago."

She huffed, her skinny shoulders straightening. "Doc Binnings didn't bar me from riding."

"The answer's still no." His words sliced through the room, and he winced. He'd come to say goodbye, not get into an argument, but there seemed to be little help for it with Ma convinced she could go riding.

"There's a letter for your sister on the dresser." She nodded toward the white envelope.

A smile slid up the corner of his mouth. "I'm carrying one from Pa, too, and another from Levi Sanders."

"Levi?" A flush tinged Ma's pale cheeks. "Samantha will like that."

"She'll like hearing from everyone, I'm sure. She'll be even happier to finally come home."

Ma stopped, her hands frozen midway through fastening the gold locket about her neck. "You're bringing her back?"

"Of course. What did you expect?"

"No. Deal with the estate as we discussed, but leave Samantha there."

Not get Sam? The thought stopped him cold. Even if he didn't need to leave for New York to settle his late grandfather's affairs, he still would have gone to fetch his sister home. With Ma nearing the end, Samantha belonged with her family. "It's time she came home."

"I read her letters. She loves that school, makes good grades, will graduate come spring. She needs to stay."

"Ma..." Luke scrubbed a hand over his face.

"I've got a letter for Cynthia, too, on the dresser over beside Samantha's. You'll take that one, won't you?"

Cynthia? His hand stilled over his eyes. He hadn't heard the name of his brother's widow for three years and didn't care to hear it again for the rest of his life.

But Ma was staring at him, hope radiating from her weary eyes.

"You know how I feel about Cynthia." And if Ma wasn't half delusional from her illness, she never would have brought up the confounded woman. "Just mail the letter yourself."

"You're not even going to see—?"

It started then, one of the coughing fits that spasmed through Ma's body. She grabbed the rag sitting beside the rose water and held it to her mouth, planting her other hand on the vanity for support.

"You should have been in bed." Luke strode forward, slipped one arm beneath her knees, and used the other to brace her back before he swooped her in his arms. The coughs racked her body, shaking her slight form down to her very bones. "Breathe now, Ma. Remember what the doc said? You need to breathe through this."

He laid her on the bed and sat beside her, holding the rag to her face. Blood seeped into the cloth, staining her teeth and lips and pooling in the corner of her mouth. The doc had also told him and Pa not to touch the foul cloths, or they could end up with consumption. But he wouldn't watch his mother struggle to keep a simple rag in place.

He braced her shoulders and gripped the cloth until she lay back against her pillows, eyes closed, stringy chestnut hair falling in waves around her shoulders, most of it knocked loose from her bun because of the jerking.

And she'd wanted to ride with him to the edge of the ranch.

He tossed the rag into the pail in the corner, already a quarter filled with sodden cloths, washed his hands in the basin, then moved back to her. The scents of rose water and blood and chronic sickness emanated from the bed.

She opened those dull blue eyes and blinked up at him.

"Are you…" *All right?* He clamped his teeth together. Of course she wasn't all right. Every day she crept closer to death. And every day Sam stayed East was a day forever lost between mother and daughter.

"Luke…promise me." Short breaths wheezed from her mouth.

"Promise you what?" He knelt on the floor, his eyes tracing every dip and curve and line of her features, branding them into his memory lest she not be alive when he returned.

She wrapped her hand around his, her corpselike skin thin and translucent against the thick, healthy hue of his palm. "Th-that you won't tell Samantha how sick I am."

"What do you mean? Haven't you told her yet yourself? Doesn't your letter explain?"

She looked away.

"Ma?" He stroked a strand of limp hair off her forehead. "You have to let Sam know you're sick."

"No." A tear streaked down the bony ridges of her cheek. "If I tell her, she'll come home. She needs to stay and finish school."

"She deserves to make that choice on her own. Deserves the chance to see you before you…" *Die.* He couldn't move the wretched word past the knot in his throat. Ma might not want Sam told about her condition, but Sam would never forgive herself if Ma passed without her saying goodbye. "Surely you want to see Sam again? Surely you miss her?"

Ma squirmed. "Let her finish her schooling, and we'll see each other next summer."

Except Ma wasn't going to live that long. "Sam needs to know. Now."

"I won't let her give up the life she loves to watch me die." She shook her head, her sunken eyes seeking his. "You mustn't tell her. Promise me."

He couldn't do it. He could barely stand to leave Ma as it was, wouldn't if he had any choice in the matter. How could he promise to keep her condition from Sam? Maybe Ma was right, and Sam wouldn't want to come home, but she should know what was going on.

"Luke? Promise?" Ma's voice grew panicked, even desperate.

Something twisted in his gut.

His twin's death three years earlier had been quick, nearly instant. Watching Blake die had hurt, but watching the life slowly drain from Ma? No one should be asked to endure such a thing.

But he couldn't very well leave her knowing he'd denied her last request.

He might never see her again. Even if he got Sam and brought her home, he might be too late.

"I promise." The words tasted bitter on his tongue. "Goodbye now, Ma."

He stood, swiped Sam's letter from the top of the

dresser, and left, taking long strides out of her room and through the ranch house before she could thank him.

Before delight from his agreement could fill her face.

Before common sense forced him to rescind his promise.

Chapter One

Valley Falls, New York

The simple cotton curtains on the classroom window fluttered with a whispered breeze, while autumn sunlight flooded through the opening in the thin fabric and bathed her in a burst of gaiety. But the warm rays upon Elizabeth Wells's skin didn't penetrate the coldness that stole up her spine, numbing her lungs and turning her fingers to ice.

Elizabeth tightened her grip around the envelope in her hand. She could open it. It wasn't such a hard thing, really, to slip the letter opener inside and slit the top. She just needed a moment to brace herself.

The envelope weighed heavy against her skin, as though it were made of lead rather than paper. She ran her fingers instinctively along the smooth, precise edges. A quadrilateral with two pairs of congruent sides joined by four right angles. The mathematical side of her brain recognized the shape as a perfect rectangle. But the contour of the paper didn't matter nearly so much as what was written inside.

She sighed and glanced down, her gaze resting on the name printed boldly across the envelope.

Miss Elizabeth Wells
Instructor of Mathematics
Hayes Academy for Girls

Forcing the air out of her lungs, she slit the envelope from the Albany Ladies' Society and slipped out the paper.

Dear Miss Wells...

The jumble of words and phrases from the letter seared her mind. *Regret to inform you...revoking our funding from your school...donate money to an institution that appreciates women maintaining their proper sphere in society.* And then the clincher. The Albany Ladies' Society not only wanted to stop any future funding but also requested the return of the money they had already donated for the school year.

And they called themselves ladies. Elizabeth slammed the letter onto her desk. Two other organizations had also asked that money previously donated—and spent—be returned. Then there were the six other letters explaining why future funding would cease but not asking for a return of monies.

This request galled more than most. If even women cared nothing about educating the younger generation of ladies, then who would? She'd spoken personally to the Albany Ladies' Society three times. Her mother was a member, and still, at the slightest bit of public opposition to the school, the society had pulled their funding.

She stuffed the letter back into the envelope, yanked out her bottom desk drawer, and tossed it inside with the other letters—and the articles that had started the firestorm.

She shouldn't even be receiving letters from donors and disgruntled citizens. Her brother, Jackson, was the head accountant for Hayes Academy for Girls, not her.

But then Jackson wasn't responsible for the mess the academy was in.

She was.

She'd only been trying to help. With the recession that had hit the area following the economic panic in March, the school had lost students. A lot of students. Many parents couldn't afford to send their daughters to an institution such as Hayes any longer. And without those tuition dollars, the school risked being seriously underfunded. So she'd written an editorial delineating the advantages of female education and girls' academies and had sent it to the paper.

She'd hoped to convince a couple families to enroll their daughters or perhaps encourage donations to the school. Instead, she'd convinced Mr. Reginald Higsley, one of the reporters at the Albany *Morning Times,* to answer her.

On the front page.

She pulled out the newspaper, the headline staring back at her with thick, black letters.

Excessive Amount of Charity Money Wasted on Hayes Academy for Girls

Since the economic panic in March and the ensuing depression, countless workers remain unemployed, food lines span city blocks, four railroad companies have declared bankruptcy, three Albany banks have failed and myriad farmers have been forced to let their mortgaged lands revert back to lending institutions. But not six miles away, in the neighboring town of Valley Falls, community and charity money is being wasted on keeping open an unneeded school, Hayes Academy for Girls.

It has long been recognized that the overeducating of females creates a breed of women quick to throw off their societal obligations to marry and raise children. It is also well-known that educated women are more concerned with employment opportunities and their own selfish wishes rather than fulfilling their roles as women....

Elizabeth's stomach twisted. No matter how many times her eyes darted over the words, the opening made her nearly retch. The article went on to compare the lower marriage rate of women with college educations to those with only grammar schooling. It examined the divorce rate, also higher among women with college educations. And then the reporter turned back to the topic of Hayes Academy's funding, questioning why anyone would waste money teaching women to throw off their societal responsibilities while the poor of Albany were starving.

Elizabeth shoved back from her desk and stood. Charity money "wasted" on keeping an "unneeded" institution open? How could the reporter say such a thing, when the academy prepared young women to attend college and qualify for jobs that enabled them to support both themselves and their families? An educated woman could certainly make a fuller contribution to society than an uneducated one.

Yet since the article had appeared, the academy had lost half of its financial backers.

A burst of giggles wafted from outside, and Elizabeth rose and headed to the window. In the yard, groups of girls clustered about the pristine lawn and giant maple trees with their reddening leaves. They laughed and smiled and talked, flitting over the grass alone or in packs, their eyes bright, their spirits free, their futures optimistic.

She sank her head against the dark trim surrounding the window. "Jonah, why did you go and die on me?"

The words swirled and dissipated in the empty room. As though she'd never spoken them. As though no one heard or cared what a mess Hayes Academy had become when its founder unexpectedly died three months earlier.

If Jonah Hayes were still alive, he would know how to get more donors. He would write an editorial on women's education, and people would listen, enrolling their daughters at the academy. And in the interim, while the school struggled through the recession, he would likely donate the money Hayes Academy needed to continue operating.

But Jonah Hayes was gone, and his estate had been tied up for three months, waiting for the arrival of his grandson heir from out West. In her dreams, the grandson came to Valley Falls, filled Jonah's position on the school board, convinced the other board members to keep Hayes Academy open, obliterated all opposition to the academy.

Of course, the heir had to arrive first.

And at this rate, the academy would be closed and the building sold before the man got here.

The students returned from lunch, a cascade of laughter and conversations fluttering in their wake. Elizabeth tried to smile, tried to straighten her shoulders and stand erect, tried to be grateful for the chance to teach her students—an opportunity that she might not have in another month.

Tried, but failed.

"Miss Wells?" The shining blue eyes of Samantha Hayes, Jonah's granddaughter and one of the academy's most intelligent pupils, met hers. "Meredith, MaryAnne and I are going to have a picnic along the stream that runs through Grandfather's estate tonight. Do you want to join us?"

Elizabeth did smile then, though it doubtless looked small and halfhearted. How enjoyable to spend the evening chatting with the girls beside the clear stream, watching autumn swirl. If only she didn't have to find a way out of the financial mess she'd created for Hayes Academy, which meant she had an appointment for tonight with the extra set of ledgers she kept for the school. "I'd best not. Thank you for asking."

"Are you feeling all right?" Concern flitted across the young lady's face. "You look pale."

"I'm fine, but…well, now that I think of it, I could use your help on a certain project tomorrow."

Samantha's eyes danced, light from the window streaming in to bounce off her golden tresses. The girl was breathtaking. More than breathtaking, really. Elizabeth smiled. Little surprise her brother, Jackson, had started courting Samantha Hayes last spring. Half the men of Albany would be courting her if they had any sense about them.

"Is it more calculus?"

She did smile then, full and genuine. If only all her students were as exuberant over calculus as Samantha Hayes. "I'm afraid not. I've some ciphering to do tonight, and I'd like for you to check my sums."

Samantha excelled at finding discrepancies in account books, whether they be the school's or Jonah Hayes's or Elizabeth's personal ledgers. "Sounds fun. Should we meet at the picnic spot around lunchtime tomorrow, then?"

If Samantha knew the state of Hayes Academy's accounts, she wouldn't be nearly so happy. Oh, well, the younger girl would find out tomorrow.

"Yes, that will be fine, but you'd best take your seat now." Elizabeth moved to the chalkboard and turned toward her students. Thirteen expectant faces stared back at her. Last year, she'd had twenty-three in her advanced algebra class.

"Today we're going to learn about…"

But she couldn't finish. How could she, with the school struggling to pay its bills and teachers' salaries? Did the girls understand how much funding had been pulled from the academy within the past five days? That they might not be able to finish their final year of high school if more students didn't enroll or if new funds couldn't be raised?

And part of it was her fault. Oh, what had ever possessed her to write that editorial?

"Miss Wells, are you feeling okay?"

"Can we do something for you?"

"Did you forget what you were saying?"

The voices floated from different corners of the room. Elizabeth plastered a smile on her face. "Forgive me, class, but I've decided to change the lesson. We'll review today."

Her hand flew across the chalkboard as her mind formed the numbers, letters and symbols without needing to consult a textbook for sample equations. "I'm giving you a surprise quiz. Take the next half hour to finish these quadratic equations, and we'll check them at the end of class." She wiped her chalk-covered hands on a rag and turned.

A shadow moved near the open classroom door, and the darkened frame of a man filled the doorway.

A man. At Hayes Academy for *Girls*. What was he doing here?

"Can I help you?"

He entered and dipped his head. "Excuse me, ma'am." A Western drawl lingered on the rusted voice.

"You're here!" Samantha screeched.

Elizabeth nearly cringed at the unladylike sound, but Samantha took no notice as she sprang from her desk and rushed toward the gentleman. "I can't believe you finally came. I missed you so much!" Samantha threw her arms around him for all the world to see.

Most unladylike, indeed. Did Jackson know about this other man? These were hardly fit actions for a girl who'd had an understanding with another man since last spring.

"Samantha…" Elizabeth drew up her shoulders and stepped closer. Their quiz forgotten, the other students watched the spectacle. "Sir, if the two of you would accompany me into the hallway. Students, please continue working."

The girls returned to their work—or attempted to. Half still peeked up despite their bent heads.

Elizabeth moved to the door and held it for Samantha and the stranger. Neither moved. She anchored her hands to her hips and ground her teeth together. Of all the days. Didn't the Good Lord know she hadn't the patience for such an interruption this afternoon?

The man hugged Samantha, bracing her shoulders with a hand that held…*a cowboy hat?* Elizabeth blinked. Surely she didn't have a cowboy in her classroom. Her eyes drifted down his long, lanky form. He wore a blue striped shirt, some type of leather vest, a brown belt and tan trousers complemented by a pair of what could only be called cowboy boots. And was that a red kerchief around his neck?

Plus he was covered in dust—whether from traveling or working with cows, she didn't know—but she could well imagine the dust embedding itself on the front of Samantha's—

A cowboy. From out West.

No. It couldn't be.

But it was. She knew it then, as surely as she knew how to solve the quadratic equations on the board. Samantha clung to her brother.

The Hayes heir.

The man who held the power to either continue Hayes Academy or close the school for good.

"Samantha?" Elizabeth's vocal cords grated against each other as she spoke, but she had to get her student and Mr. Hayes out of the classroom.

Finally, the girl pulled back from her brother and looked around the roomful of staring students. She flushed and moved into the hall, the dark skirt of her school uniform swishing about her ankles. The cowboy followed but only to crush his sister against him in another embrace.

Elizabeth wasn't sure whether to roll her eyes or scream.

Luke Hayes hadn't hugged his sister in three years, two months and thirteen days—not that he'd been counting— and he didn't plan to stop hugging her because some fancy teacher squawked at him like a broody hen dead set on guarding her eggs.

"I'm sorry, Sam. I didn't mean to get you in trouble," he spoke against her head, still unable to unwind his arms from her.

"It's all right," came her muffled reply.

She'd grown taller and curvier since he'd seen her last. Looked grown-up, too. Her hair was done up in a puffy bun, not long and free as it had been in the Teton Valley. And she smelled different, no longer of sunshine and wildflowers but like fancy perfume. He tightened his hold. He should have come and yanked her out of this school sooner, regardless of what Pa had to say about it. "I missed you. Can't rightly say how much."

Inside the classroom, the teacher said something in that stern voice of hers. Then the distinctive clip of a lady's boots on wood flooring grew louder, and the door closed with a *thunk*. "Samantha Hayes, what is the meaning of this?"

Sam pulled away from him, her eyes finding the floor. "I'm sorry, Miss Wells. I didn't mean to make a scene. This is my brother, Luke, from Wyoming."

The hair on the back of his neck prickled. Sam didn't need to cower like a whipped dog because she had hugged him. He crossed his arms and met the teacher's stare.

Hang it all, but she was a beautiful little thing, with deep hazel eyes and a wagonload of reddish-brown hair piled atop her head.

Her name should be Eve, for if ever God had created a perfect woman, she was it. Adam would have taken one look at that long, smooth face, milky skin and sparkling hazel eyes and been lost.

Good thing he wasn't Adam.

"Sir?"

He swallowed and took a step back, while Sam snickered beside him. Why was he staring? Pretty or not, she was a city woman—just the type he avoided. Citified women didn't fare well out West. They squealed when a bear meandered into the yard, left the door open on the chicken coop and complained about getting water from the hand pump—he knew. His twin brother had up and married one of the useless critters.

He scowled, but still couldn't pull his eyes from the gentle curve of the teacher's cheek or the soft pink of her lips. "Excuse me, ma'am, but I didn't catch your name."

"Miss Elizabeth Wells."

Did she know a strand of hair had fallen from her updo and hung beside her cheek? Or that she had a big smear of white—most likely chalk—smack on the front of her plum-colored skirt?

"I'm Samantha's mathematics instructor and private

tutor." She arched an eyebrow, a rather delicate and refined eyebrow.

He snuck a hand atop Sam's shoulder. "Your letters
haven't said anything about having trouble with mathematics."

Sam smiled up at him, that familiar toothy grin that
had always wriggled straight into his heart. Except the
grin didn't look quite so toothy anymore, and her lips
had a rather refined curve to them. "Oh, no, Luke, not
trouble. Miss Wells instructs me in preliminary calculus
after school. That way I can head straight into the calculus class when I attend college next fall."

College next fall? He pulled his hand from her shoulder.
"Sam, we've got a load of things to talk about, what with
Grandpa's passing an' all. Go on and gather your belongings. You're coming to the estate with me. I've already
arranged it with the office."

Her face lit up like sunlight sparkling off a cool mountain stream. "May I be excused from classes early, Miss
Wells?"

The teacher's gaze went frigid, those beautiful eyes
likely to turn him into a pile of ice. "If the office has
granted you leave, I've no authority to say otherwise."

Luke bit back a cringe. He wouldn't say the office had
said yes. Exactly. He'd just handed a letter explaining the
situation to the secretary, who would probably give it to
the boss lady.

"Thank you, Miss Wells." Samantha gave him a brief,
tight hug before pulling away. "It'll only take a moment
to pack a bag."

"No, Sam, not a bag." He slung his Stetson atop his
head. "All of your belongings. You won't be returning."

The teacher let out a little squeak, her hand flying up
to clutch the cameo at her neck. "Surely you don't mean

to pull one of our brightest students from the academy. Why Samantha's..."

He shut out the teacher's prattling and focused on Sam. Her face had turned white as birch bark.

Confound it.

He should rip out his tongue and hang it up to dry. He hadn't meant to tell Sam she was leaving like that, but he'd spent most of his trip out East pondering things. He'd promised not to tell Sam about the consumption, but he'd never promised not to take her out of her fancy school. If he could get Sam to make a clean break from this place, convincing her to come home with him should be easy as coaxing a thirsty horse to the drinking trough. She could help him sort through Grandpa's things for the next few weeks, and then she'd be off to Wyoming before she had a chance to think about missing her school.

He stepped forward and rubbed Sam's back. "Now don't go bawling on me, Sam. It's just that—"

"How could you take me from here?" Her voice quivered.

How could he?

How could he *not?* Grandpa was gone now—there was no kith or kin anywhere in the whole of the state of New York to tie her here. Surely she didn't expect to be left here without anyone to look after her. She must hanker to see Ma and Pa and the ranch. To fall asleep to the sound of coyotes yipping and awake to the scent of thin mountain air. To see Ma before she died.

"Samantha." The teacher laid a slender hand on Sam's arm. "Why don't you head to your room and freshen up? I've a matter to discuss with your brother." Her eyes shot him that ice-coated look again. "Privately."

Sam fled toward the staircase, muffling her sobs in her

hand. And something hollow opened inside his chest, filling him with a familiar ache.

"Mr. Hayes, I do not appreciate having my class interrupted or one of my students upset."

He turned back toward the teacher. Though the woman only reached his shoulder, she acted like she commanded an army. A firm line spread across those full lips, a hint of fire burned beneath her cool eyes, and her face looked as blank as a riverboat gambler's.

He'd gone and raised her hackles, all right. She probably had a hankering to sit him in the corner or send him to the office or apply some other schoolboy-type punishment.

He tipped his hat. "I'm sorry. I'd no intention of disrupting anything, miss—" or of sending Sam away in tears "—but I haven't seen my sister for a fair piece, and I wasn't keen on waiting any longer."

Not that he was about to plop down and explain the bad blood between Pa and Grandpa to the woman.

"I understand that, sir, and I appreciate your apology."

"If you'll excuse me, then." He dipped his head and shifted toward the stairs. "I best find her and get on to the estate."

"Mr. Hayes." The teacher stepped in front of him, a bold move for someone so tiny. "You can't take Samantha from here."

He crossed his arms. "My sister's not rightly your concern."

"Yes, she is. You made her my concern when you sent her here."

"Now listen. I never sent her here and neither did Pa. This school thing was all Grandpa's idea. Pa just wanted to get Sam away from the Teton Valley while we dealt with a few troubles. We figured she'd come live with Grandpa and go to the local high school hereabouts. No one ever mentioned Sam coming to this fancy school until she was already here."

But that bit of information seemed to have no effect on the teacher. Her eyebrows didn't arch, her jaw didn't drop and her eyes didn't flash with questions. Instead, she pointed her finger and shoved it in his chest. Hard.

"Be that as it may, she has been a student here for over three years without your interference, and she has done exceptionally well. I'm sure you want the best for your sister's future, and she thrives in this environment. She'll make an excellent student at Maple Ridge College a year from now."

College. There it was again. That lousy word that threatened to keep Sam out East for good rather than home where she belonged. "Look, I appreciate what you're doing here, trying to educate women and all. And if you want to teach fancy mathematics to the girls in your classroom, you go right ahead."

"It's advanced algebra."

"Call it whatever you want. But with no more family in the area, there's nothing to keep Sam here. My sister will finish her schooling in Wyoming and won't be attending college next fall. She's coming home with me as soon as I straighten Grandpa's affairs."

The teacher raised her chin, her small nose jutting arrogantly in the air. "This conversation is becoming ridiculous."

"I agree."

"I'm sure if we schedule an appointment to discuss the situation with your sister and the headmistress, we could reach a more satisfying conclusion for all affected."

Oh, he could think of a satisfying conclusion, and it involved him and Sam hightailing it out of this confounded school, never to return. "I said my sister won't be returning, and I meant it. She's got obligations at home."

"Mr. Hayes, you are making a grave and regrettable mis— Is that a *gun?*" Her voice squeaked, all semblance of propriety fleeing while she stared at the Colt .45 holstered on his right hip.

Somewhere down the hall a door closed, and the clip of shoes on flooring resonated against the walls. He shifted his weight to his left leg and cocked his right hip, purposely exaggerating the firearm's presence. Not that he wanted to scare her, but she was a sight to behold with her perfect little feathers all in a ruffle. "We use them where I come from."

Unfortunately, she didn't stay flustered quite long enough. She clamped her hands to her hips and glared. "I'd thank you to remove it from the premises at once. We've no need for guns at Hayes Academy. Why, the entire class probably saw it."

Luke crossed his arms. "I seem to recall something in the U.S. Constitution about citizens bearing arms."

"Yes, well, certainly not in a school."

"Now look here—"

"Mr. Luke Hayes, I presume."

Luke flicked his eyes toward the tall woman coming down the hall. She moved the way a shopkeeper did when suspecting someone of pocketing a gold watch—quickly and full of purpose.

The woman stopped and extended a wrinkled hand. "What a pleasure to meet you. I'm Josephine Bowen, headmistress here at Hayes Academy."

"Luke Hayes." He gave the hand a hearty shake.

"I trust there's no problem?" The headmistress slid a stern gaze toward Miss Wells.

He'd seen similar looks on teachers' faces plenty a time

in his youth. It always preceded him being dragged to the front of the schoolroom for a switching.

But Miss Wells didn't so much as flinch under the heated stare. "Mr. Hayes and I were discussing his sister's schooling. Now if you'll both excuse me, I should return to my students."

"Yes, Miss Wells." The headmistress nodded. "Do return to your class, please, and thank you for taking time to make Mr. Hayes feel welcome."

He rubbed his jaw. Hopefully the rest of Valley Falls didn't plan to "welcome" him the way the fiery little teacher had.

Miss Wells gave a tight smile as she opened the classroom door, then disappeared inside.

"Mr. Hayes, we're simply delighted to have you." The headmistress's overly bright voice echoed through the hallway, but she wasn't lecturing him on pulling Sam out of school. Then again, she probably hadn't read his letter yet, or she'd be bawling like a cow in labor.

"Hayes Academy has benefited greatly from your grandfather's generosity, and we look forward to doing the same with you," she continued.

Seeing how he'd never met his paternal grandfather, he hadn't the foggiest notion what Grandpa's *generosity* entailed. "I haven't talked to Grandpa's lawyer yet. In what ways, exactly, has my grandfather aided you?"

Miss Bowen beamed up at him. "Where, sir, do you think the name Hayes Academy comes from?"

He'd figured as much.

"Twenty years ago Jonah Hayes donated the land that this school sits on and a good portion of the funds to build it." The headmistress clasped his hand. "Three years ago we used another donation to replace the windows on the second floor and renovate the grounds. Surely you noticed the horticulture as you came in? But right now, we're simply hoping to—"

"I'm sorry, but I…" *Won't be making any donations.* The words turned to dust in his mouth. The headmistress's severe face shone with delight, and he'd already upset enough womenfolk since walking into this school. Two an hour ought to be his limit. "Settling Grandpa's estate is a mite complicated. I don't know how much I can promise."

Her shoulders sagged—if that were possible for a woman who exuded perfect posture. "Of course, I understand it will take time to fully grasp the reins of your grandfather's financial concerns. But I do hope you'll bear in mind that, while your grandfather left a wonderful legacy, in order for it to be enjoyed by future generations, we must all endeavor to keep the legacy alive. Perhaps the board members call fill you in on some of your grandfather's other contributions when you meet them."

"Board members?" This whole school business was growing a bit too involved. He took a step backward and glanced toward the stairway. The hot, stale air inside the building clung to his skin, and the hallway's white walls and dim lights were a mite too suffocating. He needed to get outside, breathe some fresh air, feel the sun on his face. What was keeping Sam?

"The school board meets once a month." Miss Bowen's grip tightened on his arm, her nails digging in a tad too forcefully. "Of course you'll fill your grandfather's seat. What a shame you missed last night's meeting, though. We truly needed someone present to keep the needs of Hayes at the forefront. Otherwise I'm afraid our precious institution gets eclipsed by the needs of the nearby college and boys' school. Unfortunately the most I can do now is provide you with a copy of the minutes."

"Uh, sure," he mumbled, then stuck a finger in his

collar and pulled, but that didn't stop the tight feeling in his throat.

"But I will be able to introduce you to the board at the banquet tomorrow night. How marvelous that you've arrived in time to attend!"

"Banquet?" he croaked.

"Yes, the annual banquet for Maple Ridge College and its two preparatory schools, Hayes Academy for Girls and Connor Academy for Boys. All are located here in Valley Falls, but as most of the board members are Albany businessmen, the banquet is held in Albany. The Kenmore Hotel. Seven o'clock."

Seven o'clock. Albany. Tomorrow night. These fancy eastern women wanted money, his gun off, his sister in school, his presence at some uppity banquet and him seated on a stuffy school board. And he'd only been off the train an hour.

What demands would they come up with tomorrow? And how was he ever going to survive a month?

Chapter Two

Mug of coffee in hand, Luke stood at the French doors in his grandpa's study, looking out over the estate's immaculate back lawn. To the west, the Catskill Mountains, shadowed in blue and gray, rose over the fields and trees like sentinels guarding the land below. Pretty enough, but not anything close to the untamed wilderness he hailed from.

He rubbed a hand over his face.

What was he even doing in New York State, standing in a fancy house that he'd somehow inherited rather than Pa?

You be careful out there, Pa had told him before he left. *Your old codger of a grandfather was awful wily. Wouldn't surprise me if he found some way to chain you to that wretched estate of his, even from his grave.* The tension had risen like an old, unhealed wound still festering between Pa and Grandpa despite one of them being cold and buried. *Probably ruined Sam in the few years he had her.*

Not once in his twenty-eight years had Pa said anything good about Grandpa. Luke had about fallen over three years ago when Pa sent Sam off to the man. But the ranch had been no place for a young girl after Blake's death, and she'd needed to go somewhere.

Someone rapped at the office door, and Luke turned.

"I'm here…like you asked."

Oh, Sam was there all right. With a face chiseled in granite.

His boots sunk into some highfalutin gold and burgundy rug as he walked behind Grandpa's desk. With lions' heads carved into eight columns and sprawling paws to serve as feet, the desk belonged in a king's throne room rather than a study and wasn't something he cottoned to sitting behind. Still standing, he gestured to her. "Sit."

Head high, back rigid, she took dainty steps toward a gilt chair with blue cushions that faced the desk. She still wore that lifeless school uniform of a white shirtwaist and navy skirt, the black armband around her right sleeve indicating she was in mourning for a man he'd never met. And yet, she carried herself like a lady. Maybe that was the problem. She wasn't so much the girl he remembered anymore, but a woman.

A *citified* woman.

He cleared his throat and placed his half-empty coffee mug on the desk.

She tilted her nose into the air. "You shouldn't set that on the wood. It could ruin the finish."

He lifted his eyes, and their gazes collided. He set his jaw. She straightened her spine. He narrowed his eyes. She raised her chin. Somewhere outside, a bird chirped and a servant called. A door closed on the floor above, and footsteps plodded down the hall. But neither of them moved.

"Since I inherited this desk, along with the rest of the estate," he said slowly, his eyes still burning into hers, "I reckon it's not your concern how I treat it."

"You shouldn't use phrases like 'I reckon,' either. It's most unbecoming."

He gripped the edge of the desk and leaned over it. "I'm not interested in being 'becoming,' Samantha. I'm interested in settling this slew of money Grandpa left me and taking you home. Where you were born, where you were raised and where you belong."

"You can't make me leave."

Figured stubbornness was the one thing that fancy school hadn't stripped from her. "Don't you tell me what I can and can't do."

"I can't tell you what to do? What gives you the right to tell me?" She jumped from the chair, her hands balled into fists at her sides. "I'm staying here and graduating, then I'm going to college to study mathematics and architecture. Because I want to be an architect one day."

Her tongue lingered over the word *architect,* and her eyes burned with a fierce passion. "Not that you've bothered to ask why I want to go to college."

He didn't know whether to laugh or bang his head against the wall. At least Sam had something she wanted to do, some reason for avoiding their family—though she'd evidently had the good sense not to mention such a ridiculous notion in her letters to him.

Had probably told Ma all about it, though.

A woman architect. Who'd ever heard of such a thing?

"Well, aren't you going to say something?" she snapped.

He rubbed the back of his neck. "That's a fine dream you've got, Sam." Or a crazy one. "But I've got to take you home before you go off chasing after college."

"You don't. Ma would want me to stay here. I just got a letter from her last week saying how much she loved hearing about how happy I am in Valley Falls."

Of course Ma would say that. But then, Ma hadn't exactly told Sam about her consumption, either. And if Ma were here, watching his conversation with Sam right now, she'd be upset with the way he was handling things.

He rolled his shoulders, trying to loosen the knots tightening his muscles. If he could manage a ranch with five thousand head of cattle, he could convince Sam to go back home while still keeping his promise. Couldn't he? "Look, I'm sorry for how I brought up your leaving at school. I didn't mean to yammer about it in front of your teacher. The words just slipped out, when you talked about packing a bag. But you can't stay in New York now that Grandpa's passed. Who would look after you? Besides I need your help around the estate for the next few weeks while we get ready to leave.

"You can start going through the things in Grandpa's room. You know better than me what should be kept or sold off. I figured Pa might cotton to a couple of keepsakes." Which was probably more a dream than anything, given that Pa hadn't talked to Grandpa in over thirty years. "The sooner we sort through this estate, the sooner we can get home."

"I cared about Grandpa," she said, nodding toward the black band around her upper arm. "And I'm happy to sort through his things, but don't you try using that as a way to get me out of school. There will be plenty of time for me to sort through things outside of school hours. Come Monday morning, I'll be back at Hayes Academy. And I'm not going to Wyoming."

Had Sam been this disagreeable three years ago? He tried to envision it but ended up with the mental picture of a sweet girl crying over her injured cat in the barn. "I happen to love you, and I happen to want my sister with me, under her family's care."

"If you loved me, you'd let me stay. I love it *here!* This place is my life."

Love it. She once said that about the Teton Valley. "What about Ma and Pa? You haven't seen them for nigh on three years." *And Ma might not be around in another year.*

She ducked her chin and toyed with the fabric of her skirt. "Do they know you're trying to take me away, trying to quash my dream?"

A fist tightened around his heart. His sister stood before him, her body tall and womanish, her eyes alive with hope and passion, her mind determined to win their argument. He'd had a dream once, too—one he shared with Blake about buying a cattle ranch. No one had told him that he couldn't. If anything, Ma and Pa had encouraged him and Blake to make their own ways in life. And they had.

And while he'd been out West, grieving Blake and seeing to the cattle ranch that now belonged solely to him, Sam had grown up, become a woman.

But woman or not, she still had a dying ma in the Teton Valley, and he had a promise to keep. Except didn't he also have a duty to reunite his sister and mother before it was too late? "I'm not trying to quash anything, Sam. Ma and Pa miss you. Is it so hard to believe they want to see you again?"

Her back went rigid as a fence post. "*They* sent me away."

"Come on now. Once you get back home and see some of your old friends, things won't seem so bad. Levi Sanders took over his pa's ranch a year back, and he's looking for a good wife who knows the ways of a ranch. Not a silly city woman who can't tell the front end of a horse from the rear. Here." He dug in his pocket and held out the creased envelope. "Levi sent you this letter."

She clutched her hands together defiantly, but her actions didn't hide the moisture shimmering in her eyes.

He blew out a breath. What was he to do with a girl who

was hard as iron one minute and all weepy the next? "Take the letter, Sam, and stop being so all-fired stubborn."

"What about Cynthia and Everett? Are you forcing them to go back, as well?" she whispered furiously.

He froze, a flood of bloody images he couldn't erase scalding his mind. "I wouldn't take them back West for all the land in the Teton Valley."

"They're—"

"Enough." He slashed the air with his hand, cutting her off. "We're discussing you, not the woman responsible for Blake's death. Now take the letter." He shoved the envelope across the desk as a knock sounded on the door.

The butler poked his head inside. "Mr. Hayes? Mr. Byron, the lawyer, is here for your meeting."

"Thank you." But his gaze didn't leave Samantha.

She huffed, stood and snatched the letter. "Fine. I'll read it. And I'll reply. But I'm not going back to Wyoming. I'm graduating from Hayes Academy, and then I'm attending college. I'm going to become an architect one day. You just see if I don't." A tear slipped down her cheek before she flew out of the room.

Luke blew out another breath and rubbed the heel of his palm over his chest, but the action didn't quell the pain in his heart. He should have never let Pa send her away, should have stood up to his sire the moment Pa had suggested Sam had to leave after Blake died. But he hadn't, and now he was good and stuck.

He couldn't drag his sister, crying and screaming, away from a place she loved. And she wasn't about to come willingly…unless he told her about Ma. But then he'd be breaking his promise, and a man couldn't just up and ignore a promise like that.

His fingers dug into the polished wood top of the desk.

If he did nothing else on this confounded trip, he'd convince Sam to come home on her own.

If only he could figure out how.

Elizabeth's head ached, her neck muscles had turned into a mass of knots and her stomach roiled as though it would heave out her lunch—despite the fact she hadn't eaten any.

She could blame most of her discomfort on Luke Hayes.

She'd grown up with a politician father. She'd seen him, her younger brother, Jackson, and even her mother wheedle donations more times than she could count. Goodness, *she* had wheedled donations before. She knew the best way to go about it. Smile. Look pretty. And agree with everything the potential donor said.

Not three hours earlier, the man who could save Hayes Academy had stood in front of her. She hadn't smiled. She'd probably looked a fright with chalk on her skirt and her hair askew. And she'd disagreed with everything he had said.

Goodbye, Hayes Academy.

She sighed. Was she was being too hard on herself? Luke Hayes had interrupted her quiz and then pulled her brightest pupil out of school. Certainly he didn't expect her to smile and say, "Yes, that's fine. Ruin your sister's future. I don't care in the least."

She opened her bottom desk drawer and stuffed into her satchel the letters she needed to work on the ledgers. He had no right to rip Samantha out of class then spout off about his sister not being her concern. Of course she was concerned—she knew exactly what the girl was going through. The battle was all too familiar.

What do you mean, you're going to college?
A pretty girl like you should find a husband.

Just because one man jilted you, doesn't mean the next will.

A college degree? What's wrong with the schooling you already have? Why do you need more?

The sharp comments twined through her memory. Why should her desire to teach mathematics matter, when she could get married and have children? People had been asking her that for six years, and now Mr. Hayes had said the same about Samantha.

Maybe if she had explained the possibilities that awaited Samantha after she had a high school diploma and college degree, he'd let his sister continue her education.

Maybe.

But how many people understood her own pursuit of mathematics? Mr. Hayes would likely squelch his sister's dreams just as so many people had tried to kill hers.

Elizabeth straightened and slipped her satchel over her shoulder. She wasn't doing herself any favors by stewing over Luke Hayes, and she needed to stop by the kitchen and inventory the recent food delivery before she even went home.

She closed and locked her classroom door, then walked down the hallway toward the large double doors at the opposite end of the building. The tinkle of girlish giggles from outside floated through the main entrance to the school, and the clear autumn sun filtered through the windows beside the doorway.

If only she didn't have the cook to meet with and ledgers to refigure, she could enjoy that picnic with her students. But some things weren't meant to be. She pushed through the doors leading into the dining hall, then weaved her way through the maze of tables and chairs toward the kitchen at the back.

Dottie McGivern, the school's cook, stood at the counter just inside the kitchen.

"There you are. Been wondering whether you were going to show up." Dottie's plump hands dove into a bowl of dough and began to knead. "We need more flour, apples and sugar."

Elizabeth sighed. Of course they did. It only made sense. She already had the ladies' society, Samantha's brother and the school's financial woes to deal with. Why not add trouble with the food order, as well?

"I'm assuming you didn't get the amounts you ordered?" *Again?*

Dottie pointed to the half-empty shelves lining the wall of the kitchen. "Now look here, Miss Wells. I've been cooking for a long time, and I know how much money it costs to feed a slew of girls. Or at least how much money it *should* cost. So when I say I need a hundred and fifty dollars each month to pay for food, I mean a hundred and fifty dollars, not the fifty dollars' worth of foodstuffs that showed up this morning. That look like a hundred and fifty dollars' worth of food to you?"

"No, it doesn't." This could not be happening again, not with the school in such dire financial straits. It seemed every time Dottie had a load of food delivered, something had gotten mixed up and only a portion of the needed food was delivered. "I don't understand. Jackson says he authorizes the food money to be released every month. You should have plenty of supplies, not be running out."

Dottie wagged a flour-covered finger at her chest. "Talk to your brother, then. Maybe you got your messages mixed up, but the delivery that arrived today wasn't no hundred and fifty dollars' worth of food."

Yes, she would talk to Jackson. Indeed, she hoped something had become mixed up. Otherwise, the academy was being cheated somehow. And not just with groceries. This was the fourth time such a thing had happened since the school year started. Jackson said enough money for materials and bills had been released, yet the gas company claimed they never received payment, the store they ordered teachers' supplies from was missing money as well, and Dottie said only a third of her food arrived.

"Miss Wells, there you are. I feared you had gone already." Miss Bowen's head poked through the swinging kitchen door, her perfect coiffure and straight suit grossly incongruous against the counters piled with potatoes, messy casserole dishes and frazzled works in the kitchen. "I'm sorry to interrupt, but I simply must speak with you. In private, that is."

Miss Bowen sent Dottie a brief smile and then disappeared back through the door.

Elizabeth squeezed Dottie's arm. "I'll be back tomorrow to figure this out."

The fiery-haired woman nodded. "Thank you."

Elizabeth headed out of the kitchen and toward the far corner of the dining hall where Mrs. Bowen stood. The lines of her gray dress looked so stiff that the woman couldn't possibly be comfortable walking. Or standing. Or sitting. Or doing anything at all. But a smile softened the creases of her face.

"I need to speak with you about the school board meeting last evening."

Of course. Why not discuss the school board meeting? It was just one more thing to add to her list of disastrous events. At this rate, she'd better not bother to go home later. She'd likely find her house burned to ashes or swallowed by an earthquake. "What about it?"

"Well, naturally the board is concerned about the bad publicity Hayes Academy received earlier this week."

Which the school board undoubtedly blamed on her, since she'd written that editorial. "Do they plan to file a complaint with the *Morning Times?* To the best of my knowledge, no one, not a school board member, nor you, nor I, nor anyone associated with Hayes Academy, was asked to defend it in an official article. I suppose it will be left to me to write something in response."

Miss Bowen blanched. "No. I'm afraid that won't be necessary. In fact, I do believe several of the board members requested you not write anything more for the paper."

"Does someone else plan to write an editorial, then?" Surely the school board didn't intend to let Mr. Higsley's article go unanswered. "Or perhaps the board could invite the reporter to the school? The man might well retract some of his comments, were he to see firsthand how beneficial—"

"The school board is considering closing Hayes Academy. Immediately." The words fell from Miss Bowen's mouth in a jumbled rush.

Elizabeth's heart stuttered, then stopped. She opened her mouth, hoping something intelligible would come out, but all she could do was stare at Miss Bowen's pale, pinched face. She should have known. She'd suspected the school board would lean in this direction, of course. But so quickly? Before she even had a chance to refigure the ledgers or write another article or find more donors?

"I see. Did…did my father…" She pressed her eyes shut, hated herself for even asking, but she had to know. "…support closing the school?"

Miss Bowen's eyes grew heavy, and Elizabeth's gaze fell to her feet. Of course Father would pull his support. He discontinued support of anything politically disadvantageous. He wouldn't care that he had championed the school during his past two reelection campaigns.

"Elizabeth? Are you all right?"

"Yes. Fine." Except her throat felt like sawdust had been poured down it, and her stomach twisted and lurched as though it would lose its contents again.

"The decision hasn't been finalized yet. There's hope in that, I suppose, though I must confess the majority of the members seemed to have already made up their minds. Still, the school board wants a detailed report from your brother on Hayes Academy's financial status by the end of next week. They're scheduling another meeting two weeks from now."

"That's when they'll decide whether to close the school?"

"Yes."

"So there's hope."

"A glimmer." But no hope shone on Miss Bowen's face.

And rightly so. One week, maybe two. That wasn't much time.

"Elizabeth." Miss Bowen touched her shoulder. "Where do we stand financially? I know several letters from our sponsors have come this week. I'm assuming your brother has received more?"

"I'm heading home to calculate numbers."

"Surely you must have some idea."

She glanced toward one of the small dining room windows. The sun still burned clear and bright outside, but the little shaft of light barely seemed to penetrate the dark, empty room. "It's not good."

"Well." Miss Bowen's lips curved into a painfully brilliant smile. "Perhaps things will improve shortly. I asked Mr. Hayes about the possibility of another donation."

Her head snapped up. "When he was here earlier?"

"Why of course. When else would I have seen him?"

Lovely timing. He'd probably pasted a grin on his face

and agreed to everything asked of him, especially since she'd just finished lecturing him about bringing a gun into school and pulling his sister out. "What did he say?"

"He didn't say no, but he didn't rush to make a commitment, either. I'm sure he just needs more time."

The headmistress's voice held a fragile kind of promise. Elizabeth rubbed her temples. She didn't want to shatter it, not when it would shatter soon enough on its own. "That's something at least. He probably doesn't realize how much responsibility for this school he's inheriting. I'm assuming his lawyer will inform him sometime over the weekend."

"I'm sure Mr. Hayes will want to continue in his grandfather's stead, or he wouldn't have come East at all. But I want you to speak with him about a donation."

"Me? Speak with him? Certainly you're in a better position to solicit funds."

"Don't be foolish, Elizabeth. You have such a convincing way about you, when you're passionate about an issue. I doubt the man will be able to tell you no."

Elizabeth raised her eyebrows. Luke Hayes certainly hadn't found saying the word difficult earlier that afternoon.

And he likely wouldn't have trouble saying it again.

Chapter Three

"Sell it all," Luke said from behind his grandfather's desk. "The companies, the estate, everything but the stocks."

The lawyer, Mr. Byron, cleared his throat. "You can't."

"Why?" Luke waved his hand over the will spread across the desk. "Is there some sort of stipulation that prevents me from selling?"

"It's not done." Mr. Byron folded his stubby arms across his chest and peered through his spectacles. "Your grandfather intended for you to continue running the companies he worked so hard to establish, not to sell them off."

Luke stared at the papers he'd spent the past two hours poring over, the lines of neat handwriting growing blurry beneath his gaze. He'd inherited nearly everything his grandfather had owned. Fifteen accounting offices with an insurance company attached to each branch, and a smattering of investments both in Albany businesses and on the New York Stock Exchange. "This shouldn't even be mine. My father should inherit it."

"Your grandfather was very clear. He wanted the estate and businesses to fall to his only living grandson."

The lawyer spoke without inflection, as though the words didn't threaten to shatter the life Luke had built out West.

The unreachable little spot between his shoulder blades started to itch. Had Grandpa thought Luke would feel obliged to stay, once he saw the vast holdings? According to Pa, Jonah Hayes had manipulated everything and everyone around him. When the old codger tried forcing Pa into a marriage all those years back, Pa left, and Grandpa disowned him. Was Grandpa trying to get back at Pa by pulling his pa's only living son back East?

Luke stretched his arm behind his back and tried to scratch the nagging itch. He couldn't spend his days in an office, staring at lists and numbers, instead of ranching. Falling asleep to the distant howl of wolves and breathing the sharp air of the first mountain blizzard. Working with his hands to brand the cattle, round them up and drive them east. Seeing the prairie change from summer to autumn to winter to spring, all while the bold, jagged Tetons to his west watched like slumbering giants.

No. He wouldn't leave the West. Not for all the wealth of his grandfather's estate. "If Grandpa left everything to me, then he shouldn't care what I do with it, and I want it sold."

"You don't realize the scope of what you ask." The lawyer shoved his spectacles back up on his nose, only to have them slide halfway down again. "Think of all the problems selling such large holdings will cause. With the economy as it is, you'll get maybe half the true value of your grandfather's companies."

Luke clenched his jaw. Beating his head against a brick wall would be easier than talking to the lawyer. "I don't care about the money. My ranch does well enough. But if Grandpa was bound and determined to leave me his estate, the least I can do is take the money from it back to Pa, who should have gotten all this in the first place."

"I appreciate that you want to reconcile things between your father and late grandfather, but you must consider some of the other people caught in your decision. What will happen to all the employees at Great Northern Accounting and Insurance if you sell?"

How was he to know? The new buyers would likely keep some of the employees. It wasn't as though he put thousands of people out of work just by choosing to sell Grandpa's companies. He wouldn't be shutting down the businesses, merely putting them in the hands of men actually interested in running them.

"And what about the staff here at the estate? Do you realize how many people's livelihoods you will be terminating with the single command to sell?"

Luke raked a hand through his hair. He hadn't thought of the servants, either. Whoever bought the estate would probably have his own slew of servants to replace Grandpa's. He'd need to have a meeting with the staff next week, explain the situation and let all but the minimum go.

No. That seemed too abrupt. Maybe he would keep them on for an extra month and give them time to find new employment.

But how would they look for other jobs if they were working here? Perhaps he should give them each a month's salary and then release them.

And where would they sleep and eat for the coming month? The servants all lived on the estate, and kicking them out meant they had no home, even if he sent each of them off with a heap of money. Would his former employees even be able to find other jobs? He didn't need to live out East to know that many of the country's wealthy had lost money since the panic had hit. People were cutting back and getting rid of extra staff, not hiring more.

"Have you ever fired a person before, Mr. Hayes?" Byron leaned over the opposite side of the desk, his brown eyes extra large behind his glasses.

Luke bristled. "Of course." Cowhands who were lazy or dishonest or lousy with cattle. But he'd never before fired a good, honest worker. It seemed a shame for decent people to lose their jobs because of a business decision. *His* business decision.

This whole affair was too complicated by half. Why had Grandpa left everything to him in the first place? He'd made a big enough mess of his own family. What made Grandpa think he could run an estate, and one of the largest insurance and accounting corporations in the East? He needed to get Sam, take her back home and see Ma through until she passed. Surely Grandpa would have understood that he didn't have time for servants and accounting companies and whatever else.

"You could look for a manager," the lawyer supplied. "Someone who would run the companies in your absence and report back to you in Wyoming. Then you could travel here every two or three years to see that things are being managed properly."

Luke rubbed the back of his neck. The manager idea wasn't half bad. It made more sense than anything else at the moment.

"You would continue to make a profit off the companies, as well." The lawyer pounced on Luke's moment of deliberation like a cougar on an unsuspecting rabbit. "Think of it as an extra source of income. It's a rather sound business decision to make. Of course, you'll have to interview potential managers while you're here. But once you've found a man, you'd be free to return to Wyoming."

"I don't want to commit to anything like that just yet."

"Why don't you ponder the decision over the weekend?"

Yes, he'd better think it through. He didn't want a lot of strings tying him to the East. And yet... "Then the employees would be able to keep their jobs?"

"All but the ones on the estate."

"I'll give you an answer next week."

"Excellent." A smile curved at the edges of Mr. Byron's pudgy lips. "Let's move on to your sister-in-law's inheritance then, shall we?"

The world seemed to freeze around him, his blood turning frigid at the mere mention of her. "My grandfather left money to Cynthia?"

"Yes, a tidy sum of—"

"I don't want to know." Luke turned away and crossed his arms, but the image came back to him like hot, glowing embers buried beneath layers of ash. Cynthia with her pregnant belly cradled between her body and legs while she kneeled on the ground. Her fiery hair tangling in the mountain breeze, her eyes shining with tears, her voice pleading with him. And lying beside her, his dead, blood-soaked twin.

"Your sister also stands to inherit a nice amount," the lawyer continued.

Luke walked to the French doors and pushed them open, then sucked in a breath of cool outside air.

"Samantha will receive ten thousand dollars either when she marries or turns twenty-five."

Luke drew in another deep breath and tried to wrap his mind around the lawyer's words. Samantha. They were talking about his sister now, weren't they? Not the woman who'd let his brother die. "Has Sam been told?"

"Yes."

He stared out into the darkening valley, rife with the music of insect sounds and toads and the faint rustle of the breeze. Returning to Wyoming beautiful and single, Sam would have been the talk of the Teton Valley. But with a ten-thousand-dollar inheritance, she'd attract every bachelor west of the Mississippi.

"In addition to her inheritance, your sister also has a separate fund to pay for the rest of her schooling."

"What?" The calming air he'd just inhaled deserted his lungs.

"The remainder of Samantha's year at Hayes Academy is, of course, already paid for. But this fund contains money for further education. College—not just a bachelor's degree but a master's program, even a doctorate, if your sister so desires."

Luke turned back toward the lawyer and stalked to the desk. Grandpa's will just kept getting better and better. "That's ridiculous. She needs to go home to her family. Not chase some dream she has little hope of achieving."

Perhaps if she wanted to be a teacher or a nurse, he could understand her desire to attend college. But architecture? She'd be laughed out of her classes. And even if she managed to graduate, who would hire her?

The lawyer cleared his throat. "Educating women was one of your grandfather's passions, and something he devoted much time and money toward. He wouldn't want any less for his granddaughter."

Educating women. Why wasn't grade school enough of an education? That was all the education he had, and he managed just fine. In fact, he'd wager Grandpa didn't have more than a grade school education either, and the man had built a financial empire.

Luke poured what was probably his third cup of coffee

and sank down behind the polished mahogany desk, brow furrowed as he stared at the pages of the will.

Why was God doing this to him? He hadn't asked to inherit this estate. He just wanted to put his family back together and go home where he belonged, but now Grandpa's will made it possible for Sam to stay with or without his approval. He took a sip of coffee and set the mug on the desk.

You shouldn't set that on the wood. It could ruin the finish.

He blew out a breath. His sister was right—not that he cottoned to being reminded. Still…he grabbed a page of the will and stuck it under the mug.

His head ached, he was covered in road dust, and his face needed a shave. What he wouldn't give for a good scrubbing in the stream, but first he needed to talk to Sam again. Or at least try talking to her. Hopefully their next conversation would go a little better than the first two they'd had. "Can we continue this discussion tomorrow? I've had about all I can take for tonight."

The lawyer turned from where he stood shuffling through his own copies of the papers. "We're about done, as it is. Let's cover the charities quickly, then you can have the weekend to look over the will. Perhaps you'll stop by my office in Albany on Monday with any further questions? Or if you wish, I can come here."

"Albany on Monday's fine." He'd walk there barefoot, if doing so would end this fiasco for the night.

"Here's the list of institutions your grandfather contributed to over the past five years." Mr. Byron handed him three sheets of paper. As though the twenty-five names on one sheet wouldn't have supplied his grandfather with enough philanthropic opportunities. "I'd expect the ma-

jority of these charities will send representatives to speak
with you about donations in your grandfather's memory."

He'd figured that much when he'd talked to the headmistress at the academy earlier. He'd probably spend a
week doing nothing more than explaining to the representatives that he would be heading West before he decided
what to do with the funds.

"This is one you need to be particularly aware of,
though." The lawyer slid yet another piece of paper across
the desk. "You may not know it, but your grandfather
was the founder of Hayes Academy for Girls and stayed
rather involved in that institution. It's assumed you'll fill
the role he vacated."

Luke frowned as he glanced at the papers for Hayes
Academy—lists of finances and supplies, students and
faculty. Easy enough to make sense of and not so very
different from the accounts he kept of the ranch. "There's
a projected deficit. Am I in charge of raising money for
my sister's school?"

The lawyer shoved his drooping spectacles onto his
nose yet again. Following the pattern, they slid right back
down. "Either that or donating it yourself."

He was never going to get back home. It took every
ounce of pride in his body not to bang his head on the
desk.

"Hayes Academy for Girls was your grandfather's
crowning social achievement. He remained rather proud
of the school and very involved in its running, right up
until his heart attack."

Luke ran his eyes over the lists of expenses on the papers again. Looked like things could be managed a little
better, but what was he going to do with the mess? He
might be able to tell his lawyer to sell an estate, but he
couldn't exactly tell the lawyer to sell a girls' school that

he didn't even own, could he? "All I see is projected expenses based on current enrollment. There's no ledger?"

"The manager of the accounting office in Albany has the official ledgers, but the mathematics teacher, a Miss Elizabeth Wells, keeps her own ledgers and reports to the accountant. You might check with her about the school's current financial state, particularly in regard to the day-to-day details. She stays more informed about such things than the accountant or the school board."

Miss Wells. Lovely. He could just imagine how that conversation would go. *Howdy, Miss Wells. Now that I've pulled my sister out of your school, I want to scrutinize every last figure you've recorded in your books.* "How much, then?"

Byron's eyebrows furrowed together. "How much what?"

"How much money did Grandpa's will bequest to them?" Luke spread the papers into a bigger mess across the top of the desk. "For all the figures on these papers, I can't find the amount."

"Your grandfather made no bequests for a single charity. Everything was given to you, with the exception of the sums for Cynthia and your sister. He probably assumed once you saw the extent of his philanthropic endeavors, you would continue donating in his stead."

Luke stuck a finger in his collar and tugged. Likely another way for good old Grandpa to trap him in this uppity little eastern town. "How much did my grandfather usually donate?"

The lawyer pointed to a number on one of the sheets.

"Two thousand dollars for *one* school year?" Luke jumped to his feet, the thunderous words reverberating off the office walls. He could understand five hundred dollars, or maybe even a thousand. But two thousand dollars so girls could learn fancy mathematics? "That seems a little extreme."

The lawyer's eyes darkened, and he jerked the paper away. "On the contrary. As I already mentioned, your grandfather advocated educating women, and it's only natural he use his money toward that end. Since its inception, the school has been very successful at seeing its graduates enter colleges across the country."

Luke leafed through the pages. "But it looks like donations are down…enrollment, too. It isn't much to say the graduates go to college, when there's no one to graduate."

"That is hardly the fault of the school," Byron insisted. "The current economic state has, of course, caused some students to delay their educations. And of late, there has been a bit of local opposition to the school."

Byron handed him two newspaper articles: An Editorial on the Necessity of Educating Young Women by Miss Elizabeth Wells, and Excessive Amount of Charity Money Wasted on Hayes Academy for Girls by a certain Mr. Reginald Higsley.

Luke let the papers fall to the desk. "The derogatory article appeared at the beginning of the week. Has the school board printed an answer?"

The lawyer shook his head. "Your grandfather always handled situations such as this personally. But if you're concerned about the articles, you may find it interesting that your grandfather was a rather large investor in the *Morning Times*."

Luke sunk his head in his hands. "I see."

And he did. He hadn't even been in Valley Falls a day, and his life had been upended, flipped around and spun sideways a couple times. He was never going to survive here for a month.

Chapter Four

"These numbers don't look good." Samantha frowned and glanced up from the ledger she'd had her face buried in for the past fifteen minutes. "Do you think the school will close?"

"I don't know." Elizabeth moved the chalk in her hand deftly across her slate, finishing up some ciphering with yet another depressing result.

She and Samantha had spread a blanket beneath a large maple tree overlooking the back fields on the Hayes estate. The afternoon sky boasted a brilliant blue, and the breeze snapped with autumn's crispness; birds circled the air above, and the nearby brook babbled gaily as it flowed over rock and sticks.

In short, it was a perfect autumn afternoon. But Elizabeth could hardly enjoy it when her time with the ledgers last night had revealed a frighteningly small amount of money left in the bank account. The academy barely had enough funds to pay teacher salaries and outstanding bills, and it was only October. They hadn't even purchased the coal for the boiler system yet.

Elizabeth set her chalk down. "The school board will

make the final decision about the academy closing. But Jackson's findings will be a big part of it."

Samantha blushed and ducked her head at the mention of Jackson's name. "That doesn't sound very promising."

"No. Did you spot any mistakes in my mathematics?"

Samantha shook her head and shifted the still-open book to the ground beside her.

Elizabeth sighed. If only there had been a mistake, an extra five hundred dollars tucked into an account somewhere. But Samantha would have caught something so glaring. Goodness, Samantha would have caught a mistake ten times smaller than that. The girl was a pure genius when it came to ciphering.

"I don't suppose it matters much either way for me." Samantha gave a careless shrug of her shoulders—hardly a ladylike gesture—and slumped back against the tree trunk. "It's not as if I'll be around."

An image of Luke Hayes, standing in the school hallway with his arms crossed and that frown on his face, flashed across her mind. "Is your brother still determined to take you out of school? If there was such a problem with your attending, why didn't he or your father protest earlier, when you first started?"

"It's not my going to the school that's the problem. It's staying in Valley Falls now that Grandfather is gone. Luke's decided I have to return to Wyoming."

The breath stilled in Elizabeth's lungs. Pulling Samantha out of school was bad enough, but to take her all the way back to Wyoming? Samantha's future would be ruined. "Why would he want such a thing?"

Samantha tucked her knees up into her chest and huffed. "Because he's a tyrant, that's why."

"I'm sure there's more to it than that." There had to be.

No one would be so cruel without a reason, not even the intimidating man she'd argued with yesterday.

"Not really. All he'll say is that Ma and Pa miss me, there's no one left to care for me here and I belong back on the ranch."

Elizabeth reached over and squeezed Samantha's hand. "Do you think it would help if I talked to him? Maybe if I explained all the opportunities graduating would give you, he'd let you stay."

"It won't work, not with my brother. Once he gets an idea into his head, he doesn't listen to reason."

Elizabeth let the silence settle between them, punctuated by the chirping of birds, the nattering of squirrels and the constant trickle of water over rocks. There wasn't much she could say, really. She'd speak with Luke Hayes, all right, do anything she could to keep Samantha here. But Samantha knew the man better than she did, and if Samantha didn't think anything was going to change Luke Hayes's mind, the girl was probably right.

"How long since you've been home?"

"Three years."

"That is rather long." Elizabeth bit the inside of her cheek. "Christmas doesn't afford a long enough break for you to travel home and come back, but maybe if you offered to return to Wyoming for a visit after you graduate, your brother would let you stay until then."

"Actually, I've been thinking of something else…" Samantha drew in a breath and fixed her eyes on the ground. "Do you think it's wrong to…to hope Jackson proposes? Then I could stay here, marry him and not bother with anything Luke says."

The meadow grew silent around them as she stared at Samantha's flushed cheeks. Her brother and Samantha certainly showed signs of being a good match. But

Samantha had dreams of being an architect, and she was still so young...

"I—I think marriage is a very serious decision, one that affects the rest of your life. If you marry Jackson, you should do so for the right reasons. Because you love him, want to spend the rest of your life with him, and will be happier with him than you'd be without him. Marrying for any other reasons will just cause trouble."

It was a lesson she'd learned far too well when she'd been Samantha's age.

A horse nickered somewhere in the distance, and the ground reverberated with the steady *thump-thump, thump-thump, thump-thump* of the beast's gallop.

"I suppose you're right." Samantha looked up from the speck on the ground she'd been staring at. "That sounds like Triton's gait, but who would be riding out this far? The stable hands don't usually head this direction."

A moment later, a rider in a cowboy hat appeared atop a magnificent dark brown steed at the far edge of the field.

Samantha scowled. "I should have guessed. My brother has to spend at least six hours of his day on a horse, or he goes crazy."

Elizabeth tried not to watch as Luke Hayes approached, but in truth, she could hardly take her eyes from him as he raced across the field. He seemed to move as one with the strong horse, his legs hugging the beast as though it were an extension of his own body. It hardly seemed possible to imagine the man stuffed into Jonah Hayes's office, going through the endless papers.

"Good afternoon." Mr. Hayes reined the horse to a stop beside the blanket, towering over them like a king; then his eyes narrowed on his sister. "You didn't say anything about coming out here, Sam."

Samantha's eyes flashed, and she crossed her arms over

her knees. "I wasn't aware I needed to ask permission to go for a walk on the estate."

He raised one of his arrogant eyebrows and scanned the blanket, ledgers and slates sprawled on the ground. He didn't need words to express the thoughts clearly written across his face: *this doesn't look like an unplanned walk.*

Samantha huffed and picked up the ledger again, interested anew in the endless columns of numbers.

"Miss Wells, I can't say I expected to find you here either, but I've a need to speak with you." He glanced briefly at the equation-filled slate on her lap, and the side of his mouth quirked into a cocky little smile. "Do you ever take time off from that fancy mathematics?"

"Do you ever take time off from being a cowboy?"

The smile on his lips straightened into a firm, white line, and he swung off his horse. "I own five thousand head of cattle in the Teton Valley. I'm a *rancher.* That's a mite different than being the hired help we call cowboys."

"Indeed." She nodded curtly and drew in a long, deep breath. With Samantha sitting beside her, she couldn't exactly persuade him to let his sister graduate, but she still needed to ask about donating money to the academy. If only she could be polite long enough to make her request.

It was going to be very, very hard.

She blew out her breath and forced herself to smile.

"Can I help you up?" Mr. Hayes extended his hand.

She stared at it for a moment, hesitating to reach for him. But really, what was the point of being rude when she still had to ask about that wretched donation? She placed her palm firmly in his.

Mistake.

His wide, callused palm engulfed her small fingers, and heat surged through the spot where their skin met. He raised her to her feet without ceremony, as though he didn't feel the impact of their touch somewhere deep inside. As soon as she was able, she tugged away her hand and shoved it behind her back, where it could stay safely away from Mr. Hayes.

The rascal didn't even seem to notice, just pinned her with his clear blue eyes. "It seems you've taken quite an interest in the business affairs of Hayes Academy here lately." Afternoon sunlight glistened down on Mr. Hayes's head and cowboy hat, turning the golden-blond tufts of hair beneath the brim nearly white.

Elizabeth forced her gaze away from his hair. Why was she staring at it, anyway? So the man had beautiful blond hair. His sister did, as well. Blond hair wasn't *that* uncommon.

Except when it shimmered like silvery-gold in the sunlight.

And she was still thinking about his hair. Ugh! "I teach at the academy. It's only natural I'd be interested in it."

"Interested enough to write editorials for the newspaper?"

Every bit of blood in her face drained to her feet, and her limbs felt suddenly cold. Did he hate her for interfering? Feel she had no business fighting for new students? Resent the negative attention she'd drawn to the school when that dreadful reporter retaliated?

The emotionless look on his face gave nothing away. His eyes stayed that cool blue, the same shade as a winter sky, without a hint of either understanding or disdain as they waited for her answer.

"Educating women is important to me."

"I gathered that much yesterday. A bit hard to miss, actually, but I'm curious about the school ledgers at the moment." He nodded toward the books, the one lying on the blanket and the other still in Samantha's lap. "My lawyer informs me you're keeping a set. I assume these are them?"

Oh, perfect. Just what she wanted to discuss. "My brother in Albany has the official ledgers. Perhaps you should talk to him."

"I intend to, but I'd like a look at yours, as well."

"No." The word flew out of her mouth before she could stop it.

Samantha slammed her ledger closed. "Why do you want them? So you can look for some excuse to close down the school? As if pulling me out isn't bad enough."

Mr. Hayes glanced briefly at his sister. "This has nothing to do with you, Sam. I'm only doing the job Grandpa left me. Miss Wells, you must be aware that since I've been given my grandfather's seat on the school's board, I can request your books at any time."

She knew very well what he could request, and what he'd likely do if he saw the books. He'd take one look at how little money was in the account and want the school closed immediately.

"Mind if I borrow your rag?"

"Excuse me?"

Mr. Hayes held up his hand—the same he'd used to help her stand. His palm was practically white, smeared with chalk dust.

Heat flooded her neck and face. She didn't need to look down to know her own hands were covered in fine powder.

"Messy place, these fields."

She reached into her pocket, grabbed a hanky—one of the ones she was forever using to wipe her chalk-covered hands on—and held it out to him. "I apologize. I don't usually forget to clean my hands."

"Thank you." He rubbed the cloth over his palm and returned it.

She wiped her hands furiously, even though she'd be back to work the second he left.

He simply watched her, a half smile quirking the side of his mouth. "You missed a spot." He pointed to her right sleeve, where a huge smear of white stood stark against the yellow of her dress.

"Thank you," she gritted.

"So can I take those ledgers now?"

"I'd—" ...*rather eat a toad!*

Could she lie? Tell him things were going well—or at least as well as they had been before the newspaper article appeared on Monday morning—and tear out the last pages of the ledgers so the school appeared to have money?

She rubbed her fingers over her temples. No, of course she couldn't do such a thing. She'd never been one to lie for convenience, and she wasn't about to develop the habit now. He'd find out the truth soon anyway; just as he'd learned of the article she'd written to the paper. Better to be honest.

No, better to ask for another donation, and *then* be honest.

Except she didn't want to ask the arrogant man in front of her for a penny.

Taking her requests to Jonah, with his kind smiles and grandfatherly manner, had been easy. But the man who had stormed into her class yesterday and torn Samantha out of school wasn't exactly grandfatherly.

Or approachable.

Or kind.

"Miss Wells?"

She stared into Luke Hayes's rigid face, his mouth and eyes stern and unreadable, and forced herself to form the words. "Actually, I've been wanting to speak to you about the ledgers and the academy. We've recently had difficulty with several of our donors, and I was hoping you could make a donation to Hayes Academy."

There. She'd said it. Surely she deserved some type of award. A medal of honor, a golden cup, a life-size statue of herself erected in the town square.

"Yeah, that would at least be something nice you could do for the school." Samantha crossed her arms over her chest. "Seeing how you're dead set on pulling me out of it."

But Mr. Hayes didn't bother to look at his sister. "Grandpa donated slews of money to Hayes Academy. I don't understand why you can't be happy with what it's already received."

She threw up her hands. The man's brain was as dense as a piece of lead. "Happy? You think I want a donation to make me happy? Girls' futures are at stake, not my happiness. It's an issue of keeping the school open, so we can train young women, not pleasing me."

Mr. Hayes rubbed his hand over the back of his neck. "Why is girls getting high school diplomas so all-fired important? I never graduated from high school, and neither did Grandpa. Yet here I am, doing a fine job of running my ranch without any piece of paper from a high school."

She opened her mouth to respond, then snapped it shut. What did she say to that? Was it true Jonah Hayes never finished school? Probably. A lot of young people left to find work before graduating even now, let alone sixty years ago.

Mr. Hayes's face remained set, his jaw determined, but sincerity filled the little sun lines at the corners of his eyes and mouth. He wasn't furious with her as he'd been yesterday but was asking an honest question.

And here she was, parading the importance of educating women in front of him, when he'd never finished his own education. Did he feel slighted or belittled? That hadn't been her intention. "Well, you see, a high school education is important because—"

"Never mind. I read your article last night. I don't need to hear some highfalutin list of arguments in person. Just give me the ledgers, and I'll be on my way."

"Oh…um…" And there again the man had her speechless. From ledgers to donations and back again, she could hardly keep up with the conversation. "Will Monday be all right? Samantha and I have a bit more work to do on them this afternoon, and I've some issues to discuss with my brother. I truly need the books over the weekend."

Mr. Hayes blew out a long, tired breath, the kind that held a world of weariness in the exhaled air. "Monday, then. Sorry to disturb you ladies." And with that, he swung back onto his horse and galloped off.

Elizabeth tucked a stray strand of hair behind her ear and sighed. The conversation surely could have gone worse. At least she hadn't stormed away in a rage, and he hadn't refused to give money to the school—

Though he hadn't agreed to give any, either.

So why did she have a sour taste in her mouth?

She turned and offered Samantha a weak smile. "I feel like I handled that wrong."

Samantha shrugged as she settled back down beside the tree. "It's Luke. Anytime you disagree with him, he'd say you handled something wrong."

Chapter Five

Covered in dust and smelling of sweat, Luke hurried through the back entrance to Grandpa's house. After spending the first half of the day sorting through the things in Grandpa's office, he'd decided to take a peek at the stable. After all, if he shut down the estate, he'd need to sell off whatever horseflesh Grandpa had acquired. But at a glance, some of that horseflesh had looked a little too good to be sold. So he'd hopped astride Triton, the finest beast in the stable, for a little ride.

He certainly hadn't expected to find Samantha and Miss Wells. He glanced down at his hand and couldn't help but smile. The white stain from her chalk dust had long since faded, but he'd never forget the memory of first looking at his hand and seeing white, then watching the color rise in Miss Wells's face.

With her bright hazel eyes, perfect mouth and head of thick mahogany hair, the teacher was just as beautiful today as she had been yesterday…and terribly determined to wheedle money for the school out of him.

Luke rolled his shoulders as he headed through the back hallway and out into the grand hall. Should he give the school some money? It wouldn't hurt anything. Grandpa had left him more than enough. And it might help Sam to see he wasn't some type of greedy tyrant.

But then, he didn't rightly know what he wanted to do with any of Grandpa's money yet, besides give it to Pa. And how unfair would it be to all the other charities Grandpa had supported if he discounted them and wrote out a bank draft to Hayes Academy because a pretty little teacher with shiny hazel eyes smiled at him?

Twenty-four hours in Valley Falls and his brain was already half mush. He had to get out of this place. Soon.

Luke strode through the grand hall toward the bright marble staircase. He'd stayed out riding Triton for too long after meeting up with the womenfolk. Now he needed to bathe fast, if he didn't want to arrive at that fancy banquet late. He could always scrub up quicklike in the stream behind the house, but this place crawled with enough servants that someone would probably venture along while he washed. Plus Sam could probably list a good ten rules about why a man couldn't take a simple bath in a stream these days.

A knock sounded behind him on the front door, not more than three feet away. He glanced around the large empty room with its glittering chandelier and polished white marble. "I'll answer it."

The butler emerged from a doorway on the left, but Luke pulled the door open anyway. A dark-haired young man stood there, dressed in a tuxedo and top hat, his skin smooth and pale as though he'd never seen a day in the sun.

The man pondered him for a moment, then a polished smile curved his lips, and he thrust his hand out. "Good evening. You must be Mr. Luke Hayes."

Luke shook the offered hand, the scent of his body's

odor rising as he moved his arm. The other man deserved some credit for not gagging.

"I'm Jackson Wells."

Wells. As in related to the mathematics teacher? Couldn't be. Miss Wells was proper all right, but she didn't come off as slick, like the spiffed-up man in front of him. "Howdy, Mr. Wells."

"I'm manager at the Great Northern Accounting and Insurance office in Albany." He rubbed the brim of his top hat.

"Nice to meet you." So this was the accountant for Hayes Academy—who also happened to share the same surname as his little mathematics teacher? He scratched behind his ear. The lawyer hadn't said anything about the accountant and teacher being related, but he supposed it was possible.

And either way, he had a couple hundred questions to ask the man, if not for needing to be ready for that banquet thing he'd gotten roped into.

"Your grandfather hired me a few years ago. I imagine you own the accounting office now? It's a pleasure. I've been wanting to meet you."

"Thanks for coming around, Mr. Wells. But I've got a banquet to get to. Let's schedule an appointment at the office on Monday. About nine o'clock?"

"Yes, sir." Wells's gaze drifted down Luke's sweat-encrusted clothing, and the man frowned. "Were you planning to travel with us tonight? Should Samantha and I wait for you?"

"Samantha and you?"

"Of course."

"Traveling?" Luke's scalp heated. The man spoke too easily, as though he expected to wrap Sam up in a blanket and haul her off to…to…

Well, it didn't really matter where the man wanted to cart her off to. The dandy was too old for his sister. "Sam's not taking visitors today."

Something flashed in Wells's eyes. A challenge? It was gone too soon, replaced by that overly polished face once again. "Is there some trouble with Samantha accompanying me to the banquet tonight?"

Samantha at the banquet? Luke slammed the door in Wells's face. "Sam!" He grimaced as his shout echoed up the polished stairs.

"Mr. Hayes, sir." The butler stepped forward. "Perhaps I can show Mr. Wells into the gentlemen's reception room, where you can discuss the situation."

Luke turned to the butler. What was his name again? Stebbens? Stevens? "Thank you, no."

Sam appeared at the top of the stairs, dressed in a long silvery-lavender gown. "Is Jackson here?" A thousand bursts of sunlight radiated from her face.

He should speak, send her a look, do something to show his displeasure. But he only stared as her beautiful figure descended the stairs. It couldn't be his sister. Her hair, a mixture of honey and spun gold, piled atop her head in curls, a few of which hung down to frame her soft face. Her cheeks glowed the perfect shade of pink and her lips… she'd dyed them red with something.

Sam glided to the base of the stairs, an uncertain smile curving the corners of her mouth.

A fist pounded on the door.

The butler cleared his throat.

His sister sniffed the air. "Goodness, you stink, Luke."

"Where did you get that dress?" His voice was too hoarse, and try as he might, he couldn't look away. Oh, he knew she was of marrying age. Had handed her a letter from Levi just yesterday, likely with a proposal inside. But giving her a letter from an old friend was a far cry from letting her traipse around town dressed like that with the spiffed-up stranger outside.

"Grandfather ordered it made for a ball earlier this summer. I didn't attend, of course, after his heart failed, but I was able to have the color switched from blue to lavender. It's appropriate for attending the banquet, with my still being in half mourning, don't you think?" She spoke eloquently and smoothly, with a gentle lift of the shoulder here, and slight ducking of the chin there. She was practically a grown woman, wearing that beautiful gown and honoring her late grandfather.

But none of that changed the two most important things. She was still his sister and… "Did you say you were going to the banquet, the one *I'm* attending?"

He opened his mouth to add she was too young, then stopped and attempted to blow out his frustration in one giant breath.

It worked great—until his shoulders tightened into knots.

Sam frowned. "No. I'm wearing satin to a banquet in the town park. Yes, the banquet you're attending. I gave Jackson my word. Now, if you would please step away from the door so Stevens can let Jackson inside. He came all the way from Albany just to pick me up." Her dress swished, catching the light from the chandelier as she waved toward the door.

Luke raked his hand through his hair. Mourning indeed. Why couldn't the gown be some other color? A bright childlike yellow or pink. Not shades of lavender and silver that shimmered in the lighting and caused her skin to look as creamy as warm milk. He wanted his old sister back. The one that skinned her knees trying to climb trees and didn't cry when she fell off a horse.

Again, the knock.

Luke gritted his teeth and looked between his sister, the butler and the door. He'd give his grandfather's estate away in a second, if he could be instantly back in Wyoming, Sam by his side. But since that wasn't an option, what else could he do? Keep the slick-looking man outside, and haul Sam upstairs to hog-tie her to her bed for a day or two?

She'd never speak to him again. "Stevens, please show Mr. Wells into the…" He snapped his fingers, the name of the room escaping him.

The butler raised his eyebrows. "The gentlemen's reception room, sir? Or would you prefer the drawing room since the lady is present?"

Wasn't one room the same as another?

"The drawing room will do nicely." Samantha moved toward the double doors on the right.

Luke followed her into the room and nearly had to step back out. The carpet. The molding. The drapes. The furniture. Gold gleamed at him from every direction, and the few things that weren't gold were white. Someone had painted the walls a blindingly pure shade, and the white cushions on the furniture looked so bright they'd likely never been sat on. A large marble fireplace, also white, dominated the far wall, while floor-to-ceiling windows sent shafts of sunlight into the room.

He narrowed his eyes at his sister, who stepped daintily across the room. "Hang it all, Sam. Why didn't you tell me you were going to this banquet earlier?"

Samantha sat on a small fancy sofa thing with perfect cushions, her chin quivering slightly. "I didn't feel like being yelled at."

"I'm not…" *Yelling.* Though he was close. He pressed his lips together to keep from saying more.

"Mr. Hayes." Stevens stood in the open doorway. "Miss Hayes. May I present Mr. Jackson Wells."

Wells cast Luke that too-polished smile but walked straight to Sam. "Ah, Samantha, your beauty this evening is riveting." The man settled onto the dainty couch, somehow confident the fragile furniture would hold two people.

Luke eyed the chair beside them. Those spindly gold legs would likely collapse if he sat down, and if the chair didn't break, his filthy clothes would ruin the cushions.

"Thank you, Jackson. It's lovely to see you, as well." Samantha sent the dandy a smile despite her still trembling lips and extended her hand, palm down, which Wells kissed.

Kissed.

He should burn the man's lips off.

"Luke, allow me to make introductions." Samantha sniffed, her nose tilted into the air, but something wet glinted in her eyes.

Certainly he wasn't being a big enough fool to make her cry, was he?

"This is Jackson Wells, son of our esteemed local assemblyman, Thomas Wells. He also works for you, as manager of Great Northern Accounting and Insurance's office in Albany."

"I know he works for me." And the knowledge didn't curb his urge to chase away the scoundrel with his Colt.

"Jackson." Samantha's smile seemed more genuine as she glanced at her suitor. "This is my brother, Luke Hayes."

Wells's gaze, sickeningly friendly, rested on Luke. "We've spoken."

"Mr. Wells." Luke nodded, his voice vibrating like a dog's low growl. Probably wouldn't do to fire the man just for being sweet on his sister, but it was tempting.

Wells leaned forward and whispered something in Sam's ear, and she laughed softly.

Luke flexed his fingers. "Don't eastern folk ask permission from the man of the family before they start courting a lady?"

Samantha stopped midwhisper, and Wells stood. "I spoke with the late Mr. Hayes before he passed. He was thrilled when I requested to call on Samantha. He and my father are acquainted, of course, and—"

Luke cut the boy off with a wave of his hand. "And you expect to take her to the banquet."

"Yes, sir."

"Plans have changed. Samantha is accompanying me. You can meet her there."

Sam sprang from her seat. "Luke, you can't—"

"Perhaps you're concerned about a chaperone?" Wells interjected. "My sister is awaiting us in the carriage. She's a spinster and a perfectly acceptable chaperone."

"Miss Wells, Luke." Sam held her chin at a determined angle, but she blinked against the tears in her eyes. "The mathematics teacher you met at the academy yesterday."

So Miss Wells and the dandy were related after all. And that also made her the daughter of the local assemblyman. No one had bothered to tell him that, either.

What was the daughter of a politician doing teaching mathematics like some spinster?

Not that it mattered. Nope. Certainly not. Whatever Miss Wells chose to do or not do, whoever she happened to be related to or not related to, was no concern of his.

Luke rubbed his hand over his forehead and glanced back at his sister, only to find more tears glistening in her eyes. Confound it. Why did she cry at everything he did? Made him feel like an ogre—which he most definitely was *not*.

Or so he hoped. Maybe he had some questions for Sam, and needed to have a long chat with her suitor, but now was hardly the time to go into all that. Clearly Sam and Wells had arranged to attend the banquet, and it hardly seemed fair to stop them just because he'd arrived in town and hadn't known about their plans.

But he still didn't cotton to the idea of Sam going off without him. "How about this. Sam and I will go to the banquet together. Sam, if your *friend* and the mathematics teacher want to tag along, so be it."

Sam bit her bottom lip and sent him an uncertain glance. "Does that mean you're going to change clothes?"

Chapter Six

Elizabeth scooted toward the far side of the carriage, giving the *rancher*—not cowboy—more room as he sat beside her. She hadn't considered that he and his sister would attend the banquet together, or that he would insist they take his carriage, not Jackson's. She didn't want to share a carriage with the man after offending him earlier that afternoon.

Though she still wasn't sure how she'd offended him. Surely the man couldn't be upset because she'd asked for a donation, could he?

She clasped her gloved hands together on her lap. What had Jonah been thinking, anyway, to leave the estate to his grandson? It would have been much simpler had Jonah divided up his legacy before his death and donated everything to charity. Then again, maybe he'd planned to do that in a few more years. No one had been expecting that sudden heart attack.

"Good evening, Miss Wells." Mr. Hayes's voice rumbled from beside her.

She glanced his way, then down at her lap. My, but he did look dashing in a tuxedo, all the wild strength of the

West, thinly veiled in dark evening attire. Now if only he would trade in that cowboy hat for a proper top hat.

But cowboy hat or not, he'd still be the most sought-after man at the banquet. He had too much money and too-fine looks for people to ignore him. Not that she cared in the least.

And she'd best find something productive to talk about, lest she sit here contemplating his appearance for an hour. "Jackson, about our previous discussion, have you—"

"Not now, Elizabeth." Jackson flicked his hand as though getting rid of a fly. "I'm sure Mr. Hayes has more pressing things to discuss than your preoccupation with food costs at the academy."

"I'm not—"

"Mr. Hayes." Jackson nodded at the rancher. "Please accept my sincere condolences about your grandfather."

Mr. Hayes's hands gripped the edge of the seat, and his body tensed as though he would vault from their bench and squeeze between the courting couple across the carriage. The man was quite good at issuing threats with his eyes, and this one read: *Jackson Wells, touch my sister, and you'll regret it.*

"Jonah Hayes was a great businessman," her brother continued. Whether oblivious to Mr. Hayes's disapproval or purposely ignoring it, she couldn't tell. "Not to mention one of my father's most faithful and generous supporters."

"Yes." Mr. Hayes's eyes glinted with studied coolness. "I understand my grandfather was a faithful supporter of a great many things."

Jackson laughed, the overly loud sound bouncing off the carriage walls. "Have you considered following in your grandfather's footsteps and donating funds to one of New York's longest sitting and most popular assemblymen? My father has personally passed legislation that…"

The sun cast its fading orange rays inside the carriage while the familiar discussion about politics and campaigning swirled around her. Elizabeth shifted in the seat and made herself comfortable as the carriage wheels rumbled over the road.

If they were exactly 5.2 miles from Albany and they reached Albany in 56 minutes, that meant they traveled at a rate of 5.474 miles per hour. So say the wheels on the carriage were twenty-four inches in diameter, what would be the wheels' rate of rotation? She closed her eyes, letting the numbers and equations dance before her.

But even with her eyes shut, the scents of grass and sun and musk emanated from the person beside her, and the seat dipped ever so slightly in Mr. Hayes's direction, making him rather unforgettable—even with her equations.

It was going to be a long ride.

As the carriage threaded through the crowded streets of Albany, Mr. Hayes and Jackson continued to discuss Father's politics. Jackson talking about Father's campaign and funding for an hour wasn't unusual, but Mr. Hayes not agreeing to give away a penny?

Amazing.

Across from her, Samantha stared blindly out the carriage window, bored with how Mr. Hayes had kept Jackson's attention away from her this whole time. An intelligent man lurked behind the rancher's cowboy hat and country slang—now if only he shared his grandfather's passion for educating women.

Instead it seemed he'd come into town convinced he needed to undo half of his grandfather's strides in that area. Elizabeth folded and unfolded her hands in her lap.

"Are you looking forward to the banquet?" Mr. Hayes's breath tickled her ear.

She turned to face him. Had he and Jackson finally finished their conversation? They must have, because he was leaning over, his attention riveted to her.

"Yes, of course."

The bright glow of streetlamps shone through the carriage window, bathing that bold, handsome face in a mixture of shadows and light, while subtle wisps of cologne teased her nose. She stared at the ceiling. She could breathe. Nice calm breaths not remotely affected by the fragrance of sun and grass and musk tingeing the air. "I... um...thank you for your concern."

"I'd like a word with you once we step inside," he whispered as he leaned closer.

Her heart pounded. She wanted words with him, too— about keeping Samantha in school, about contributing to Hayes Academy. But not at the banquet.

"I'd like to discuss things, as well." She glanced across the carriage as it rolled to a stop in front of the Kenmore Hotel. The lovers whispered together much the way she and Mr. Hayes did. She edged as far away as she could, pressing herself against the wall. "But not tonight."

His eyes narrowed and blood throbbed in her ears.

She averted her gaze and focused on a streetcar clunking past, but she didn't let out her breath until he shifted away. How foolish to let him bother her. First with getting her ire up that afternoon, and now by acting so polished and intelligent she could hardly think. A man hadn't stirred her this way since her former fiancé.

But she was older now, and stronger, no longer a child to be swayed by flattering words and handsome looks. She'd even gone to college and gotten her mathematics degree to avoid being trapped into a marriage with someone like David again.

"Miss Wells?"

She glanced up.

Mr. Hayes stood in the doorway of the now empty carriage, his hand extended, his eyes assessing. Did he know what went on inside her? How handsome she found him? How hurt she was by his disregard for anything and everything concerning Hayes Academy?

Of course not. He could only see what the lights illuminated, which was precious little, as she clung to the far corner of the conveyance and shadows filled the space between.

"Are you all right?"

Of course she was all right. She was Miss Elizabeth Wells, daughter of the esteemed and long-standing assemblyman, Thomas Wells. Educated woman and teacher of mathematics. And she wasn't about to let a few whispered words from Mr. Hayes bother her. She leaned forward and gave him her hand.

"I'm sorry for barging into your class yesterday and disrupting the test, and for that comment this afternoon about a diploma not being important. I didn't mean to upset you. Not either time." His low voice rolled over her, smooth as polished glass.

She nodded slightly as she climbed down from the carriage. "You apologized about interrupting class yesterday."

He rubbed a hand over his chin. "Didn't exactly mean it then, but I do now."

She couldn't stop the smile that curved her lips. "Thank you, sir. We've still much to discuss, but I'm afraid this evening simply isn't the time. Now we'd best head inside."

"As you like." He took her hand and placed it firmly on his arm.

She glanced around and tried to tug free. But Mr. Hayes only settled his other hand atop hers, giving her little choice but to follow him into the Kenmore. She didn't intend to let him escort her. She had plans for the evening, and they involved speaking to the school board members about keeping Hayes Academy open, not standing around on the arm of a rich bachelor and fluttering her eyelashes every time he deigned to look her way. Arriving at the banquet together had been merely a matter of convenience, hadn't it?

Once inside, Mr. Hayes helped her with her cloak before she could take it off herself, and handed the garment and his hat to the clerk. When he extended his elbow this time, she stepped back.

"If you'll excuse me." Her heart thudded slowly, as he turned those cool blue eyes—eyes that always seemed to see too much—on her. "There is a gentleman I must speak with. Do forgive me if I slip away."

Before he could answer, or take her hand again, or stare into her eyes for too long, or do something else equally unnerving, she turned and hurried toward the banquet hall, alone.

The room held the dimly lit, quiet ambiance of formal dinners but lacked some of the usual glamour. The rich array of women's dresses should have looked beautiful beside the men's crisp tuxedos, but the gowns and suits appeared old and overworn. That only made sense, as her own dress was more than four years old. No one had money for new dresses or properly tailored tuxedos these days.

Even the hall itself reflected the hotel's attempt to save money. On the tables, crystal goblets glittered beside sparkling china plates and polished silverware. But the tablecloths weren't bright white, more gray in hue with an occasional faded stain, and the chandeliers and windows looked in need of a good scrubbing.

The depression had hit New York hard, and her family

felt it more than most. The force of the panic struck home last April, when a mob had descended on her father's bank. Nearly all her parents' campaign financing and personal savings had been lost, along with the trust funds set up for her and her brother—which she hadn't been able to access until she married anyway. Indeed, few people had escaped the panic and depression unscathed. Fortunately for Luke Hayes, his grandfather had been one of them.

Elizabeth weaved quickly through the room, searching for a board member not already engaged in conversation. She finally spotted Mr. Wilhem standing beside a window and surveying the crowd. Perfect.

"Elizabeth. Don't you look becoming this evening." Mr. Wilhem swirled the wine in his glass as she approached.

"Thank you, sir. You're looking rather fine yourself."

The middle-aged man chuckled, his bushy black-and-gray-specked eyebrows rising. "Come now, child. There's no need to flatter an old man's vanity."

Child. The word struck her in the stomach. He didn't think her that young, did he? But then, he'd known her since she was a little girl. "I wanted to let you know how much the students at the academy are enjoying their studies this year."

Mr. Wilhem patted her on the shoulder, much like a grandfather would. "Are they now? Always a pleasure to hear students are excited about learning. Though I must admit, I'm a little concerned about those newspaper articles, both the editorial you wrote and the one the reporter penned in response. Did Miss Bowen tell you—"

"Samuel, there you are."

Elizabeth turned as Mr. Taviston, the head of the school board, approached.

"Good evening, Charles." Mr. Wilhem extended his hand to Mr. Taviston. "Miss Wells and I were just discussing Hayes Academy. It seems the students are enjoying their studies."

A thick, wooly sensation wrapped itself around her tongue. She hadn't anticipated any trouble discussing the benefits of keeping the academy open with an old family friend. But the head of the board of directors?

Mr. Taviston watched her like a fox would a rabbit.

"Thank you for allowing the school to stay open," she managed. "The students are doing quite well, and I've spent time working on the books this weekend, looking for ways to allow the school to function on a reduced budget."

Mr. Wilhem smiled, but Mr. Taviston ran his gaze slowly down her body, his eyes observing every subtlety of her blue silk gown. A flame she couldn't stop started at the base of her neck and licked onto her face.

"I don't understand how students being happy will help the school to stay open, Miss Wells. But I'm very interested to see your brother's report in another week. I doubt we've enough money to keep the school running for the remainder of the year."

"Of course we'll be able to keep things running." Her voice sounded overly bright, even to her. "We'll find a way."

"Are you aware how many letters board members have received from the public since those articles appeared? I've gotten over a dozen myself from people imploring us to find better use for our funds. It seems the people of the Albany area are very much of the opinion that young women should marry and have children, not fill their heads with calculus formulas and astronomical charts, which any good mother would find rather useless, wouldn't you agree?"

If he thought education useless, why was the man on the board of directors? But she knew the answer. He thought educating *women* useless, but not men. And he was a businessman who would invest in a girls' school if he saw the potential for immediate profit. If the profit disappeared, so did any vision for the school.

"No, I wouldn't agree," she mumbled.

"Well, it certainly seems to be in the best interest of both our banking accounts and society as a whole to close Hayes Academy."

"Of course we should close it. Was there any doubt after the meeting a couple nights ago?"

Elizabeth nearly cringed at the familiar blustery voice. Father wedged himself between her and Mr. Taviston, his wide shoulders and thick middle forcing her to take a step back. "Good evening, Father."

"Daughter, you're not discussing business with these gentlemen, are you?"

If a school banquet wasn't an appropriate time for her to discuss school business, when was? "Just Hayes Academy, where I happen to teach."

"I'm sorry to say we must close it, dear. The public is simply outraged after the appearance of that reporter's article, which you encouraged by that ridiculous editorial you wrote. Have you any notion how furious your mother was when she saw what you'd penned? It isn't appropriate for a lady like yourself to express your opinions in such a public way." He spoke the words without so much as a glance her direction.

"Well said," Taviston interjected.

"You're aware you should have gotten consent from the school board before you published such a thing, aren't you?" Mr. Wilhem patted her shoulder again.

Elizabeth licked her lips and took another step back. Was there any point attempting to argue? The men had already made up their minds. "Yes, I'm sorry. I see I made a mistake. But I was only trying to help boost enrollment."

"Help?" Father adjusted the lapels on his tuxedo. "We can't afford that kind of *help.* It cast the school board and others involved in a bad light, and hurt the public's opinion of us."

You mean hurt potential voters' opinion of you. She bit the inside of her cheek to keep from spewing the words. And to think, she'd already agreed to give a speech to educators for her father in a little over a week, to help convince them to support her father in next year's election. Yet when he stood here now, he tossed any and all support for her school aside.

She should have never told him yes when he'd asked. "I think closing the school would be a great disservice to both young women and society as a whole."

Father glared. "Elizabeth, I believe Edward needs to speak with you. Why don't you go seek him out?"

Oh, sure he did. Her father's head of staff always needed to see her when she started causing trouble, which seemed to be every time she was with her father these days.

"Gentlemen. Elizabeth."

Elizabeth sighed at the sound of the crisp English voice. One would think, after thirty years in America, the accent would mellow, but Mother still sounded as though she recently stepped off the ship from London.

"Mother." She offered the group a tight smile as Mother squeezed into the foursome.

"Good evening, Mr. Wilhem, Mr. Taviston. Hasn't the weather been wonderfully mild for October? I trust you're taking the utmost advantage of it." Mother looked elegant in a new rose-colored gown, likely one Father couldn't afford.

"Why of course, Mrs. Wells," Mr. Wilhem responded. "I've enjoyed several walks with my wife during the evenings."

Mother smiled, a flawless half curve of lips and slight raise of eyebrows. "Have you gentlemen met the Hayes heir? I was informed Elizabeth arrived with him this evening, and I think I smell romance in the air."

Elizabeth's entire body grew rigid while four pairs of eyes turned to her. If only she could grit her teeth and pretend she didn't know the woman beside her. Instead she kept her forced smile in place. "Mother, my arriving with Mr. Hayes is not what you make it seem. He decided to chaperone Samantha, and as Jackson had already asked me to chaperone, we traveled here together. Mr. Hayes and I are merely…" *friends?* No, too strong of a word. "…acquaintances."

Mr. Wilhem raised those bushy eyebrows once again. "Then you're not seeing Mr. Hayes?"

"No. I'm not accepting any suitors. Now if you gentlemen will excuse us, Mother and I have some important matters to discuss." She squeezed her mother's elbow so hard the woman's perfect smile pinched.

"Yes, do excuse us, gentlemen."

Elizabeth pulled her mother away, leaving the men to whisper furiously, probably about how soon they could announce the closing of Hayes Academy. Why even ask Jackson for a report when they'd already made their decision?

"Dear, you should have had something special made for this evening." Mother's lips sank into a frown as Elizabeth led her toward a vacant corner of the room. "That dress is so old I'm afraid you'll not attract a single man."

"I'm not here to attract men." This time she couldn't stop her teeth from gritting.

Mother reached up to touch a stray wisp of hair at the side of her face. "Really, Elizabeth, a girl of your wealth and beauty should be married."

Wealth. That was laughable considering the money her family had lost in the panic. And if her beauty wasn't enough to keep a suitor faithful, then what good was it? "I'm a mathematics teacher, Mother, and a rather good one according to my students and the headmistress. I don't plan to stop what I'm doing."

She should have expected the crestfallen look, the way the light deserted her mother's eyes and turned them a dull green. But something inside her deflated anyway.

"We never should have let you walk away from marrying David when you were younger." The tone of lecture in Mother's voice, the hint of implied guilt, the soft way her eyes entreated Elizabeth to agree all coalesced into a giant wave of regret. Did Mother stand in front of the mirror and practice these speeches? "You were so young, and I thought we were helping, that maybe you should wait another year before you married. Now it's been eight years and I see how foolish a mistake we made."

"No. The mistake would have been marrying David. I'm happy remaining a spinster and teaching."

"I expect you to care about your family's happiness, not just your own. You're still a Wells, after all." Mother's face paled beneath her face powder and rouge, and she blinked an absent tear from her eye. "And it…it happens that your family needs you right now."

Her family needed her? Since when? They always seemed to manage fine on their own. Elizabeth reached her hand out and clasped her mother's. "What's wrong, Mama?"

"Oh, do forgive me, dear. I didn't intend to get so overwrought." Mother wiped another tear from beneath her eye and fanned her face, though the jerky movement did little good in the overly stuffy room. "It's nothing really. At least I think it's nothing. But well…oh, how I worry about your father. He's not been the same since the panic, losing all his savings and having to mortgage the house, so he can build his other assets back up. Some of the voters are speaking out against politicians, claiming people like your father were responsible for the panic itself. He's under so much strain."

Elizabeth patted her mother's hand. "Father may have happened upon hard times, but he'll ride it out. He always does. A year from now things won't seem nearly so terrible, but if there's anything I can do, you know I'll help."

"Do you understand how much a good marriage could aid us in a time like this? You know I married your father because of the benefit it brought my family, even though it meant I had to leave England. Every daughter should be willing to make such a sacrifice."

She dropped her mother's hand. The argument was far too familiar. "I want to help Father, but I'm not willing to spend the rest of my life chained to someone like David. It's unfair of you to expect such a thing."

"But what if your father can't make payments on the house? What if he loses it?" The whispered words hung in the air between them. "We'd lose everything then."

"No." Elizabeth spoke the word quickly, almost harshly. In her mind, she drew up an image of the century-old stone home she'd grown up in, the room in the top right corner that even now held some of her things. "That won't happen. It's ridiculous to even think it. Father's been managing his own money and investments since before I was born. Perhaps the panic set him back, but he's still a smart businessman."

The lines around Mother's eyes and mouth only deepened. "Don't you see? This is why we need you, dear. You say your father won't lose the house, but it's possible. If you were to marry someone who could help support the family, everything would be taken care of. I've invited several guests to dinner next weekend, and you should have a new gown made for the occasion. It's a time to look your best."

Elizabeth rubbed her temples. "I'd be there, you know I would. But I told you last week, the school play is that Saturday."

Mother's shoulders slumped, as though the very world would end if her daughter missed one of the weekly family dinners. "The guests are coming specifically for you."

Lovely. She so enjoyed being paraded around like a horse for auction. In fact, she could almost hear the auctioneer's announcement. *Marry Elizabeth Wells, and you'll land yourself a spinster mathematics teacher with an overbearing mother and debt-laden father.* "Why don't you reschedule for the following week?"

Mother sighed, the unladylike sound only further evidence of her distress. "Elizabeth, dear, I have your best interest in mind by wanting you at that dinner. Your family should be more important than your students."

She wanted to scream. She wanted to howl. She wanted to beat her head against the wall. And she would have, if any of it would make Mother understand. "You are, but this play is only once a year. I'll attend dinner the week after next, I promise."

"Sometimes I hardly know what to do with you," Mother huffed. "Now, just look at the Hayes heir over there. He would make a choice husband."

She glanced at Mr. Hayes, standing among a small crowd, tall and devastatingly handsome with layers of sunbleached hair falling around his tanned face. Mr. Brumley, the manager of the orphanage, spoke with him, while several others circled like vultures waiting to descend upon his vast inheritance.

If Mr. Hayes's handling of Jackson was any indication, he wouldn't be giving away a penny.

Directly beside him, Mrs. Crawford stood with her daughter, a young lady Samantha's age, wearing pink and flounces. Indeed, every mother in the room seemed to keep one eye trained on Mr. Hayes, waiting for that perfect chance to introduce her daughter.

"He'll return to Wyoming," Elizabeth muttered, more to herself than anything.

"He can't." Mother's face pinched. "He'll need to stay and manage his grandfather's estate, unless he wants to see Jonah Hayes's life's work run into the ground."

As though that would bother him.

"You simply must go over there and stand beside him." Mother gripped her shoulder and nudged her forward. "The man escorted you here, and now he's not paying you the least attention. It's nearly scandalous."

Probably wiser not to tell Mother *she* ignored *him,* not the other way around. "The man didn't escort me anywhere. We—"

The announcement for dinner interrupted her.

"What excellent timing. Come along now. I've already arranged for him to sit across from you."

Chapter Seven

Luke shifted sideways ever-so-slightly in an attempt to put some space between himself and the gentleman crowding his left side. Unfortunately that placed him a little too close to the girl wearing butter-yellow and ruffles standing on his right. He looked around the banquet hall. With dinner and the speaking long finished, people sauntered toward the exits.

But for all the people leaving, he stood surrounded. He stuck a finger in his collar and pulled. Four hours of chattering. Meet him, meet her, donate money to this, donate money to that. He needed a break.

And he spotted his excuse to escape, right by the back double doors. Jackson stood in a corner alone with Samantha, far too close and looking ready to eat his little sister for dessert.

Where was Miss Wells? Wasn't she supposed to be chaperoning? He glanced around the room. There she was, on the far side of the hall, engaged in a fierce conversation with an older gentleman. The woman probably wouldn't be paying attention to Jackson or Samantha anytime soon.

Luke shifted his gaze back to the rotund man earnestly yammering about beds and quilts for the hospital. "If you'll excuse me, sir. There's a matter I must see to."

The man's mouth dropped slightly. "Yes, well, can we look forward to that donation, then?"

"I'll speak with my lawyer." Luke dipped his head and scooted toward the door, their shirts brushing as he squeezed past. He didn't glance back at the girl in yellow, but another mother waiting with a different young lady gave him a furious glare.

Reaching Jackson and Sam, he grabbed Jackson's shoulder and jerked the younger man backward. The city boy landed against his chest with an *umph.* "You best step back from my sister. Or you'll not be seeing the likes of her again."

"Yes, sir," Jackson squeaked.

Samantha scowled at him. "Let him go, Luke. He wasn't doing anything wrong."

"He doesn't need to stand so close." Luke let go of the slippery accountant, and with another three steps, he burst through the doors and into the yard. Muted voices from inside floated to his ears, horses clomped past on the road and an electric railcar clunked along the street. No one else appeared on the patio, but he stood awful close to the banquet room. Anyone who stepped outside could see him, and one of those calculating mothers was sure to send her daughter out. He ducked around the far side of the hotel, where shadows shrouded the ground.

A gate or wall of some sort blocked the far end of the pathway leading to the street. Probably a wise decision on the hotel's part. One too many men had likely gotten bored with a fancy to-do and escaped thataway. Hang it all, *he* would escape if he didn't have two women to escort home.

He leaned against the brick and inhaled the thick city air, not nearly as stale as the air inside that banquet hall, but a far cry from the clean air of home. At least he had a break from all the badgering. How many young women could a man be expected to meet in one night? He didn't remember what half the ladies looked like, let alone their names.

And he wouldn't go back inside until he figured out some way to stop the constant requests for donations. Maybe he could be generous with some of his money before he returned to Wyoming—Grandfather had evidently been so—but a man needed a chance to breathe, didn't he?

A door thudded and footsteps clattered against the stone pavers.

"Don't be infantile. You know we must have the money back."

Luke grimaced. Probably time to show himself and get back to the banquet.

"You simply can't revoke the funding from the school. Half of it's already spent."

The steely voice laced with sugar stopped him. Was Miss Wells out here? Alone with a man?

"Well then, unspend it." Frustration grew in the older masculine voice.

Luke rubbed his chin. He should make himself known. But wouldn't it look strange, him appearing from the side of the building with no good reason for being there? Still, whatever was going on between Miss Wells and the other man wasn't his business.

He shifted farther down the wall. Maybe he could hop over that gate near the street, then make his way back to the banquet through the front of the building.

Crack. A snapping sound reverberated against the brick building. He'd stepped on a twig. Now the arguing voices would come around the hotel and spot him plain as day. Then he'd have a heap of explaining to do.

Except they kept right on talking. He raked his hand through his hair and slumped against the wall. Did more twigs litter the ground? Maybe there was an old can he might kick? Anything else that would draw attention his way? Looked like he'd gotten himself good and stuck.

"It's public money, already approved and given to Hayes Academy. How are we to give the money back?"

"Cancel whatever you ordered with it," the male voice blundered. "Surely you understand why this must be done. Your father's in a precarious political situation, and those newspaper articles have made the academy widely unpopular. If the public were to find out the school received state funds, your father's reputation might not recover. We need the money returned by the end of next week. Your brother understood perfectly when I explained the situation to him yesterday."

Luke held his breath. Miss Wells's *father* was taking money away from the school? What kind of father took money away from his daughter because of some embittered newspaper article? If Sam needed a large amount of money for building a house in Wyoming or saving her husband's ranch or some other cause, he'd give her the funds in an instant. Of course, she would have to be home where she belonged before he gifted her any such thing, but still, he'd never be able to hand her money one day and take it back the next.

"My brother doesn't care about the academy," Miss Wells's voice quivered, whether from rage or tears, he couldn't tell. "The school's no more than a nuisance to him. Besides what will you do with the money after we return it?"

"As a matter of fact—"

"No, just leave. I don't want to know what frivolous things it'll be wasted on."

"It won't be wasted."

"It's not being wasted now."

"There are differing opinions on that."

"Yes, I see there are. Good night, Edward."

Elizabeth pressed her back to the cold brick wall and stared up at the sky, vast and dark with only a handful of bright stars shining down. The chilly night air wrapped around her, causing gooseflesh to rise on her arms, but she couldn't seek the warmth inside. Not when curious eyes and wagging tongues filled the banquet room.

Dreams were a bit like stars, weren't they? Most swallowed up by the city lights, and only a few so bright they shined through all the busyness trying to snuff them out. She'd once thought her dreams were brilliant enough to sparkle on their own—graduate from college, get a teaching job, train young women. But even after achieving so much, her dreams risked falling pale and dry to the ground. Father remained too busy to know she had dreams, Mother wanted her married despite her dreams and Jackson smiled and promised to help with her dreams, then ended up doing nothing at all.

She'd thought she'd been following God, pleasing Him in some way by refusing to marry a man like her ex-fiancé and then training to be a teacher. She'd thought she'd be helping young women not too different from herself when she'd gotten her teaching position at Hayes. She'd thought she'd been helping the academy when she'd written that editorial about female education. But somewhere along the way, she'd ceased helping anyone and started causing trouble. When had she strayed from the path God intended for her?

Father, what have I done? She sunk her head into her hands, a foolish move, since the jostle to her precariously positioned coiffure sent the side of her hair cascading down. Lovely. Just lovely. Now when she appeared back inside, the people present would think she'd been in the yard with a man.

She felt about for the loosened pins still stuck in her tresses. She could probably shove her hair back atop her head and arrange it in a manner that wouldn't attract too much attention.

If only fixing her other problems was as easy as jamming pins into her hair. Maybe she should stop fighting for the academy and tell the board she would abide by their decision if they closed the school. Tell Mother she'd attend that dinner next Saturday and meet whatever gentlemen had been invited. Tell her students they couldn't return after the semester break because no one cared enough to defend the school they attended.

"Miss Wells?"

The unfamiliar masculine voice sent a chill down her spine. She looked toward the patio doors. A tall figure in a painfully crisp suit approached, his dark hair gleaming in the lamplight though his face remained shadowed. She took a sudden step back.

"May I help you?" The night seemed to swallow her words, leaving only emptiness around them.

"You most certainly may. I'm Reginald Higsley from the Albany *Morning Times*."

He didn't need to say where he worked. His name had imprinted itself on her mind, when it first appeared beneath the headline of that wretched newspaper article.

"Why are you here, sir?" *Outside? Alone with me?* Though her stomach twisted, she raised her chin. "At an event to which you weren't invited?"

"I was indeed invited. Your father asked me to attend."

Betrayal blazed through her gut. Of course Father

would invite the reporter and try to schmooze good publicity from him.

"I've hoped for a word with you all evening." He moved close, so close the sleeve of his coat brushed her gloved arms and the soft puff of his breath on the chilled air floated into her face.

She took another step back, bumping the wall. "Would you like a statement, then, for the paper?" She cringed at the quiver in her voice. "Perhaps next week you're going to run an article on the importance of educating young women rather than the dangers of it?"

His mouth curved up into a shadowed smile. "Yes, I suppose you could say that."

"Very well, then. I believe the importance of educating women cannot be ignored despite the current economy. Young women are not to blame for the panic or the recession. Why should they be the first to suffer?"

"So you feel women should be educated at all costs, even at the expense of feeding hungry children?"

She ground her teeth together. This was why she hated reporters. "I think both causes are important, and one shouldn't be sacrificed for the other."

"So you would starve children if it allows you to keep teaching trigonometry?"

Advanced algebra. First her mother tried fixing her up with Luke Hayes, then her father revoked the funding from Hayes Academy, and if that wasn't enough, now this polished reporter was twisting her words. It was enough to drive even the most sane of people mad. "I didn't say that. But how like a reporter. You ask questions fifteen different ways until you get an answer you half like. Then you go on your merry way and make up false quotations for all the world to read the next day."

And she'd just ruined any hope of Mr. Higsley's next

article repairing the damage from the last one. Oh, why couldn't she keep better control of her tongue? It was like she had a little monster inside her mouth, popping out and saying whatever it willed at the worst times.

"I don't appreciate being called a liar." The man loomed over her, barely contained fury radiating from beneath the lines of his stiff suit.

She shrank back against the wall. Yes, she should cut out her tongue for all the trouble it got her into. Tongues were such a useless part of one's anatomy, anyway. One didn't need them for practical things like quadratic equations or theorems or integration.

Except one could use a tongue to scream when in danger. A sure benefit in her current situation. But if she cried out now and someone came, everyone would see she'd been outside with a man. And with her hair in such a state of disarray, it would appear that…that…

Well, the incident would get her fired.

"Tell me, Miss Wells." Mr. Higsley placed one arm on either side of her, trapping her against the cold bricks. "Does it feel good knowing that students at your extravagant academy continue their education in luxury while most young women their age work ten-hour days to bring bread home for their families?"

"Leave the lady alone."

The reporter jerked back as though stung.

Elizabeth felt more than saw Mr. Hayes approach from the far side of the building. Trembling, she blew out the air in her lungs and took a hesitant step away from Mr. Higsley, only to have her next breath clog in her throat. Had Mr. Hayes been there this whole time? Listening around the side of the building?

But then, perhaps his eavesdropping wasn't so terrible.

At least he wouldn't assume she'd set up a secret rendezvous with the reporter.

Mr. Hayes stopped beside her, his gaze narrowed on the reporter. "Why don't you take yourself back to whatever hole you climbed out of. The lady's spent enough time with you."

Mr. Higsley extended his hand. "I'm Reginald Higsley, sir. And I'm afraid this situation is not as it appears. You see, I'm a reporter for the Albany *Morning Times,* and I just stepped outside to get a—"

"You could be President Cleveland for all I care. If the lady asks you to leave, you leave."

"I'm sorry, sir, but I didn't catch your name." The reporter's voice turned icy.

"Because I didn't give it. Now go." The growl in Mr. Hayes's voice must have convinced the other man to obey, because he departed.

"Are you all right? Did the scoundrel hurt…?"

Luke's words fell away as he turned to face Miss Wells. He'd thought her beautiful before. She *had* been beautiful before, in that midnight-blue gown that reminded him of the sky just after sunset and with her hair swept up into that mass of fat curls. But now half of those thick mahogany locks fell about her shoulders and shimmered under the lighting.

She wasn't simply beautiful, she was magnificent. Beyond magnificent. Luke edged closer, compelled partly by a desire to ensure she was safe and partly by some invisible pull he didn't understand.

He should be drawn and quartered for leaving her unprotected with that man for so long. But she didn't seem harmed. Her body didn't tremble nor did tears streak her cheeks. If anything she seemed more courageous than before.

"No. I'm not hurt, and I can explain," she answered, but she refused to meet his eyes.

"Go on, then." His fingers itched to slide up into those burnished mahogany tresses. Surely they couldn't feel as soft as they looked. He crossed his arms solidly in front of his chest—a good way to make his hands stay put.

She began to babble then, a torrent of words about not doing anything untoward with the reporter, and being upset earlier and grabbing her hair, at which time half of it fell down. Then she claimed if he just went back inside, she'd take a few minutes to set herself to rights, and they could leave for home.

Her brain had plumb run off and deserted her body, if she thought he'd leave her alone again. After he'd overheard her conversation about the money for the academy, he peeked around the side of the building to find Miss Wells still outside, clearly distressed. Then he'd wandered over to the gate near the street to try getting out somehow. A crying woman hardly needed to know that a man she despised had witnessed her being humiliated.

But the exit had been shut up tight, with no way to break the lock, short of putting a bullet in the thing. And since he didn't rightly want to climb the fence and mess up his fancy getup, he waited awhile, figuring to give Miss Wells some time to herself. He hadn't thought some brute might approach her.

"So if you please, Mr. Hayes?"

If he please what? Had she asked him something?

"I only need a moment of privacy."

Oh, so they were back to him leaving again. "Not likely."

She took a step away from the wall, maybe to chase

him off, maybe to head somewhere herself, but the bricks at the back of her head must have pulled something loose in her up-do. The moment she moved forward, the rest of her hair tumbled down, a waterfall of velvet glinting traces of red and brown where the lights touched it.

She gasped, the quiet sound clambering through his head as though she'd screamed, and she started sifting through the heavy locks. "Oh, I've done it now. I'll never be able to get this back up. I'm terrible at putting it into anything but a twist, you see. This is why most women who attend such events have maids. To pin up their hair properly, so it doesn't fall at the slightest bump. But I simply must become a better hairdresser, living on my own as I do." She sank to the ground, her hands still moving frantically about.

"What are you doing?"

She glanced up. "Searching for pins, of course."

Searching for pins. She'd just been told her father was taking back money from her beloved school, then a reporter nearly accosted her, and she became upset over her hair?

Most times women made little sense, but at moments such as this, they made no sense at all. He hunkered down to help anyway.

"The things are impossible to find in the dark." Her hand brushed his, slender and warm even through her glove, then went about searching the ground. "And I can't go back into the hall with my hair like this. Everyone will assume your hands have been in it, or worse, and—"

She stopped and stared at him, then pressed a hand over her mouth, her eyes rounding. "Oh, no. I didn't mean it like that. Forgive my tongue. It gets carried away far too often."

"Calm down." He laid a hand over hers. "If you can't

go back through the banquet hall, we'll go 'round the side of the building and have the carriage brought out." He'd find some way to break the lock on that gate if it meant saving the woman from rumors. Then again, maybe there wasn't a gate on the other side of the building.

"Oh." She breathed the word like a sigh. "I hadn't thought of that."

He would have released her hand and drawn back, but she held him with her eyes, those wide, vulnerable orbs shimmering with a tearless pain that pulled words from him before he even realized he'd opened his mouth to speak. "I'm sorry about your evening—the money, the reporter, the whole lot of it."

Her face hovered so close to his that her breath warmed his neck. His gaze drifted to her lips, full and dark in the night. They'd taste as sweet as that fruit-and-sugar voice of hers. He'd give up his Colt .45 and saddle if he was wrong.

The breeze stirred, and a strand of hair fanned across her cheek. He swept it away and anchored it behind her ear, then let his fingers linger at the tender spot behind her earlobe. Did she know how beautiful she looked in that dress? Bathed in moonlight? With her hair falling to her waist?

Her jaw trembled slightly. Would she tremble more if he pressed his lips to hers?

"Mr. Hayes."

Her whisper, soft as it was, slapped him. He pulled back and dropped his hands. Here he thought about kissing the woman senseless, and she called him Mr. Hayes.

"It's Luke," he said, his voice rough as gravel. "And we best be going." Because if he stayed here any longer with her, he was going to kiss her—the woman who didn't want to let Sam come home and lectured him for wearing his gun.

Yep, that would have been a disaster, all right. He stood and extended his hand. "Let's get you to the carriage, then I'll go hunt up Sam and Jackson."

She hesitated for the briefest second, something unreadable flashing across her eyes, before she placed her gloved hand in his.

Confound it, did that have to be small and delicate, too? Couldn't the Good Lord have made some part of the woman undesirable? Blessed her with a big nose or unseemly freckles? Carrot-orange hair or a laugh that sounded like a pig snort?

He swallowed and helped her up, brushing his thumb over the top of her knuckles. Shafts of silvery moonlight filtered through the sporadic clouds above, illuminating the gentle curve of her pink cheek, the fragile column of her creamy neck, the spilling waves of her mahogany hair.

Disaster. Kissing her would be a disaster. He'd just keep repeating it until he and the woman were safely surrounded by a slew of other folk, and he forgot all about his urge to kiss her.

Because he would forget—he hoped.

"Come on," he said a bit too roughly and pulled her forward. She followed silently, her dress swishing softly over pavers, then grass, as they rounded the far side of the building.

He led her down the narrow dirt path between the Kenmore and a similarly massive structure. Darkness shrouded the walkway, and moonlight barely slanted through the small space above. But streetlights illuminated the far end of the path, a good sign there wasn't a locked gate before them.

A gasp. A rustle up ahead. He quickened his pace, tugging Miss Wells behind him. Through the shadows, a silhouette of two lovers locked in a passionate kiss emerged.

Getting around them in this confined space would be interesting, if not embarrassing.

A breathy sigh filled the air, and the man pressed the woman's back against the building while her hands clutched at his hair. Heat stole across the back of Luke's neck.

He shifted farther in front of Miss Wells, hopefully blocking her view of the careless couple. Then falling gold curls caught the dim light, and fury rushed his blood, a swelling tide he'd no desire to stop. He dropped Miss Wells's hand, strode forward and heaved Jackson back by the collar.

Jackson gagged, the sound similar to the noise a man made as a noose tightened about his neck. Luke jerked the fabric harder, and Jackson gagged again, his hands flying up to loosen his shirt. Well, the man deserved to choke for a bit after touching his sister.

"Jackson?" Miss Wells gasped.

"Luke!" Samantha cried.

He didn't glance at either woman but leaned his head close to Jackson's ear. "Don't you *ever* touch her again. Don't you *ever* come calling again. And don't you *ever* try contacting her again."

He released Jackson's shirt enough so the man could suck air. "Say 'Yes, sir.'"

"Luke, stop. You're hurting him." Samantha rushed forward and gripped his arm, trying to yank it away from Jackson.

"Luke, please release my brother and let's discuss this." Miss Wells, ever calm, appeared behind Samantha.

"He was touching Sam." Maybe the boy didn't deserve to die, but so help him, Jackson Wells wouldn't touch his baby sister again.

He finally let go of Jackson. The other man stumbled forward, and Samantha rushed to his side.

"I love her." Determination carried on Jackson's voice.

Luke stared into Jackson's eyes, his stomach sinking. Not his baby sister. She wasn't old enough to be loved by a city slicker like Jackson Wells. She was just a girl at heart, a beautiful girl caught in a woman's body. Not big enough to be kissed that way, touched that way. "If you loved her, then you wouldn't take advantage of her."

"I wasn't taking advantage. It was merely a kiss."

"It was more than a kiss."

"Luke, I'm sorry. We didn't mean to. We just…got caught up." Samantha tucked herself beneath Jackson's arm.

Did she fancy herself in love with Jackson, too? Luke closed his eyes as tiredness flooded him. *Please, Father, no. How will I ever get her to come home if she's moonstruck?* "Say goodbye and get to the carriage." His voice, soft but firm, carried through the air. "You'll not be seeing him again."

"No, wait. You can't do that. I said I was sorry." Samantha wound her arms about Jackson's waist, and Jackson settled his hands around Samantha's back in return.

Luke raked a hand through his hair. How had he gotten into this mess?

"Jackson, obey Mr. Hayes. You were wrong in kissing Samantha like that. Even if you do love her," Elizabeth stated from beside him.

But Jackson didn't obey, and why should he? The way he and Sam had wrapped themselves around each other, nothing short of an army could pry them apart.

Luke could still hear Samantha's gasp echo between the buildings, still see the way her hands dove into Jackson's hair. She had no business kissing a man like that until after she was married. "Jackson, we'll discuss this further on Monday. How convenient we already have an appointment scheduled. And, Samantha, if seeing him meant so much to you, you'd not have kissed him."

"Oh, like you've never kissed a woman before," Sam shot back. "Or maybe you've forgotten about the time I found you and Mary Baker behind the barn."

"Jackson was devouring you." Luke thrust his hand toward the spot where he'd found them against the wall. "That was a heap more than some stolen kiss behind a barn."

"You've still got no right to keep us apart."

"Watch me." Luke rubbed the back of his neck. Where was his sister's guilt? Or Jackson's? Oh, Sam had apologized, but more because she'd been caught than because she felt she'd done wrong, and now she stood defending herself. Had Samantha and Jackson done this before? Exactly how familiar were they with each other?

"Samantha, go to the carriage." Miss Wells's firm voice stole over them.

"Tell my brother, Miss Wells, tell him he's being unreasonable."

Miss Wells edged forward and laid a gentle hand on Samantha's upper arm. "It's best you and your brother discuss this tomorrow, when you've both calmed down."

"But what about Jackson?" Sam's words tumbled out, caught somewhere between a sob and a whine.

"Jackson's a grown man, accountable for his own actions. You, on the other hand, are still under your brother's protection."

Sam glared at Miss Wells, but the look mellowed into calculation as she swept her eyes over the teacher's hair. "And what, dear brother, were you doing between these buildings with Miss Wells?"

"I'm wondering the same thing." Jackson scowled at Miss Wells.

"That's not your business." Luke crossed his arms. No need for Samantha and Jackson to know what type of evening Miss Wells had.

"No?" Jackson asked in a deceptively quiet tone. "It appears Samantha and I are getting into trouble for the very thing you were doing with my sister."

"I didn't…" *Touch her.* Except he had. Not in the way Samantha and Jackson implied, but he'd held her hand, stroked behind her ear, almost kissed her. *Almost.* "…do anything inappropriate." The words sounded pathetic even to him.

"Elizabeth?" Jackson watched his sister like a wolf watching a deer before it pounces.

"She looks as though you mauled her." Samantha slapped her hands on her hips and tapped her shoe impatiently on the ground.

Luke rolled his eyes. Where had his sweet, innocent sister gone? The woman who stood before him couldn't possibly be the same girl he'd taken to the train station three years ago. "Get to the carriage, Sam. Jackson, hire a hansom cab to take you home. I'll see your sister back to Valley Falls."

"I'm not going anywhere," Samantha declared. "And I won't let you stand there and berate me for kissing the man I love while you were trysting with a woman you haven't known for more than a day."

The man she loved. The words packed a wallop to his gut.

"Samantha!" Shock seared Miss Wells's voice. Whether because of Sam's accusations or her attitude, he couldn't tell. "You mustn't blame your brother. It's my fault. I got myself into some trouble, and then I accidentally knocked my hair askew when I put my head in my hands."

Luke took a step toward Miss Wells. "You don't owe—"

"Your brother came to my aid," she continued. "Yes, my hair is down, but if not for your brother stepping in, I may well look worse."

"Are you all right, Elizabeth?" The words were appropriate, but doubt tinged Jackson's voice. Instead of going to his sister's side, Jackson wrapped his arm tighter about Samantha's shoulders. He didn't ask why her head had been in her hands or if anyone had tried to hurt her, didn't even sound like he believed her.

Miss Wells raised her chin a notch, masking whatever she felt beneath that polished veneer of calm. "Thank you, I'm fine."

So she claimed. But she swallowed as she stood there. So still, so alone, his arm ached to reach out and pull her against him.

A bad idea to begin with, and definitely not something to attempt with Jackson and Samantha around. Still... couldn't Sam hug the woman or something? Then she wouldn't seem so abandoned.

"Right." Sam's gaze darted between Miss Wells and him, and the hairs on the back of his neck prickled.

Samantha and Jackson were in the wrong, not Miss Wells and him. And he wasn't about to stand around while someone else threw accusations at the poor teacher. "We're leaving, Samantha. Now." He pointed toward the front of the building, then turned to Jackson. "You'd best say goodbye. You won't be seeing my sister for a while."

The finality in his voice must have resonated with Jackson, because the younger man reached up, touched the side of Sam's face, and whispered against her ear.

Luke scowled. Something still told him this was the

first time Sam had been caught, not the first time Jackson had kissed her that way. But as he took Samantha's shoulders and steered her toward the street, he couldn't block the sound of her quiet sobs.

Chapter Eight

"How could you?"

Samantha's whimpers floated from the opposite side of the carriage. Elizabeth shifted uncomfortably and glanced out the window while the conveyance rocked and swayed toward Valley Falls.

"I love you, Sam." Tenderness filled Mr. Hayes's—she couldn't bring herself to call a man she'd known for so little time by his first name, even if he'd asked her to—voice. "I'm trying to protect you."

Indeed he was. After sneaking off with Samantha and kissing her that way, Jackson deserved a belt to his backside.

"I don't want your protection." Tears, rather than venom, choked Samantha's voice.

Through the darkness shrouding the opposite side of the carriage, Elizabeth made out the combined silhouette of the two siblings: Mr. Hayes holding Samantha on his lap and the girl crying into his chest.

The moment seemed oddly tender, and something she'd no business witnessing.

"I'm your brother. I can't just stop protecting you or caring about you."

"But I love him."

"I'm sure you love him, Samantha. But you're only seventeen," Elizabeth said, then licked her lips. The same age she'd been when she had fancied herself in love with David. "You've much to learn yet."

"You don't understand." Samantha sniffled. "Neither of you do. You've never been in love."

Elizabeth's heart twisted. If only she didn't understand. If only she'd never been in love. "Perhaps so. But your brother is simply trying to help."

"If he wanted to help, then he'd let me see Jackson rather than tear the two of us apart."

"Samantha, it's not like that," Mr. Hayes rasped, his voice a mixture of tiredness and frustration.

Fabric shifted across the carriage, likely Samantha moving away from her brother, and Elizabeth sighed. The girl didn't realize how blessed she was to have a brother willing to protect her from ill-intentioned suitors. If her own family had been half as concerned about her as Mr. Hayes was about Samantha, then breaking off her engagement with David all those years ago might have worked out better. Namely, her family wouldn't still think her a villain for her decision.

Instead, she'd had to fight her family to get away from David, rather than fight to be near him.

"Do you mind?" Mr. Hayes appeared from the shadows and settled onto the seat beside her. "I'm not exactly welcome on the other side of the carriage at the moment."

His presence seemed to fill the entire bench, which was ridiculous, as he only took up 33 percent of the black leather seat. Though it seemed like more with the way the mixture of grass and sunshine and subtle cologne filled the air.

Elizabeth shivered. Because of the draft creeping in

from under the carriage door. Not because Mr. Hayes shifted subtly closer. Not because he watched her with those piercing eyes. Not because he smelled so good she wanted to lean toward him.

"Why don't you tell me what's putting those worried lines around your mouth and eyes?" He spoke gently, that deep, rusted voice full of concern.

The carriage rocked and bumped—common, lulling movements—and somewhere outside coyotes yipped. Across the conveyance, deep, rhythmic breathing had replaced Samantha's soft sobs.

Elizabeth picked at a speck on her dress, unwilling to meet his eyes. "It was a long night."

"Because you learned your father's revoking public funding from the academy?"

"You overheard."

"Not intentionally."

Embarrassment flooded her anyway. "Yes, in part because of Father, but even more so because of that reporter." She folded and unfolded her hands in her lap. "You see, with the panic last spring and now the recession, enrollment at the academy is down, and—"

"My lawyer explained the situation. Why do you think I asked for your ledgers?"

"I'm afraid you still don't understand. The reason I didn't want to give you my ledgers…that is, well…a lot of donors have pulled their funding from the school… like, like my father." She could barely force the last words over her tongue. Maybe if she said it over and over in her head, it wouldn't be so hard to speak it aloud. *My father revoked our funding. My father revoked our funding. My father revoked our—*

"Your father shouldn't have pulled your funding."

She stared at him. "I beg your pardon?"

"I said your father shouldn't have pulled money out from under you."

"Why would you be bothered by such a thing, when you're taking your sister out of school without so much as a thought about her desires?"

"Because no father should deal with his daughter like that."

Her lungs suddenly stopped drawing air. Was he defending her? This man who'd come into town with a will of iron and a desire to make everyone bend to his wishes?

"It's cruel enough to give you something and then ask for it back. But the old man didn't even tell you himself. He sent his little minion to do it." Resentment dripped from Mr. Hayes's voice. "Then that reporter appeared, and where was your father? Or your brother? Not keeping an eye on you. Not making sure you were safe. Your brother wasn't even concerned you may have been hurt. Instead, the scoundrel thought I'd taken your hair down and refused to listen when you tried to tell him otherwise. No person should suffer that kind of treatment from family."

Something thick rose in her throat, and she looked down toward her feet. Surely her family didn't treat her as poorly as he made it sound. They were just caught up in their own lives and wanted her to support their endeavors rather than her own.

So how should she answer Mr. Hayes? Say she was used to it, that they'd treated her this way since she had called off her engagement? "Thank you for your concern. But I'm a spinster. It's ridiculous to expect my father or brother to watch me as though I were a debutante."

"I wouldn't have figured you for a spinster." He shifted forward and moved a strand of hair from her face. Then he trailed his fingers beneath her jaw and tilted up her chin.

Her skin burned beneath his touch, tiny agonizing fires

that paralyzed her, despite her mind screaming to slap him
or push him away.

"Well, I am." And being one was better than being a
wife to the wrong man.

"You don't want a husband? Children? A family?"

She used to. And maybe somewhere deep inside, she
still did. She'd had numerous opportunities to marry, good
men whose faces lit up like the sun when she'd walked into
the room. But no matter how kind or interested a gentleman might seem, her experience with David had taught
her that she wouldn't be able to keep him happy. The man
would probably be content with her for a year or so, then
lose interest. After all, David hadn't been engaged to her
half a year, and he'd found himself a mistress. "No. I'm
quite comfortable remaining a spinster. Thank you."

Mr. Hayes released her jaw, though the pressure of his
fingers against her skin still lingered. "Why? You're still
young enough to have a gaggle of little ones."

She looked away. Of all the things to discuss, why her
spinsterhood? "My marital status isn't your concern."

"Is it teaching, then? Does that mean so much you'd
give up a family?"

The inside of her mouth turned painfully dry. The man
didn't understand. Teaching was all she had, her only escape from life with an unfaithful husband. And if the academy closed, she would lose the little security she'd found.
"We've discussed enough about me. Now what about you?
Tell me what you'll do with your vast inheritance. Obvi-
ously you're not planning to give to charities or to further educational opportunities, like your grandfather did."

"Sell what I can and go back home."

He said it so simply, as though he was discussing the
dinner menu or the weather rather than his grandfather's
life work. "All of it? Even the companies and estate? You

could keep something in your name for an investment, at minimum."

"Every bit and as quick as I can."

"Oh, that's noble. What happens when you get home? Do you sit around on your pile of money and congratulate yourself on a job well done? You sold a man's life work in record time. What a hero you are."

"I wouldn't expect you to understand."

"No. Rest assured I don't. You're planning to yank your sister away from her dream and run back home when you have opportunity to do so much good here. Did you know Samantha wants to study architecture?"

"Yes, and it's ridiculous."

Rage burned under her skin, flushing from the tips of her toes up to her hairline. How dare he say such a thing and of his sister, no less. "Why, because she's a woman? A woman can study architecture as well as any man."

"I'm sure a woman can. And let's say for just a moment that you're right. Let's say that Sam doesn't go home, where she belongs, and goes off to college instead. What happens after college? Does she graduate and get a job? As an architect? No architectural firm is going to hire a woman. And even if she does get hired, how would she deal with the builders? You think a crew of men is going to listen to her when she tells them they have the wrong dimensions for a parlor, or that they need to frame a doorway at a different angle?"

Elizabeth swallowed. He had a point, of course. Most of society would agree that architecture was hardly an acceptable field of work for women. Women could do things like nurse and teach, but becoming something like an architect or lawyer was a bit different. Still, Samantha shouldn't have to give up her dream so easily. The goal she'd set for herself would be difficult to achieve but not impossible. "Louise Blanchard Bethune is a professional architect. She even lives in the state."

"A woman as a professional architect?" Mr. Hayes snorted. "She probably runs an architectural firm with her father or brother."

"Husband. But that doesn't mean she couldn't run one on her own."

Mr. Hayes gripped her wrist, his fingers closing around her skin until she brought her eyes up to meet his. "It does, Miss Wells. No businessman in need of architectural work is going to hire a woman for such a thing."

"So, because of that, what some man might tell your sister in the future, you'll deny Samantha the chance to be an architect? She could end up like Louise Bethune. Even if Bethune works with her husband, she's still doing the thing she loves. It's wrong for you to steal such a dream away from your sister and force her back home."

He released her wrist. "I don't have a choice."

"But you do."

The muscle in his jaw clenched and unclenched. "No. I don't."

The man was three sides of stubborn and an oaf on top of it. "How can you say that?"

"It's not just about me or Sam. It's about my ma…" His eyes dipped down to his boots, nearly shrouded in the darkness. "She has consumption."

Consumption. The word echoed through the dark carriage, the heaviness behind it seeming to drain the very life from Mr. Hayes.

"If Sam's going to see Ma before she dies, Sam's got to get home soon."

Elizabeth drew in a long, slow breath. She'd assumed the man beside her was being selfish in demanding his sister return to Wyoming. She hadn't thought, hadn't expected, hadn't dreamed something so serious drove him.

"I—I'm sorry." The words sounded inane. A paltry offering that couldn't begin to make up for the grief Mr. Hayes must be feeling—or the pain Samantha would feel once she found out.

"Yeah, me, too."

Elizabeth glanced at the other side of the carriage, where Samantha's breathing had grown deep and even with sleep. "She must have no idea. You clearly haven't told her yet, or she'd be packing her bags and heading West on the next train."

Mr. Hayes's hand clenched around her arm again, squeezing so tightly her hand grew pale and cold. "I can't tell her and neither can you. My ma and I aren't fools, Miss Wells. We read Sam's letters and know she likes her schooling. Neither of us wants to take her away from something she loves. That's why Ma made me promise."

Promise? What kind of promise could he be talking about? Likely not a good one if it prevented Samantha from finding out about her mother. "What did you promise?"

"Not to tell Sam about the illness. The doc says Ma's got a year to live. She's ailing faster than that. Everyone can see it. Pa, me, any of our friends, but she's gone and convinced herself she has plenty of time, so Sam doesn't need to come home until she graduates. Then she thinks Sam will spend the summer with her before she passes.... But she won't last until summer."

Elizabeth clasped her hands together on her lap and glanced down. His mother was dying, and he and his sister were stuck two thousand miles away. What must that feel like? For all the antics she put up with from her own mother, she'd be devastated were her mother to become seriously ill. "So instead of telling her about your mother, you're not giving her any choice in leaving."

"Yes."

The clomp of the horse's feet and rumble of the carriage wheels grew louder as the carriage moved from the dirt road onto the cobbled streets of Valley Falls. A few more moments, and she would be home, the conversation finished whether she'd spoken her piece or not.

The soft moonlight filtering through the window cast Mr. Hayes's hair and eyelashes in a silvery glow, outlining half of that strong, handsome face while leaving the other in shadows.

She understood him now, at least partly. It made sense that this man would storm into Hayes Academy and announce his sister had to leave, made sense that he'd want to sell everything and get back to his mother's bedside as quickly as possible. She'd do the same in that situation. And yet, Samantha was trapped between his desires and his mother's wishes, and all the answers she needed were being withheld. "You need to tell your sister anyway. She deserves a chance to decide for herself what she's going to do."

"No man with any bit of character can just up and break a promise like the one I made to Ma."

"Then maybe you shouldn't have made the promise in the first place."

"You try telling the woman who raised you no, while she's lying on her bed coughing up blood."

The carriage rolled to a stop in front of her house, and Elizabeth took her reticule and stood as the coachman opened the door. "If you don't tell Samantha, you'll end up breaking her heart in a worse way than Jackson ever could."

His eyes widened even as his jaw took on that famil-

iar, determined set. She turned and stepped down from
the carriage before he could think of something else to
say, because in the end, her words would turn out true.
He knew it. She knew it. And even his mother, sick and
dying back in Wyoming, had to know it.

Luke's boots sank into the plush carpet as he carried
Samantha across the floor and laid her on her bed. Lavender and lace decorated the room, from her bed to her curtains to the wallpaper. Girlish colors in a childish room. He
swiped a hand over his eyes, trying to dispel the image of
Sam kissing Jackson, but it clung to his mind like a wood
tick on a buffalo.

Sam's dress rustled as she curled on her side without
waking. Lamplight spilled off the silvery-blue material,
making it glisten in the half-lit room. He should probably
rouse a servant to help her change. But she looked so rest-
ful he could hardly wake her.

Her face lay peacefully against a white, flowery pillow. Tears had streaked the black around her eyes and the
pink smudged onto her cheeks. He rolled his shoulders and
took a clean handkerchief from his pocket to dab her face.

The girl was too young for makeup, and too young to be
kissing Jackson. She'd looked like a gullible child beside
the accountant. But society deemed her old enough to attend the banquet, old enough to find a husband, old enough
to graduate from school. And she seemed so grown-up in
that confounded dress, such a mixture of girl and woman
he hardly knew what to do with her.

She wasn't supposed to start crying when he protected
her from a man. Wasn't supposed to claim she loved the
scoundrel. And she wasn't supposed to come out East and
make plans for her life that didn't include her family. She
should chafe for home at that ridiculous academy, not want

to graduate. Not think about going to college or becoming an architect. Luke raked a hand through her hair. He didn't want to crush her dreams or the life she'd built in Valley Falls, but to protect her. If her dreams were doomed to fail, then wouldn't she be better off back home, with her family looking out for her? Wouldn't she be happier in Wyoming, the place where she belonged and where she'd have time to spend with Ma before it was too late?

Maybe Miss Wells was right, and he should tell Samantha about Ma's consumption, regardless of the promise he made. But that felt wrong somehow. He'd only been in Valley Falls for a day and a half, and he needed to try to honor his promise for more than two days.

But would anything short of the truth draw his sister away from here?

I love you, Jackson. The scene beside the Kenmore flashed across his mind once again. The tremble in Sam's voice. The tears in her eyes. Getting her away from Jackson Wells was going to be harder than starting a campfire during a rainstorm, especially with her accusing him of being so unreasonable. It was *not* unreasonable to protect his sister from a wily city slicker. Why couldn't she see that?

Then again, him pulling her out of school with little explanation probably had something to do with her anger.

What if he went ahead and made that donation to the academy? That might temper Sam some, at least convince her that he didn't hate her school and wanted the best for her.

An image of Miss Wells rose in his mind. Her eyes soft and vulnerable as she explained that her father had pulled state funding away from her school. No, it couldn't hurt to make the donation.

And what was he thinking? He was *not* going to pledge

away two thousand dollars of his grandfather's money just because a pretty teacher had gotten misty eyed with him. Something was happening to his brain. He'd been clearheaded and competent enough to run a ranch for the past decade, but put him around Miss Wells, and his mind suddenly turned to mush.

He rose and left the room, taking the stairs down to the grand hall two at a time. "Stevens!" He'd consider giving money to the academy, but he'd do so based on sound logic—and the possibility of it helping his relationship with Sam—not because of a pretty mathematics teacher.

And before he gave a dime, he was going to learn everything he could about the woman asking for the money. He walked into the drawing room and blinked against the bright lights glinting off the gold and white furnishings.

"You called, sir?" Stevens appeared in the doorway.

"What do you know of Miss Wells?"

"Miss Wells? The mathematics teacher and daughter of Assemblyman Wells?"

"That's the one." Luke leaned back against the wall and crossed his arms.

Stevens pursed his lips together and paused, as if trying to reach into the back drawer of his mind for information. "She thinks rather highly of female education, and went off to college instead of marrying her intended several years ago."

"She had an intended?" His pulse accelerated. He'd been daft not to see it sooner. With her family and looks, the woman had probably been offered more proposals than there were men in the Teton Valley.

"Yes, sir, one of the most acclaimed men of Albany. He's in Washington, D.C., now. A congressman."

"How convenient for her father." He could imagine it all too clearly, Miss Wells in a shimmering silk gown like tonight, her hand tucked gently into the arm of her politician husband as he smiled and schmoozed and cajoled. And after growing up in a politician's home, Miss Wells was surely practiced at playing the perfect role of supportive female. Yes, on the surface, she would make a fine politician's wife. "Why didn't they marry?"

Stevens kept his face set in austere lines. "It's not my business to speak of it. Perhaps you should make your inquiry to Miss Wells herself."

A servant that didn't like gossip. Just his luck. "You know something. Tell me."

"Really, sir. I'd prefer not to—"

"Stevens!"

Stevens cleared his throat. "Ah, yes, sir. I don't know much of the situation, but before Miss Wells was to marry Mr. DeVander, it is my understanding that she learned the gentleman kept a mistress, so she refused him."

He stilled even as his blood began to simmer. What type of cheating crook would do such a thing? "I assume the family ran off the scoundrel with a shotgun."

"No, sir."

He glowered at the butler, who again didn't seem inclined to give more information. "What do you mean, no?"

"The family didn't seem to mind Mr. DeVander's indiscretion. He had a rather large bank account and a bright political future."

"So she stood up to her family." That made sense. He could almost picture her telling her father she wouldn't marry a cheat as she stood with her chin high, her shoulders back and her gaze cool.

"She would have still ended up married had your grandfather not stepped in."

"What?" Now that he couldn't envision. Especially since the old codger had tried forcing Pa into a similar marriage. Oh, as far as he knew, the bride picked out for Pa hadn't been a cheat, but Pa hadn't loved her. Marrying her would have been nothing but a business transaction, arranged for Jonah Hayes's benefit. Grandpa would have been more likely to help the Wells family marry Elizabeth off, not protect her. "Doesn't seem like it would even be his business."

"Your grandfather and Thomas Wells were rather close, and he was always something of a godfather to the Wells children. They seemed to replace the grandchildren he never saw, until Samantha arrived, that is."

Luke glowered. As though he needed to be reminded that he'd never met his grandfather. "Go on."

"I never inquired into your grandfather's motivations regarding Miss Wells, sir. It wouldn't be proper. He did smooth things over with her parents regarding the broken engagement, however. And he was most supportive of her studies. It pleased him greatly to see her teach at the school he'd founded. And then, in his will, he gave her the house she'd been making payments on."

"Grandpa did all that for her?" Luke scratched his head. This didn't seem like the man Pa'd told cruel stories about, but hadn't the lawyer said something about giving someone a house when they were going over the will? He just hadn't been paying much attention.

"Perhaps you should speak with Mr. Byron about it, if you have any further questions. All I know of the situation regarding Miss Wells is what I've overheard."

"Thank you, Stevens. You may go."

"You're welcome, sir."

The butler turned and left, and Luke rubbed the heel of his hand over his bleary eyes, his blood still boiling at the thought of what her former fiancé had done.

And why should his blood boil? Why should he care at

all? She was just a teacher who wanted a donation from him. No different from any of the other people who had asked him for money tonight.

So why couldn't he get those fiery hazel eyes out of his mind?

Chapter Nine

Elizabeth's breath clogged in her lungs, and the air around her turned thick and heavy. One would think she stood held at gunpoint, with the way her heart raced and her body went from hot to cold and back in an instant. Instead she stood in church, exactly one pew behind Mr. Hayes.

People filled the small sanctuary, their voices singing and bellowing and crooning on this bright Sunday morning. Smiles radiated from faces as though heaven itself had descended and implanted a spark of divine joy in the hearts of the worshippers. But she could hardly focus on singing with Mr. Hayes blocking her view of the song leader—and everyone else.

She held the hymnal open and scanned the page. She'd known the words to "Rock of Ages" since childhood, and the song rolled over her tongue with little effort. Maybe that was the problem. The hymn proved too familiar to offer a distraction.

Not that being distracted from those muscular shoulders would be easy. She glanced around the small church. A handful of farmers carried themselves the way Mr.

Hayes did, with wide shoulders and thick necks and strong bearings.

But the farmers looked rough in their coveralls and flannel shirts, while Mr. Hayes's tailored suit lay smooth against his body. And if she leaned close enough to Mr. Hayes, she could probably even smell the sun and grass and cologne that had entranced her last night.

She looked around the congregation as the pianist continued playing. Every woman present, whether married or single, watched Mr. Hayes—not that she was paying attention. If the man decided to sit right at the front of the church, of course women would stare. He was likely the richest man within a hundred miles.

But he hadn't held another woman's hand last night. And he hadn't rescued someone else from the reporter. And he hadn't smoothed hair from another woman's face or stared into another woman's eyes. She swallowed. He had looked at *her* as though she mattered. He'd caressed her jaw and pinned a strand of hair behind her ear, his face close enough that his breath warmed her cheek.

And she would have kissed him. Oh, why hadn't he leaned forward just a bit? Let their lips brush? Then she'd know how his mouth felt on hers and wouldn't be left wondering.

And *what* was she thinking? Why kiss at all when he would leave in a few weeks?

The minister motioned for the congregation to sit while the pianist played the introduction to "Amazing Grace." Elizabeth sang the opening line, letting her soprano voice ring out above the others.

Samantha turned and looked at her, giggles sounded from the pew behind, and Mrs. Weldingham, seated to her left, glared. Elizabeth looked around. Was something…?

She clamped her mouth shut as more snickers erupted.

A rich alto voice filled the air. *One* rich alto voice. She shifted to see past Mr. Hayes. Indeed, one woman stood at the front of the church, singing the solo Elizabeth had tried making into a duet.

Elizabeth pressed her eyes closed until the last strains of music faded away, and she could open them to find everyone staring at the pastor rather than her.

"Take your Bibles, and turn with me to 1 Samuel 15." The aging minister's voice filled the crowded church. She flipped through the delicate pages of the pew Bible, then followed along as the minister began to read.

An invisible band tightened around her chest. Minister Trevnor wasn't preaching on Saul disobeying God. He couldn't be. But the pastor's voice boomed through every wretched word of the passage, causing one verse to reverberate through her mind, the verse Mother had quoted when she'd refused to marry David DeVander eight years earlier. *Rebellion is as the sin of witchcraft, and stubbornness is as iniquity and idolatry.*

"We're going to examine what the Bible teaches about obedience and disobedience this morning," the minister continued. "The Bible promises happiness to those who obey God and His commandments, but sorrow and punishment to those who disobey. When God looks at you, does He see obedience or disobedience? Children, do you obey your parents? Laborers, do you obey your bosses…?"

Elizabeth crinkled the pages of the Bible between her fingers. She didn't need to hear a sermon on obedience, not now.

Have you any notion how furious your mother was when she saw what you'd penned? It isn't appropriate for a lady like yourself to express your opinions in such a public way. Father's words from last night about the newspaper articles flashed through her mind.

Had she disobeyed some unwritten law, some sacred commandment, by writing that editorial? Mother and Father seemed to think so.

Her parents had also said she was disobedient and rebellious for refusing to marry David. No matter what she did, what grades she'd gotten in college or how far she went out of her way to please them these days, she was somehow always "disobedient." She likely would be until she married a suitable man. And by "suitable" her parents meant some rich public figure who would help her family's political connections. Her husband could behave in countless despicable ways beyond the public's eye, so long as he looked good in the papers. And she was disobedient for refusing to comply.

She fidgeted and looked about as casually as she could manage. She ought never to have made a habit of sitting in the third pew from the front. How easily she could slip out if she sat nearer the back.

Mrs. Weldingham eyed her again, and Elizabeth straightened, staring ahead and trying to shut out the sermon.

Certain words slipped through anyway. *Disobeyed. God. Punished. Destroyed.*

Was God punishing her for not obeying her parents? Was that why Hayes Academy would likely close? Because she'd written an editorial rather than sitting back and accepting whatever happened to the school? Was that why her parents never seemed happy with her? Because she'd disobeyed them by teaching rather than marrying?

Her head began to throb, and she glanced toward the front of the church. But instead of seeing the minister, rambling about the horrors Saul's family faced because of his disobedience, Mr. Hayes filled her view.

He already knew she disagreed with her father about

the school's funding, and he hadn't condemned her. Nor had he said anything about how she shouldn't teach last night. He'd simply said her family should treat her better and then had asked if she wanted to start her own family. Would his opinion of her change if he knew how she'd defied her parents by not marrying? Or if he knew her intended had found her so unsatisfying he'd run into the arms of a mistress before they'd even married?

And why did Mr. Hayes's opinion matter so much anyway?

Luke entered the drawing room and stopped. He hadn't expected there to be so many people. Sure, he'd seen a servant moving about the premises here or there, inside the house or on the grounds. But to have everyone in the same place—why there were nearly twenty of them.

And they looked terribly uncomfortable. Not a one sat on the dainty furniture—not that he could blame them—but half of them tiptoed about as though they'd never even seen the drawing room before.

Had he told Stevens to assemble them in the wrong place? Where did one meet with his servants? The kitchen, perhaps? Or the servants' dining room?

Stevens stepped up to him. "Everyone's in attendance, as you requested."

Luke cleared his throat and moved to the front of the room. "Thank you all for taking time from your usual duties to be here."

The milling and soft chatter stopped, and every eye turned his way. Fear and dejection filled most faces. Some eyes burned hot with anger, while others shone dull with resignation. But all knew why they stood there.

"Is he the new master?" A girl of no more than twelve or thirteen whispered to the maid beside her.

The woman made a shushing sound and cut her gaze toward him, her cheeks pale.

Luke looked away and surveyed the other workers in his grandpa's employ. No, not Grandpa's employ, *his* employ. "I know you all worked hard for my grandfather, Jonah Hayes, and I appreciate that. As most of you are aware, some changes need to be made. The estate is being put up for sale, and I will not be staying long in Valley Falls. I'm sure whoever buys this home will want to hire his own staff, so I…"

The words crusted in his mouth. Confound it. He couldn't do this. He'd planned to only keep on six of them and give the rest two months' salary plus a month of room and meals while they looked for other jobs. Now it hardly seemed enough.

What do you plan to do with your vast estate? Miss Wells's words from last night ran through his mind. *What happens when you get home? Do you sit around on the pile of money that got handed to you and congratulate yourself on a job well done?*

Luke rubbed the back of his neck. He might not want this estate, Grandpa's money, responsibility for the servants, or the rest of the mess that had been handed him, but hang it all, it was *his* mess, *his* duty. And he wasn't going to put nearly two dozen good workers out of a job because he found cutting back convenient. Let the next owner fire them, but he wouldn't have that on his conscience.

"Sir?" Stevens sidled up beside him. "Are you unwell? Do you need something? A glass of water, perhaps?"

"No." He didn't need anything another person could offer. He was the one who needed to do something, to provide for those Grandpa had left in his care. "As I was saying, whoever buys this house will most likely hire new staff, but your job here is secure for as long as I remain owner. I also have a monetary gift of two months' salary for each of you, as a thank-you for the years you spent serving my grandfather. Stevens and Miss Hampstead will distribute the envelopes accordingly."

The servants hushed completely, creating an awkward silence as gazes riveted on him. He turned on his heel and left before he could think too hard on what he'd just done.

The sun was just rising in the eastern sky as Elizabeth stopped before the four brick walls of Hayes Academy. She stared up at the towering three-story school and flicked her gaze over the windows. Her classroom and Miss Torneau's, Miss Bowen's office and the dining hall.

She didn't need to step inside to know how the classrooms looked, painted the standard white with blackboards at the front, the desks filled with bright-faced students. She could almost smell the chalk and wood polish, hear the giggles of young ladies and the clip of boots against flooring.

An empty dream.

The school would close at Christmas. The board may not have made their official announcement yet, but they'd already decided. Without the report on finances from Jackson. Without thought for where she or Miss Bowen or any of the other teachers would work next. And without concern for students themselves.

Mr. Taviston would likely have the blackboards, desks, beds and other supplies sold within weeks of closing the school, and then he'd sell the building itself.

Who would buy it? Another school? Not likely, with the way private institutions were struggling in the midst of the recession.

The Hayes Academy would probably go to some company who needed a warehouse. The inner rooms would be torn down, the walls stripped of any remembrance of the school, and the structure would become a simple building, not a place that held girls' futures and cultivated their dreams.

A breath of cold air teased her face, and she shivered in her coat. The morning was cool, with frost crusting the grass and birds slow to start their songs. She wasn't dressed to be outside long, hadn't planned to come here at all. But when she'd opened the door to retrieve the morning paper, she simply kept walking, the academy calling to her from the end of the street. She'd needed to say goodbye, here in the quiet light of dawn, without anyone to interrupt her.

But now she'd best get home before someone saw her and asked questions. Saying goodbye to a building? She could only imagine the look she'd get if she attempted to explain.

She turned, headed down the sidewalk, wrapping her coat tighter about her and not looking back at the brick structure that would soon stand empty. Instead, she looked ahead toward her house, the yellow paint and protruding turret barely visible between the stately trees lining the road. What would she do with it after the school closed? Sell?

No. She could never do such a thing. She was blessed to own her own home. Indeed, most teachers spent their lives renting rooms in houses that belonged to someone else. And those teachers who did manage to buy their own property, well, they weren't nearly as young as she was.

After she'd started teaching at Hayes Academy, Jonah Hayes had approached her about buying a house, specifically the one which she and two other teachers had been renting from him. He'd said she needed the property in her name for investment purposes, and she could make monthly payments to him. She'd nearly swooned when the lawyer came to her house after Jonah's death and told her that he'd left her the house in his will.

She lingered a moment on the walkway and gazed up at the two stories. Hers, from the peak of the gabled roof to the flower beds at the base of the walls. And she took care of it, tending the lawn and gardens, calling a repairman at the first sign of trouble, filling the interior with furniture and decorations.

She climbed the steps to the porch, the paper she'd passed earlier still resting on the wooden planks beside the door. Sighing, she picked it up and unrolled it. At least nothing about Hayes Academy was printed on the first page. She opened to the second page, and the letters stood bold and stark at the top.

Hayes Academy for Girls Employs Bribery and Accusations While Continuing to Waste Money
Charitable organizations and taxpayers have already wasted an exorbitant amount of money on Hayes Academy for Girls. Yet in the face of our current economic depression, that institution seems determined to waste more. Saturday evening…

And Higsley went on to describe the banquet. "Overly elaborate," he called it. "Wasteful…a disgrace to the area's needy," with his own invitation to the event derided as "an attempt to bribe him into silence." Then he claimed to endure the rudest behavior and most harrowing of accusations from a certain Miss Wells.

Surely this teacher's qualifications must be examined, as no one with such a venomous mind ought be allowed anywhere near society's young ladies.

She gulped air and fanned her face with the paper, even as tears stung the back of her eyes.

Venomous mind? Qualifications examined? What nonsense. Yet if people believed the raving reporter's words this time, as they had his previous article, the wretched man might well see her fired before the school even closed.

The front door opened and Miss Loretta Atkins, the literature and drama teacher, poked her head out. "Oh, there you are, dear. Miss Torneau made some oatmeal for breakfast, but we couldn't find you."

"I just…" she fisted her hand in the paper "…went for a morning walk, is all."

Miss Atkins's eyes landed on the *Morning Times*. "Oh, no. That reporter didn't print another, did he?"

Elizabeth handed over the paper. No point in hiding what the rest of the world would be reading in another hour or two.

"My, my." Miss Atkins clucked her tongue. "You don't think the school will close because of this reporter, do you?"

She watched the older woman, her forehead wrinkled as she glanced at the article. It would be nice, just for a moment, to be like Miss Atkins—a pleasant old spinster who had never fallen in love or had any suitors, to hear her tell it. She'd started teaching decades ago, always living in a house or apartment somebody else owned. She smiled gently when she heard news, whether good or bad, and never took it upon herself to take a stand or push for change. In another week or two, when she learned the school would close, she would frown and cluck her tongue. Perhaps she would say something like "such a shame, that is" and then go about her daily routine.

Elizabeth swallowed. Would it be better to live out her days like Miss Atkins? Not overly involved in anything?

Not caring when she failed because she never tried to achieve anything in the first place? Maybe she should attempt it, the calm complacency, the blind acceptance of whatever was handed her.

"Do you mind if I take this back to the kitchen? Miss Torneau will want to see it."

"Fine," Elizabeth croaked.

Miss Atkins stepped back inside and held the door open. "You come in, too, dear. Those fingers look to have a touch of frostbite."

She glanced down at her red chapped hands, nearly numb from the cold. "I'll be in shortly."

The door closed, and she leaned against the post, sucking the chilled air deep into her lungs. She needed one moment, maybe two, of peace before the whirlwind of her day began. Miss Bowen would have seen the article, as well as the students, the other teachers, the school board members. Goodness, but the article might well bring a couple board members to the academy today. If only she could hide in bed and claim she was ill. It wouldn't be a lie, not really. Because somewhere deep inside, where her heart beat heavily and her stomach twisted into knots, she was very, very sick.

Chapter Ten

"Sir, I'm afraid your sister is missing."

Luke turned from where he stood in his bedroom, threading a tie around his neck. "What do you mean, 'missing'?"

The butler handed him an envelope. "Well, sir, she wasn't in her room this morning, but this letter was resting on her bed."

Luke knotted his tie and tore open the letter. Sam had gone straight back to the school he'd told her to stay away from. Stubborn girl. He looked out the north-facing window toward town. Morning sunlight danced off the frosted grass and painted the maple trees an even brighter red, while silhouettes of whitewashed houses darkened the horizon. "What time does Hayes Academy start?"

"In about half an hour."

Confound it. He had a half hour to catch the train to Albany as well, and he needed to make that appointment with Jackson.

"Did she go to the academy, sir? Would you like someone to bring her home?"

Luke set his jaw and stared out the window again, in the direction Sam would have walked. He'd embarrassed her on Friday by pulling her out of class, and he didn't cotton to doing it a second time. Maybe he'd talk to her when he got home later and set some boundaries. Calm, reasonable boundaries. Like she couldn't leave her room again until they headed West, or see any friends, or study any mathematics books.

Hang it all, he may as well beat the girl for smiling— not that she'd done much smiling since he showed up.

Luke sighed. Maybe Miss Wells was right, and he just needed to tell Sam about Ma. Perhaps Sam would hate him for doing so, perhaps Ma would hate him even more for not keeping his promise, but things were getting ridiculous. Sam was already close to detesting him, and leaving Valley Falls was going to break her heart. Ma thought she'd been doing Sam a favor by hiding the truth, but didn't Sam deserve to know what was going on?

And somehow he'd gotten himself stuck smack-dab in the middle of the mess. "Sam wants another chance to see her friends. She can attend the academy for the day."

"Yes, sir." Stevens dipped his head and left.

Luke slid into his suit coat and glanced in the mirror. Had Grandpa liked always getting duded up? Because Luke looked like a corpse in the rigid black and white garments. But he couldn't help pausing, lingering an extra moment at the too-familiar face in the mirror.

If only he and Blake hadn't looked so similar, hadn't shared the same bright blue eyes and sun-streaked hair. If only he could change his face and replace it with another. Black hair. Gray eyes. Less prominent cheekbones. A softer chin. Anything so he didn't have to stare at his brother's face whenever he looked in the mirror.

"I'm sorry, Blake," he whispered into the empty room. And indeed he was. Sorry for Blake's death, for the sudden way Pa had sent Sam out East afterward, sorry for not trying harder to keep his family together. Something had shattered the day of Blake's death, and the pieces of that tragedy still lay like splintered shards on the hot Wyoming ground.

He straightened his tie and suit coat as best he could without looking back at the mirror. He didn't have time to think about Blake or the way his family had been torn apart after his twin's death. He had a train to catch, more meetings scheduled than he wanted to think about and a scoundrel to scare away from his sister.

Luke's boots hit the wooden platform as the train that had returned him to Valley Falls hissed and steamed behind him.

"Mr. Hayes, sir, your carriage is ready." A young coachman instantly appeared by his side.

"Thank you." He spoke absently, then followed the boy to the conveyance.

A certain part of him, the part that loved the Teton Valley, wanted to say he'd hated his day and found the meetings dull and stifling. But while sitting round a table with a bunch of other suits wasn't near as fun as riding the range, it wasn't terrible. He'd never been slow at ciphering, and the columns of numbers he'd glanced over made sense. The businessmen he'd conferenced with hadn't been half bad, either. They were, after all, still men underneath their fancy getup. And the meetings weren't much different than managing a crew of cowhands around a campfire.

In fact, sitting in those meeting rooms, making decisions that would affect other people's lives, was almost kind of nice. Like how to offer a home insurance plan that was affordable and yet would provide adequate coverage in case of a fire or flood. Or sending a corporation-wide memorandum out to all Great Northern Accounting and

Insurance employees explaining that there would be no change in operations or job layoffs at present. A lot of his workers would return to their homes happy after getting news like that.

All in all, hadn't been bad in the least—which made that familiar spot between his shoulder blades start to itch.

The lawyer, too, had been thrilled when Luke told him to go ahead and start interviewing men for an overseer's position. If he was going to keep the house staff on for as long as possible, he could at least find an overseer to manage the accounting and insurance offices. If the setup didn't work after a year or two, he could always come back to Valley Falls and sell the companies.

But campfires and managers and meetings aside, he now had another stack of paperwork to get through, and he still needed to have that conversation with Sam. "Did my sister enjoy her day at school?"

The boy turned back to him, a frown plastered across his face. "Wouldn't know, sir. I don't usually ask her such things. And besides, she hasn't returned yet."

Luke stopped, despite the people milling in the crowd around him. "She hasn't returned? As in she's still at school?"

"No, sir. She's at Miss Wells's house for her calculus lesson. Goes there every Monday and Wednesday, she does."

"And no one thought to fetch her home?"

The boy shifted nervously from one foot to the other and glanced at his boots. "I wasn't aware I needed to."

Luke scrubbed a hand over his face. So help him, he should shove Sam on the first train West. Here he was trying to be nice by letting her go to school one last time, then she up and headed to a lesson without so much as asking. There was no keeping the girl happy. "And where does Miss Wells live?"

"She owns a place just down from the academy. Rents rooms to two of the other teachers."

"You'd best take me."

The coachman nodded and scampered toward the carriage.

The conveyance took him to a quiet tree-lined street where neighbors sat on porches and children played in the yards. Just the sight of the two-story house, painted a buttery-yellow with soft green shutters and gables, calmed him. He could well imagine Miss Wells up in the little turret on the north side of the house, knitting or painting or doing some other ladylike craft while she looked down on the street below. Not that he needed to think about Miss Wells all cozy in her home.

He headed up the walk and knocked on the door, then waited.

Nothing.

He knocked again, a little louder this time.

Still nothing.

Turning the door knob, he slipped inside. Muted female voices floated from the doorway on his left. He followed the sound, trying to force his boots to step quietly through the otherwise silent house.

Samantha sat at a writing desk against the far wall of the parlor, while Miss Wells stood beside his sister, her shoulders and head bent, her soft voice filling the room with odd sounding words: *derivative, function, linear approximation, tangent line.* Sam's head bobbed back and forth as she scrawled something across a slate.

A teacher. The woman standing beside the far wall surely was one. She'd said as much to him the other night in the carriage when she'd insisted she was content to remain a spinster and had refused to answer his questions about why she didn't want a family. When he had first seen her at the school, she'd been so beautiful he couldn't envision her doing anything but marrying a distinguished gentleman.

But would she marry if it meant she'd spend her days at home rather than lecturing or whispering encouraging words to her students? Rather than covering her hands with chalk dust?

He walked closer. They'd have to hear the rustle of his suit or the floor creak beneath his feet. But with their backs to him, neither woman noticed until he stood close enough to touch.

"Mr. Hayes?" Surprise lit Miss Wells's eyes.

"Luke." Sam turned, guilt rather than astonishment etching her face. "What are you doing here?"

He crossed his arms. "Seems I should be asking you that."

Sam stiffened. "I'm studying calculus with Miss Wells, like I do every Monday. Grandfather never had a problem with it."

Miss Wells's gaze flitted between them, her lovely hazel eyes filled with questions. "Samantha, did your brother give you permission to be here?"

Sam hunched back over the desk. "I understand the first one. It's this second derivative I can't quite grasp."

"No." Luke shifted and tapped a finger against the slate, filled with as many letters and symbols as digits. How did they even call this stuff mathematics if it hardly used numbers? "She didn't have permission to be here or at school today. She was supposed to sort through Grandpa's room. I need her help at the estate, if we're going to make it home anytime soon."

"Oh. I'm sorry." And the round, sad look in Miss

Wells's eyes showed she truly was. "When I saw Samantha this morning, I assumed that you…well…had become more sensible about your decision and had given her permission to attend classes until she left Valley Falls."

"My decision's perfectly sensible." He not only needed Sam's help at the estate, he needed to break her away from the things she'd grown to care about here and get her excited about going home. None of that would happen if she spent her days at school, fixated on heading to college. "Sam, get to the carriage."

"Mr. Hayes, if nothing else, please let her continue these private lessons with me. It's the least you can do, if you're going to be taking her away soon." Miss Wells looked away, blinking and biting her lip.

He swallowed a groan. The last thing he needed was for the woman to start crying.

"I understand that you miss your sister," she went on, her shoulders straightening. "And I realize you have reasons for wanting her home. But can't you wait a few more weeks? Maybe she could return home with you at Christmas, after the end of the semester."

"Go home at Christmas? Now *you* expect me to leave, too, Miss Wells? I'm not going to Wyoming at Christmas or anytime after that." Samantha gripped the back of the chair, her knuckles whitening. "You'll have to drag me to that train, and I'll scream the entire way. Then I'll—"

"I don't care how much screaming you do." What was the point in being reasonable with the girl anymore? Nothing he did made a dent in Sam's stubbornness, and he could be just as mule-headed as she. "And I'm done trying to be nice about it. You're on a train West as soon as I find a chaperone to take you."

"No!" Horror filled his sister's face. "I'll turn around and come back, I swear it. I'm finishing school. I want to graduate and go to college. I want to be with Jackson. He says I can still attend college after we marry."

Luke balled his hands into fists. "You're not marrying that scoundrel."

Miss Wells gasped, and heat burned the back of his neck. Probably shouldn't have called the lady's brother a scoundrel while she was present. But what else was he supposed to do while Sam was hollering at him?

"This is about Blake, isn't it?" Sam sprang from her chair.

"Blake? You've gone daft." He'd been about four years old when he figured out most women were batty, but nothing illustrated it better than Sam's cockeyed statement.

"I'm just going to slip into the kitchen and make some tea," Miss Wells squeaked and scurried through the doorway.

Sam held his gaze. "I'm not daft. You're not happy I left after he died. You never wanted me to leave, and now that you see me here and happy, you can't stand that you were wrong about me leaving the Teton Valley."

She'd gone haywire. Sam needed to go home because of Ma, not because of something that had happened in the past. But her words brought back the memories anyway, an image of his twin's body lying on the blood-soaked dirt.

Blake had discovered some things missing around the ranch, and when he'd pegged the thief as one of their seasoned cowhands, Blake had fired him. The man had ridden up to Blake's place the next morning, called for him while he was sitting at breakfast with Cynthia, and shot him the moment he stepped outside.

Luke's stomach twisted at the image in his mind, and an insatiable well of regret opened inside him. He hadn't known what was happening to Blake. His brother's cabin was on the other side of the ranch property, out of view from the big house, but when Blake hadn't shown up in the stables at his usual time, Luke had ridden out, only to find Cynthia crying over his bloodied twin.

He'd jumped from his horse and kneeled beside the body, ripping off his shirt to stanch the bleeding. *"Who's riding for the doctor? Why don't you have rags here to stop the blood?"*

Cynthia shook her head while tears coursed down her face—a face she'd powdered that morning, as though she still lived in Boston rather than the Teton Valley.

"I tried. The horse..." She hiccupped. *"I couldn't... h-he wasn't hitched to the wagon."*

"Answer me, Cynthia! Who did you send for help?"

"No one was around. I tried to saddle the horse, but..." She broke off in a fresh torrent of sobs while the sticky warmth of Blake's blood soaked his shirt and coated his hands.

"I'm not going home," Sam spoke quietly from somewhere above him.

Luke looked up at his sister. Somehow, he was sprawled in the green wingback chair by the front window of Miss Wells's parlor, though he didn't remember moving there or sitting. "You don't have a choice, Sam."

"You should give me one instead of ripping me away from the place I love."

Luke didn't even glance at her, just watched the street through the lacy window covering. It was time. He couldn't keep putting off the truth about Ma if it was going to destroy their relationship. "Ma needs you. You have to go home."

But Sam didn't ask what he meant about Ma needing her. Instead, she thrust a finger into his chest. "No. It's not Ma. It's you. You don't like that mathematics makes me happy. Or that I want to marry Jackson. You don't want me to go to college and become an architect.

"You storm back into my life and try taking everything away." Sam tossed her head to the side and blinked furiously against the moisture glistening in her eyes. "Well, I won't let you. I have dreams, too, Luke. And they've got nothing to do with a cattle ranch in some forgotten valley. If my going home had to do with wanting family to be together, you'd be taking Cynthia and Everett home, too. Goodness, you have a nephew, Blake's very own son, and you've never even seen him."

Luke clenched his jaw. Why did Sam keep dredging up Cynthia when Ma was dying? "Confound it! You're not listening. Coming home—"

"No. You're right. I'm not listening to you anymore." Sam stormed past him and out the parlor door.

Luke followed her into the hall as the sound of the front door opening and then slamming echoed through the house. He buried his forehead in his hands and groaned.

How had he messed that up so badly? He was only trying to help, only attempting to tell her about Ma.

"Mr. Hayes?" Miss Wells emerged from the door at the far end of the hallway, a tray with tea service balanced in her hands. "Is everything all right?"

He rubbed the back of his neck. "Yeah, yeah. Look, Miss Wells, I'm sorry about all this…." He gestured toward the parlor. "We should have saved our shouting match for the ride home."

"I don't mind so much. Truly." She swayed gracefully inside the room, set down the tray, then returned to the doorway leading from the hall to the parlor. "Every family has words at one time or another. I'm sorry about your brother, though. I can tell he meant a lot to you, and I can't imagine how hard it must be to lose your mother, as well."

"You're a blessed woman, Eliz— I mean, Miss Wells. To still have your family alive and well."

She sighed, her chest rising and falling with the motion. "I suppose you're right. My family might not be overly supportive of my teaching, but they're all living."

"You should cherish that."

A sad smile tilted the corner of her mouth. "I should. More than I do at times."

"Right." He looked away but couldn't help seeing her as she'd been the other night. Those full lips so near his own, the soft curve of her cheek in the moonlight, the mesmerizing swirl of gold and green and brown in her eyes as she had stared up at him.

"The knot in your tie is lopsided," she stated, those beautiful eyes filled with somber thoughts.

The knot in his tie? He nearly choked. "I hadn't noticed."

And he hadn't.

Then again, most men looked in the mirror when knotting them, because most men didn't see their dead brother's face staring back from the glass. He lifted a hand and fumbled to straighten the offending piece of cloth.

"Mr. Hayes—Luke. Can you try doing something for me?"

There was a hint of deliberation in her voice, a vague trace of calculation. His hand stilled on his tie as he narrowed his gaze. Miss Wells's large, perfect eyes; her full, pink lips; the sincerity in her face. This felt like a trap, if he'd ever seen one. "Depends on what you're wanting."

"Can you try working out something with the school? For Samantha, that is. Perhaps your sister could arrange for a long break at Christmas and travel home to see your mother then. Or maybe she could still attend classes for the length of time you remain in Valley Falls and try to graduate early. Whatever you decide, you have to do something, if you want to make peace with her. I'm sure exceptions can be made, if you'll talk to Miss Bowen."

Luke rubbed his hand over his forehead. The woman was a teacher through and through, always thinking about her students over anything else. "This isn't a simple situation."

"No, but it would help if you found some way for your sister to graduate."

"Tell you what. I'll let Sam go to classes at Hayes for as long as we stay." One of the servants could probably sort through Grandpa's bedroom, or even him—if he ever dug himself out from underneath all the paperwork in Grandpa's office.

Miss Wells gasped, a small, happy sound, and her hands flew up to cover her mouth. "You mean it, then? You'll really let her come back to school? And you'll speak to the office about arrangements after that so she can graduate?"

He scowled. "You care an awful lot about my sister graduating."

"I care an awful lot about every student graduating. Have you thought anymore about making a donation to Hayes?"

"Yes," he grumbled. Far more than should have.

"Yes? As in you agree? Or as in you've thought of it?" Miss Wells's hands gripped his forearm, her tiny nails digging through the fabric of his sleeve. Her eyes sparkled with hope, and her lips curved in a full-out grin.

And how could he say no when she looked at him like that? He was making a new business policy, here and now. No more decision making when womenfolk were around. They could get a man to sign over his entire life's holding by looking at him thataway.

"Yes, as in I've thought on it, but I'll have to do some more thinking before I've got an answer."

"I understand." She released his arm and stepped away, her brilliant smile fading.

And now he'd just let her down. Teach him to open his mouth and answer without thinking while she was around.

Miss Wells shifted from one foot to the other, as though suddenly nervous, and gestured to the parlor and tea service. "I would offer you tea and discuss the possibility of a donation further, but, um, my housemates are still at the academy, and with Samantha gone, your being here is hardly proper."

He looked around the quiet hallway and parlor. Yep, they were alone all right, and he'd probably broken a couple dozen rules of society by coming here at all. "I'll get on home."

But as he turned, he knocked an already-open newspaper off the small table in the hall. "Sorry about that." He bent and reached for it, then his eyes landed on the headline, and he sprang back up. "He did this? That scoundrel of a reporter published another article?"

Miss Wells's eyes seemed to dull even more. "What did you expect Mr. Higsley to do after Saturday evening?"

"Turn tail and run. What else?"

"That's not the way reporters work. Indeed, one can't have a worse enemy than a reporter."

"Perhaps if I hadn't scared him off…"

"My tongue angered him before you arrived." She wrapped her arms around herself. "I anticipated an article such as this."

He ran his thumb over a crease in the paper, his eyes scanning the basics of the article. "He attacked you personally."

She shrugged, the gesture small and hopeless for a

woman comprised of steel and fire and determination. "It's nothing new."

"Does this mean the board will close the school?"

"I told you as much on Saturday."

But he hadn't quite believed her then. Holding this paper, with an article he could have prevented had he cared to, made the situation more real. More his fault. He glanced at the writing desk against the far wall, where Miss Wells had been not twenty minutes ago, instructing Samantha in a subject too complicated for him to comprehend. "You're so concerned about Samantha not graduating. What will happen to the other girls in Samantha's class if the school closes? Will they be able to finish out the year?"

"There are sixteen other students in Samantha's class. And I don't know what will happen to them. The school board will decide that, not me."

"But you think they'll just close the school and wish the girls well, as they find various other places to finish out their last semester of high school?"

"Yes, very much so."

"That doesn't seem fair."

She shrugged. It was the first time he'd seen such an unladylike gesture from her. "I hardly think treating the students fairly is the board's foremost concern."

And suddenly it became clear. Like it had yesterday, when he'd stood in the drawing room filled with his servants, and today when he'd told Mr. Byron to start finding potential managers for the insurance and accounting corporation. He could stop Hayes Academy from closing, at least for this school year. The school was as much his responsibility as the corporation and his servants— at least until he returned West and handed the reins to somebody else. And he wasn't going to be responsible for sending nearly a hundred students off in the middle of a school year.

"I think I'll be making that donation after all, Miss Wells. And having some visits with a few of the school board members."

Chapter Eleven

"I know you say there should be money here, Miss Wells, but I certainly can't find it." Samantha raised her head from where she sat in a chair in Jonah Hayes's office—or rather, his *former* office. The office now belonged to the man with sun-streaked blond hair standing on the other side of the room with his lawyer.

Elizabeth pulled her eyes away from Mr. Hayes and frowned at Samantha. There should be several hundred more dollars. Somewhere. If only she could find the mistake buried in the endless columns of numbers. Here she was, a mathematics teacher defending the need for higher-level academics to people like her parents and Mr. Hayes, and she couldn't even add. "You're certain?"

"Maybe it's in one of the other accounts? The food money could have gotten mixed up with the funds for teacher supplies or something."

Elizabeth flipped back several pages in the ledger on her own lap and ran her eyes down the columns once again. "I've already checked twice. There's nothing extra."

But the missing food money had to be tucked somewhere. Either that or the school's food supplier was cheating them out of produce.

"Are you saying the school's missing money?" Mr. Hayes glanced up from the paper he'd been studying with Mr. Byron.

"No." Or if so, she certainly couldn't prove it. She scratched the side of her head, causing a lock of hair to tumble down from its pins. "The books balance perfectly."

Which would be fine, if she was getting a hundred and fifty dollars' worth of food delivered to the school each month, and if she didn't have letters from the gas company and general store saying they'd never received payment for overdue bills. The books showed every expense paid in full.

She simply must have made a mistake somewhere. She'd probably recorded a donation in the wrong place and thus had incorrect fund levels in several of her accounts. If only she could find the discrepancy.

Sam flashed a bright smile at her brother. "See, nothing to worry about."

Elizabeth forced herself to nod, but Mr. Hayes's sky-blue eyes riveted to hers, as though he knew something wasn't quite right.

"Operating on a budget as tight as the one at Hayes Academy, I'd expect you to have some difficulty spreading your funds around to pay outstanding bills, am I correct?" Mr. Byron shoved his sagging glasses back up on his nose.

"Something like that," Elizabeth mumbled.

Mr. Hayes scowled at her. "You realize that if I'm going to convince the board to keep the school open, I have to prove it to be financially stable?"

"Yes, of course. I—"

"If you've any concerns, you should talk to Jackson Wells about this." The lawyer shifted closer to Mr. Hayes. "His books are likely in better order."

Samantha jabbed a finger at Mr. Byron. "That was uncalled for. Miss Wells can answer your questions better than Jackson, and I should know, since I'm close to both of them. Hayes Academy is just another client to Jackson. He doesn't pay its ledgers anywhere near the amount of attention Miss Wells does."

"Yes, Mr. Byron—and I regularly check my books against my brother's." Elizabeth stood, her face burning. She didn't need to sit here and be accused of mismanaging the ledgers after already giving Mr. Hayes and Mr. Byron three hours of her afternoon. "You'll find both sets of ledgers match perfectly. Now if you gentlemen will excuse me, it's growing late, and I've tomorrow's lessons to prepare."

She set the ledger on the ornate desk dominating the far side of the office and headed for the door. Mr. Hayes and the lawyer could spend their time attempting to make sense of the pages if they wished, but she was done for the night.

And possibly forever, if Mr. Hayes didn't manage to charm the school board.

"I'll see you out." Mr. Hayes appeared by her side, extending his elbow her direction.

She nearly groaned as she slipped her hand onto his arm. She must look a fright, with her hair starting to fall from its pins, and her skirt rumpled after a long day of teaching and studying books, and…she looked down. Yes, the front of her plum-colored skirt sported a large patch of white chalk dust.

A fright indeed.

"I appreciated your help tonight." Mr. Hayes led her down the large hallway filled with floor-to-ceiling windows, sparkling chandeliers and elaborate gold trim. The sky outside had darkened to a deep blue, turning the view from the front of the estate into a perfect scene for an artist's canvas.

"I'm happy to assist."

He sent her a lopsided grin, the kind that transformed his entire face from handsomely serious to irresistible. "You're lying."

She couldn't help but smile back. "Not really. I mean, yes, the afternoon was long, and perhaps a bit frustrating, as I feel like I've done nothing to prove the school's financial stability. But I'm willing to do whatever you need, if you think you can convince the school board to change its mind."

He placed his other hand atop hers, strong and warm over her small fingers. "I'll convince them. Don't worry."

"But how?"

He stopped at the top of the marble staircase leading down to the grand hall and turned her to face him. "You're not one to trust people, are you? I tell you that I'll take care of things, and you need to see a detailed battle plan before you'll believe me."

She paused, the words striking somewhere deep in her chest. Not one to trust people? Perhaps she trusted her students or even her fellow teachers. But not men, no. "I didn't mean to offend you. Do forgive me."

His gaze latched on to hers, watching, probing, as though looking into her very soul to find…what?

"You don't even deny it, do you? Just apologize and hope you didn't cause any hurt feelings. But you've no intention of trusting me the next time around, either."

She had no answer she could give to that, not without lying, so she smiled weakly and looked away.

"Somebody's hurt you before."

She attempted to tug her hand away from his, but he only settled those wide, callused fingers more firmly atop hers. "Really, Mr. Hayes—"

"You can call me Luke."

She glared at him.

"You just spent an entire afternoon in my study, working with me and my sister. It's entirely appropriate that you call me by my first name. Just like it's appropriate for me to start calling you Elizabeth."

Her face turned slightly warm at the sound of her name on his tongue. "Fine, then. Luke…but I hardly see how my past, or what we call each other, pertain to keeping the academy open."

"If I get the board to keep the school open, will that convince you to trust me a little more?"

"Probably not." She'd trusted a man once before, and it wasn't something she planned to do again.

Elizabeth slipped out the front door on Friday morning, picked up the paper, and nearly dropped it back onto the porch boards. There it was, written in black lettering across the bottom corner article.

Hayes Academy Creating Jobs and Opportunities for Women

Mr. Hayes—or rather, Luke—had done it. Not only had the school board members been curiously silent throughout the week, but now the paper itself seemed to be retracting its first two articles.

Her hands trembled as she glanced over the specifics. Another reporter had written this one, and Luke had been quoted as pledging five thousand dollars to the academy.

Five thousand.

And then inviting others to do likewise.

She pressed the paper to her chest and grinned up at the sky. "Thank you, Luke."

Chapter Twelve

"Miss Wells, your mother's taken ill."

Elizabeth stared at her parents' coachman and gripped the molding along the doorway until wood dug beneath her fingernails.

"She's asking for you directly," he added.

Giggles and squeals rang out from the parlor of her house behind her, where would-be actresses dressed in costumes and applied makeup for their production of *The Taming of the Shrew.* Miss Atkins's calm voice tempered the insanity of laughs and chatter—when it could be heard above the noise.

"Ill? How ill? What's wrong?"

"I was merely sent to fetch you, miss."

"Yes, of course." Something hard fisted in her chest. Mother's illness would have to be consuming for her to cancel the dinner party tonight. She'd hosted such events before in spite of fevers, headaches and nerves. Unless…

Mother wouldn't be using some illness as a ploy to get her away from the play, would she? Mother had a way of getting what she wanted, but surely a weekly dinner party wasn't important enough to pull antics such as this.

"Miss Wells?" the coachman asked.

"Is she truly ill? Not feigning something?"

The coachman shifted back and forth on his feet. "As far as I know, miss."

Elizabeth licked her lips. "Did you see her? Was she lying down?"

"I only see your mother when she needs use of the carriage."

"Yes, of course." Elizabeth glanced down at the tips of her shoes, part of her ready to bolt outside and head to Albany, and another part aching to ignore the summons and return to her students. The tinkle of feminine voices and laughter rose from behind her. But what had Luke said earlier, about her having family? Something about her being *blessed* to have family alive and well and close at hand?

Yes, that was it. She had family, and she needed to cherish it, because one day she might find herself in a situation like Luke and Samantha, with her brother in the grave and a parent heading there. "Just give me a moment. I'll be right out."

The coachman nodded and moved down the steps. She closed the door, reached for her coat, then headed into the parlor.

MaryAnne, dressed in trousers and a waistcoat for her upcoming role as Petruchio, stopped her at the entrance. "Miss Wells, are you all right?"

"Pardon? Oh, yes…I'm f-fine, dear. But I'm afraid I'll have to miss your performance this evening."

The students nearest them fell silent, and MaryAnne inched closer. "Then you're not all right. Something has to be wrong, or you wouldn't miss the play."

"You're leaving?" Miss Atkins asked from across the room.

Elizabeth swallowed. The chaos existing only moments before turned to heavy silence as every student's gaze riveted to her. If only she could find some way to be both here and in Albany. Some way to see the hours of work and effort acted out on the stage while also supporting her mother.

"You promised to stay backstage and help with the scene changes," Miss Atkins insisted.

"I'm sorry. I just…" Elizabeth blew out a long breath. Mother wouldn't want rumors spread if whatever ailed her could be easily treated. But how else to explain leaving? "A family emergency has come up. I'm terribly sorry, but I must go to Albany immediately. Please forgive me. I know you've been working hard, and I so wanted to help with your play." She turned and hurried outside before more accusing words could be flung her direction.

"Miss Wells. Wait!" Samantha rushed into the yard, a dish of powder and a cosmetic brush still in hand and more makeup spread across her dress. "It's not Jackson, is it? I was supposed to see him at the dinner party tonight, but decided to help with the play instead."

"No, no. Mother's fallen ill and sent for me. I can only assume the dinner party is canceled. But please don't speak of it. I don't yet know what ails her, and I might arrive to find it something so slight as a headache."

Concern clouded Samantha's flawless face. "I hope everything turns out all right."

Elizabeth swallowed. "I hope so, too."

And with that, she turned and climbed into the carriage.

"How is Mother?" Elizabeth demanded as she burst through the front door of her parents' Albany home.

Connors, the butler who had been serving their family since before she was born, raised his eyebrows at her. "Quite well. She is in the drawing room."

"The drawing room? She's not in bed, then? Has she

taken a turn for the better?" Without waiting to be announced, she rushed into the drawing room—and then stopped cold.

Mother sat on the settee, her face round and healthy, and a beautiful gown of green silk draping her figure. Jackson, dressed in a suit, lounged in a chair opposite Mother. And Father stood by the fireplace, deep in conversation with...

No. Anyone but him... Her body trembled as her eyes latched on to the "dinner companion" leaning against the mantel.

"Good evening, Elizabeth." Mother smiled brightly.

She should excuse herself, rush from the house and never step foot in it again. And she would, if her tongue didn't weigh like lead in her mouth and her stomach didn't lurch until it threatened to heave its contents. Instead she stood planted to the floor, staring at the one man she forever wanted to blot from her memory.

He turned slowly. "Ah, Elizabeth, darling. How kind of you to join us. A bit late though, aren't you? And..."

The eyes of her former fiancé skimmed down her. She didn't need to follow his gaze to know what he saw: a plain white shirtwaist and serviceable blue skirt. Both probably dusted with a mixture of chalk from a calculus lesson and stage powder. And her hair...she shoved some of the loose strands hanging about her face behind her ears.

All while Mother sat there, wearing soft silk and a hopeful smile.

"...a bit underdressed, perhaps," David finished.

"Mr. DeVander." Scanning the room again, she raised her chin. "We seem to be missing your wife this evening. Is she not joining us?"

Surprise lit his deceptively handsome face. "She passed away. A carriage accident over the summer. I assumed you'd heard." His voice sounded like coffee, rich and deep and entirely too smooth.

"I'm sure you were devastated," she snapped.

"Elizabeth, that was uncalled for." Mother fanned her face. "Do forgive my daughter, David. Sometimes her tongue gets the better of her."

"I was, actually. Quite devastated." David glanced at his feet, as though truly pained.

Elizabeth sighed. Perhaps she was being unfair. He may well have loved his wife. Simply because he hadn't loved Elizabeth when they'd been engaged didn't make him incapable of loving anyone else. "I'm sorry for your loss then. Truly."

"Thank you." He flicked his gaze over her once again, lines of disapproval wrinkling his forehead and mouth. "You'll want to clean up for dinner, I'm sure. We'll wait for you before we adjourn to the dining room."

The controlling snake. He was a guest here, yet he had no scruples at hinting she wasn't good enough to dine as she was. He may have lost his wife, may have even been upset by the death, but the man hadn't changed. "Mother, I'd like a word with you. Now."

Mother straightened. "Surely any conversation we have can wait until after we eat, dear."

"No." She clenched her teeth. "Either we talk now, or I leave."

"You're not leaving, when we've waited the better part of an hour for you to get here," Jackson piped up. "I'm famished."

"Yes, daughter, is this truly necessary?" Father added.

She gripped her skirt in her hands and turned. "Then watch me leave."

"Very well, very well." Mother stood slowly, as though trying to temper Elizabeth's quick movements with her own languid ones. "This won't take but a moment, gentlemen."

Elizabeth marched straight across the hall and into her father's office.

"Really, child. You're going to ruin your chance with David all over again." Mother closed the door behind her. "'I'm sure you were devastated'? You don't say such things to a man grieving for his late wife."

"If he still grieved, he wouldn't be here, expecting to have dinner with me." Fury built inside her, an angry storm of rage and betrayal and past regrets. "You lied. I had plans for this evening, a play to help with, and you deliberately misled me to get me away from it."

"Oh, don't be so dramatic." Mother sank fluidly into a chair. "I had a headache when I sent for you, and it cleared up before you arrived."

"You didn't send for me because of a headache. You sent for me because you wanted me to have dinner with David while he was in town."

"Why you're here hardly matters now that you are. So stop blabbering, fix your hair and come in to dinner. Wait. Don't you have one of your dresses here, up in your old room? That ivory velvet?"

"Hardly matters? Have you gone daft?" She paced in front of Mother's chair. How could the woman sit and wear that guileless smile after what she'd done? "No, don't answer that. You must have. Or you wouldn't have called me away from my commitments. My students have been working since the beginning of the school year on the production, and I promised I'd be there for them.

"Maybe the play and how I got here hardly matter to you. But they matter a great deal to me." She stopped her pacing and headed straight for the door. "Good evening, Mother. I'll see myself out. Thank you."

"No, you won't." Mother sprang up, a terrifyingly quick movement for someone so elegant, and rushed to the door. "You'll go into the dining hall and eat with the rest of us. You have a responsibility to aid your family, not spurn it, and this is your opportunity to do so."

"Opportunity? For what? I know you didn't want me to walk away from my engagement to David all those years ago, but that's over and done. And you *did* let me. Why do I suddenly have to marry now, when you've survived the previous twenty-six years of my life with an unwed daughter? And don't tell me it's because I wrote an editorial in the paper. I'm not a fool."

"We're going to lose our house if you don't marry him."

She barely refrained from rolling her eyes. "Yes. You told me so at the banquet. But I highly doubt it's going to happen tonight, so that still doesn't answer my question."

"No. You don't understand. The bank sent a man to… to our house yesterday. He was here when I returned from the Ladies' Society meeting. He apparently spoke with your father and assessed the value of the property. There were papers from the bank and…and…I don't know." She waved her hand, as though the simple gesture would shoo the problem away. "I had hopes of you and David reuniting while he was in town. What mother wouldn't dream of such a thing? But after your father told me about the bank man…"

Mother's lips tightened into a straight white line. "I had to get you to dinner. I didn't want to lie, but there seemed no other way."

Elizabeth gripped the bookshelf behind her for balance and pressed her fingers to her temple. Could her parents truly lose the house she'd grown up in? At the banquet, it had seemed like an idle threat, another of Mother's endless dramatics to try to keep her in line. But Mother's face had gone pale beneath her cosmetic powder, and her eyes pleaded for understanding.

"Things can't be that bad," Elizabeth argued. "Look at you, you're dressed in a fine gown and still maintaining a full staff here. If there was so little money, wouldn't Father be cutting back?"

"Oh, stop with this ridiculousness about expenses and cutbacks. I've never paid attention to how your Father manages his accounts. I simply trust him to do so, as any good wife would. And I know what he told me this morning, that the bank will take our house before Christmas if we don't come up with money. Which is why we need you."

The worry in Mother's eyes faded into a dreamy sheen. "David DeVander has money and position. The panic barely touched him. And he needs a wife. Someone elegant and refined, someone who can charm the crowds in Washington and here at home. He's willing to marry you and willing to help your father get back on his feet."

Elizabeth wrapped her arms around herself and stared at the plush blue carpet beneath her feet. Mother couldn't understand how deeply David had hurt her. If she did, Mother would have never asked such a thing. "I can't, Mama. He cheated on me."

"Don't you see, dear? David would take you back."

"He would take *me* back?" She paced across the floor again, four steps to the fireplace and four steps back. She had to do something to burn off the fury raging inside her. "How very gracious of him, but I refuse to take *him* back. I can't ignore what he did."

"Well, you should. Any woman of breeding ignores—"

"Ignores what? That her husband sleeps with other women?"

"They're called mistresses, Elizabeth."

Mother spoke calmly, so coolly, that Elizabeth stilled, all her fury draining from her at the mention of that one terrible word.

"Father has one, doesn't he?" The whispered accusation slipped from her mouth. Her lungs felt as though they would shatter if she breathed wrong, and a steel band, heavy and unbreakable, tightened about her heart. But still, it couldn't be true. Father wouldn't take a mistress. He couldn't. Perhaps he had his faults—she'd be the last person to proclaim him perfect—but he wouldn't betray her mother, her family, in such a manner.

A faint blush rose on Mother's cheeks. "Your father is very discreet, both personally and professionally. How should I know whether he has a mistress?"

"Don't lie to me. You know." Oh, goodness, she wanted to be sick. But she couldn't, not here in front of Mother, not with David and Father and Jackson across the hall. "A woman always knows that kind of thing."

She had with David. She'd just been too young and trusting to pay attention to the warnings inside her head.

"Don't you understand why you need to marry?" Mother stepped close, her eyes framed with unfulfilled dreams and glittering like bright, hard diamonds. "Mistresses don't matter, not in the grand picture of things. But a good marriage can take care of both you and your family."

Obey your parents. Honor them. The minister's words from Sunday's sermon curled like smoke around the recesses of her mind. But surely honoring her parents didn't mean she had to spend the rest of her life married to a man like David. Surely God wouldn't ask that of her, would He? "I'd never be able to keep him happy."

"Happy? What has happiness to do with duty?"

"You speak as though I neglect you, but I help the family whenever an opportunity arises. I make appearances with Father, attend your social events and give speeches on his behalf. I'm even giving a speech next week. Why can't that be enough?"

"We're going to lose our house, and you have the ability to stop it from happening, yet you refuse. Oh, dear, you're going to make me cry." Mother blinked her eyes frantically, but two large tears streaked down her cheeks. "Have you a hankie?"

Elizabeth reached into her pocket and handed Mother a chalk-dusted handkerchief.

"Thank you." Mother sniffled and dabbed at her face, unwittingly smearing the tears, cosmetic powder and chalk dust together into a pathetic mess on her skin. "I simply don't understand why you can't marry David and leave that wretched teaching job."

Elizabeth sighed. No. Mother didn't understand, not how important teaching was to her, or how miserable she'd be if she married David.

Perhaps Mother didn't understand because she didn't care to, or perhaps she was simply incapable of recognizing that some women had dreams which extended beyond marriage to a prominent husband. So round and round they went. Mother would never look at her life and see success, would never say, "Well done, Elizabeth. You're making a difference." She would only, always, see the world through her unchanging, marriage-hungry eyes.

"Good evening, then. I'm quite done here." Elizabeth hurried out of the study and to the front door, not stopping to ask for her coat or reticule. The cold air cloaked her as she rushed outside and down the steps. Then she halted, staring at the empty street.

The carriage. How could she have forgotten she'd ridden here in her parents' carriage? Mother certainly wouldn't offer to have the coachman return her to Valley Falls, and without her reticule, she could hardly pay to take the train home.

"No way home?" a cool voice asked from the steps.

Her body tensed. If only she could find some way not to turn around, some way not to face the man she'd once promised to wed. But that would involve walking down the street and into the night without either her coat or reticule. Her knees trembled and her hand locked onto the iron railing beside the steps as she turned.

"If you'll please step aside, I need to retrieve my things." She tried to move around David, but he shifted to the middle of the steps and extended his hands until they touched both railings, completely barring her way.

"You've changed."

"Yes. A great deal." She shivered. Didn't he realize that she needed her coat?

The lantern on the porch slanted down, illuminating David while his eyes narrowed and traveled down her once again—as though he hadn't learned enough from his earlier perusal in the drawing room. "I'm trying to determine if the change was for the better."

She stared into the smooth face, the hair black as midnight, and the brown eyes full of secrets. Most would call him handsome, but then, most people saw his outward charm rather than the blackness within. "And what about you? Have you changed? Or do you still keep a mistress in the house around the corner?"

He laughed, a bold, raucous sound. "Still upset about that, darling? No, if you must know. I tired of her long ago."

"And moved on to another, no doubt. Probably one who stays in Washington. Tell me, did you bring her with you on your trip here?"

"Come now, Elizabeth. No gentleman discusses his mistress with a lady. You know that."

No. You only discuss your mistresses with other gentlemen. The old wounds, long buried under the busyness of her current life, opened fresh as she stood before him, David DeVander, the man who had caused her untold hours of tears and heartache.

The man who had taught her never to trust another man again.

Of all the nights to have this conversation, all the times to face him, did it have to be now? Tonight? After Mother's lie and news of the house and missing her students' play?

She glanced down at her skirt, still splotched with chalk and cosmetic dust, and her shirtwaist tucked crookedly into her belt.

"I'm not much of a lady anymore," she whispered. Was it a bad thing?

"You would make any man a fine wife and if you marry me, I'll see that your family is taken care of. I'm sure you know your father's about to lose his house."

She tried to breathe, clean deep breaths that would calm her, allow her to think rationally. But the air choked off in her throat, and her entire body turned cold, then hot, then cold again. Mother had given her the same ultimatum inside, so why did the words seem more terrifying coming from David himself?

Perhaps because David's offer laid the choice bare in a way Mother's hadn't. Mother was always imploring her to marry one man or another, but never before had her family's house been at stake. Never before had someone made her so clear an offer: Marry and save your family or refuse and…and what?

She looked up at the house, the strong brick walls that

had sheltered her family for nearly thirty years, the bed-room in the upper left corner where she'd spent the first seventeen years of her life, the room that her parents shared on the opposite corner of the second floor. She could save it, allow Mother to keep her silks and Father to keep his dignity. Just one single, tiny word. *Yes.*

She licked her lips. The word wasn't hard to say, not even two syllables. So why did her tongue refuse to form it?

Because she didn't want a marriage based on a busi-ness contract. Perhaps some young ladies married for the reasons David delineated. But her? She'd shrivel up and die. Was the sacrifice worth it, her family for her soul?

"What are you thinking?" David's dark voice pierced her thoughts. "Tell me."

She took a step away from him. "You wouldn't want me. I've changed too much."

"You know how to behave, even if you've been off on this…" he twirled his hand in the air as though too bored to find the right word "…teaching escapade for several years. Your recent antics with newspaper articles have been a little much of late, but they merely prove a woman like yourself ought not be living on her own, without par-ents or a husband to answer to. It's nothing a solid hand couldn't correct once you're wed."

Solid hand. Correct. Did he think her some errant child?

"Furthermore, my late wife left me with two young sons. They need a mother. I need someone to host dinner parties and appear at political gatherings. You're a rather good orator and would do well speaking to ladies' groups and so forth."

A mother. A hostess. An orator. All the things he required in a wife. Still the man said nothing about *her* as a person. What she dreamed of, what she liked or disliked.

Because he didn't know. She'd been raised with him, their families were longtime friends. Then they fell into courtship and got betrothed at the proper ages. But he only knew her in the way one knew an objet d'art. A person could study the lines and forms of a sculpture, the position and facial expressions. But a statue was only clay or stone or marble, incapable of feeling or emotion, of behaving in any way other than what the sculptor designed.

That's what David wanted: a marble wife.

His golden-tipped words would have been enough once. But she'd changed; David was right in that assessment. And she'd rather spend her life teaching mathematics and offering her students a glimmer of hope instead of hanging on the arm of David DeVander or anyone of his ilk.

"I thank you for your compliments, Mr. DeVander. But truly, I must be going. Now if you'll let me pass so I can fetch my belongings." She tried to brush by him, but he grasped her shoulder and turned her face to his.

"You're beautiful, Elizabeth." He tucked a strand of hair behind her ear.

She lurched away, the feel of his fingers so near her face burning despite the cold seeping through her clothing. "Don't touch me."

He tightened his grip and dragged her closer. "I leave for Washington in two weeks. I need a wife before I return, and your family needs money. You think I don't know how badly off your father is? He can barely keep his house and staff and you can change all that—if you marry me."

"Elizabeth?" a rusty voice called from the direction of the street.

Elizabeth gulped a breath and closed her eyes. She'd imagined the voice, she must have. Luke couldn't be here, not now. She merely needed to open her eyes and see that no one stood on the walkway, particularly not a tall, lean man wearing a cowboy hat.

"What's going on here?" the voice growled.

She opened her eyes and took in the shadowed figure in the unmistakable cowboy hat. There was no denying Luke was here, all right, staring straight at her.

Luke wasn't sure whether to run up and yank Elizabeth from the scoundrel who held her on the steps or turn and head home. When he'd left Valley Falls an hour ago, he'd figured on finding any number of things at the Wells's house, but Elizabeth standing outside, practically in the arms of another man, wasn't one of them.

She tried to step down, probably to greet him, but rather than release her shoulder, the other man pulled her back against his chest. Luke curled his fingers into hard fists.

"Can I help you?" the dandy asked in a voice as smooth and liquid as water itself.

Luke flicked his gaze to Elizabeth. "Since you're not keeping vigil near your mother, I assume she's feeling a mite better."

"Yes, I—"

"The students were worried, especially Samantha. I volunteered to come check on you. Though I see they got their dander up over nothing."

"Is that what your mother did to get you here?" The other man laughed, a chilling sound. "Sent word she was ill?"

The laugher must have loosened his hold, because Elizabeth jerked away and headed down the steps. "It's not funny. My students were counting on me."

"I'm sure they were, darling. I'm sure they were."

She stopped before Luke, and he stilled as the words

sank in. Her mother had tricked her by sending word she was ill? Why would she do such a thing? Surely Mrs. Wells didn't begrudge her daughter helping with a play.

Luke shifted closer, running his eyes down Elizabeth's slender form. Her face didn't carry the flushed look of anticipation one might expect from a woman meeting with a lover, but glowed pale and taut with tension in the dim lamplight. Lines etched the corners of her mouth, while smudges haunted the hollows beneath her eyes, and her dirty, serviceable clothing hung limp and twisted on her frame. Not the way a woman would look if she had a rendezvous with a man.

She shivered under his gaze—no, not under his gaze. She was freezing. Hang it all, he'd been too all-fired frustrated to notice how cold she was.

"Where's your coat? Did you leave home without it?" He shrugged out of his and wrapped it about her shoulders. "And why are you outside without something to keep you warm?"

"My coat's inside with my reticule." She hunched her shoulders against the cool air and stretched the coat tight around herself. "I was heading inside to retrieve them when I was…intercepted."

He glanced toward his carriage, then back to her disheveled form. "You need a ride home?"

"She most certainly does not," the other man interrupted. "She's coming inside to dinner. Aren't you, darling?"

"Stop calling me 'darling.'" Her body stayed slumped as she spoke, as though she hadn't the energy to straighten and raise her chin in that familiar, haughty angle. As though the man on the steps had already defeated her.

"Aren't you going to introduce me to your friend, *darling?*" Something sharp glinted in the man's eyes.

Luke shifted in front of Elizabeth as the scoundrel came forward.

"Mr. DeVander, this is Luke Hayes, grandson of the late Jonah Hayes, whom I'm sure you remember." Gone was the usual steel behind Elizabeth's voice, replaced by a small quiver. "Mr. Hayes, this is David DeVander, United States Representative of our congressional district."

DeVander. The name set off warning sounds. Luke looked the scoundrel up and down, from the top of his sleek black hair to the tips of his shiny shoes. Where had he heard…?

DeVander. Luke hardened his jaw while Stevens's words echoed inside him. This was the man who had offered to marry Elizabeth and then taken a mistress.

"The Hayes heir." DeVander straightened and extended his hand, his eyes assessing, probably trying to figure whether he could hit up the new heir for a donation. "It's a pleasure to meet you."

Luke stared at the offered hand and pushed some spittle around in his mouth. If only the lady wasn't present…

He settled a hand on Elizabeth's shoulder instead. "Do you want to leave? I can take you in my carriage and send a footman later for your things."

"I already said she was attending dinner," DeVander barked. "And she can hardly ride back to Valley Falls with you unchaperoned."

Unchaperoned in a carriage. Did that break one of the social rules? Probably. Simply breathing was enough to break half those highfalutin guidelines. But at the very least, he could take the train and give Elizabeth his carriage.

"As though you would complain if I rode unchaperoned in a carriage with you," Elizabeth snapped at DeVander, then turned. "I appreciate your offer, Luke. I can use a ride home."

Luke extended his arm, and she took it.

"Very well, Elizabeth." DeVander glowered at them through the darkness. "I'll be waiting to hear your decision."

A shudder rippled down her slender frame as she headed to the carriage.

Chapter Thirteen

"What happened back there?"

Elizabeth's bottom had barely touched the carriage seat before Luke asked his question.

What *had* happened? She pressed her shaking fingers to her temples. She wasn't sure. Mother had deceived her and arranged an engagement to David. Father had a mistress—which evidently wasn't a shock to anyone but her. And David had proposed.

No it wasn't just a proposal. David had offered to help her family out of their current disastrous situation *if* she married him. The hard timbre of his voice as he made his offer resonated through her memory.

"Elizabeth?" Luke's fingers, firm but warm, took her chin and lifted it up until their eyes met.

She pulled back and sank deeper into the carriage seat. If only she could be home. In her own bed, that sat in her own room, that was part of her own house, surrounded by her own soothing things, in the comfortable world she'd created for herself.

She would be there in a little over an hour. She just had to endure the ride home with Luke first.

The carriage lamp burned above them, casting the inside of the conveyance in a soft orange glow. She shrank farther away from Luke. Why did it have to be lit? Darkness had cloaked their ride back to Valley Falls after the banquet, but now he could see everything about her, from her dirty clothes to her falling hair to the tears brimming in her eyes.

She shouldn't be in the carriage with him at all. David had been right in that respect. She'd get in trouble if someone at the academy found out she'd ridden alone with Luke Hayes, and David would likely announce her lack of propriety to the world if doing so served his purposes. But still, letting Luke, with all his assessing looks and uncomfortable questions, escort her home seemed a small difficulty compared to walking back inside her parents' house.

The carriage wheels clattered against Albany's cobbled roads. Snorts, groans, creaks and shouts from all manner of conveyance, beast and persons echoed through the space she and Luke shared, but the noise from outside didn't thwart the quiet that lingered between them.

She looked down at her hands, curled atop the soft brown leather of his duster, and settled deeper inside the warmth it offered. The scents of sunshine and grass and Luke Hayes clung to the material, as though she need only close her eyes and she could be with him in some Wyoming meadow, the sun beating down upon her back and wildflowers surrounding her. So very far away from the chaos her life had become.

"Elizabeth?"

She glanced up. Luke leaned forward, his eyes intent upon her face, probably still waiting to hear what had happened that evening. She could evade, of course. Change the subject or flat-out refuse to speak of the evening. Except she couldn't ride the entire way to Valley Falls with his gaze boring into her and silence strangling the air.

"My family…" she started, but tears welled up to choke her throat.

"Your family is the biggest bunch of conniving rats I've ever met."

She gasped and blinked against the burning in her eyes.

"Your ma tricked you out of helping with the play so you would come here and have dinner with that snake DeVander. Am I right?"

She looked away.

"But you didn't stay."

She sank her head in her hands. "Oh, goodness, what have I done? I was so disrespectful. Mother will never want to speak to me again. And Father, how will I ever stand up and give that speech for him?"

She was still supposed to speak to her fellow educators in two days' times. And now that David was in town, he was sure to be there as well, giving a speech on the benefits of education. His attendance had likely been planned—and concealed from her—from the beginning.

She couldn't do it. It simply wasn't possible for her to stand up and smile and speak to educators on David's behalf.

Luke's fingers gently wrapped around her wrists, tugging her hands away from her face. "You did the right thing. You shouldn't have stayed, not when your ma used deceit to get you there."

"You heard the sermon on Sunday. 'Children obey your parents. Rebellion is as the sin of witchcraft, and stubbornness is as iniquity and idolatry.'" The scripture tasted bitter on her tongue, and try as she might, she couldn't stop a tear or two from slipping down her face. "Mother's right. I'm a terrible daughter."

"No." He wiped one of her tears away with his thumb. "You're a strong, courageous woman. A tad bit independent but beautiful for it. You like teaching and helping your students. You challenge those girls to be better, more educated people than they were before you met them. You've got nothing to be ashamed of."

His words swirled around her. Supportive and hopeful and kinder than anything she'd heard all night, probably even all month. Was her independence truly beautiful? Did she mean that much to her students? And if so, how could she mean so much to them and so little to her family? "You don't understand."

"No?"

"Maybe my students appreciate me, but according to Mother, I'm sinning by refusing to marry someone who will support Father until…until he can…"

The torrent of sobs building inside her chest broke in one violent gush. She pressed her hand to her mouth, trying to stem the swelling flood.

Luke watched her for a moment, then pulled her against himself and held tight. Tears dampened the front of his shirt, and her petticoats crinkled awkwardly against his legs; but he didn't unleash a harsh rebuke about puffy eyes, unlady-like behavior or tears ruining his clothing. He only tightened his hold, his muscled arms offering strength and protection, his solid chest lending stability and support. She buried her face into his shoulder and cried until she had no tears left.

Then she cried harder, after the tears refused to come but her soul still ached.

He simply held on.

"Hush now, there's nothing wrong with you. I doubt you're disobeying God."

The words soaked through slowly, seeping in layer by layer, and filling the icy cavern inside her chest.

"What does God want for your life?" He stroked his

hand down her back then up again, gentle, soothing movements. "We're to obey God over men. Have you read the story of Jonathan in the Bible? He didn't always obey his parents. He was best friends with his father's worst enemy, but he still honored God by saving David from his father's hands."

"Jonathan." She sniffled. "Mother always quotes that verse about Saul and rebellion. And here God's answer lies in Saul's son."

"There're consequences for disobeying your parents. The Bible tells us to obey both God and the family He's given us. If God and family are at odds with one another, the person caught in the middle will have heartache, to be sure. But we ought to always obey God first."

She wiped her face with his coat sleeve. "I hadn't considered Jonathan, my parents and God being at odds, any of it."

"And now you have." His hand continued to rub up and down her back, comforting even though her tears had stopped. "Feel better?"

"Yes, thank you," she croaked, her voice hoarse and froglike.

He shifted to offer his handkerchief, and with the simple movement, his side pressed hard into hers.

Entirely too hard.

Where was she sitting? *How* was she sitting? She glanced down and found herself nearly on his lap, with her head touching the crook of his shoulder and his arm tight around her back.

She scrambled away. "I'm sorry. I shouldn't have…that is, it was very improper for… I mean…"

He laughed, actually laughed. Not a raucous sound at her expense like David's cackles but an encouraging guffaw from deep inside. "No need to get your feathers in a ruffle. I can keep a secret."

"Thank you." She glanced down, then back up. "It seems that's all I'm doing this evening, thanking you and then apologizing."

His lips slid into that lazy half smile and he handed over a handkerchief. "Everyone's allowed a bad night once in a while."

She glanced away, her cheeks suddenly hot.

"You feeling a bit better after that cry?"

She nodded without looking up.

"Good. So now we've got that business over your parents settled, tell me about this DeVander fellow."

She dabbed her face with the hankie. "Nothing much to tell, really. Just my mother's latest suitor for me."

"Who you were once engaged to."

Her eyes snapped to his. "How'd you know?"

"My butler told me."

"Why would your butler—?"

"I asked."

"You just happened to ask if I had any former fiancés?" Ugh. She could just imagine that conversation.

The side of his mouth twitched up into that smile again. "No. I asked why you weren't married."

"Oh…"

The carriage rumbled over the road that had turned from cobblestones to dirt. A faint draft stirred around the boxed-in conveyance, and a coyote yipped in the distance. She stared down at her lap, folding and unfolding her hands, unable to bring her eyes to meet his. "And why would you ask about a thing like that?"

"Seemed relevant."

"I can assure you, it's not."

"Then why were you standing outside with your former fiancé?"

"Because Mother…Mother…" Should she continue? And why was she even tempted to blurt her life's troubles to Luke Hayes?

She slid her eyes toward him, his firm jaw and solid shoulders. The man seemed strong enough to carry any burden she unveiled—and determined enough not to let her out of the carriage until she answered.

"David's wife died recently. So he needs another, you see, for appearance's sake. Mother wants it to be me. Did you know Father lost a lot of money in the panic?" She swallowed. "Actually he lost everything. His bank collapsed, and his campaign finances, his personal savings, his investments in the railroad… Everything is gone.

"So after the panic, he mortgaged his house, thinking that he only needed a little time to build his investments back up. But now Mother and Father are through that money and on the brink of losing their home and… um… David is still well off. So if I marry him, he would take care of my fam—"

"No." The single word sliced through the carriage.

She stared down at her hands, still curled in Luke's coat. "He can save my parents."

Luke shifted close, so close his broad shoulders blocked the carriage lamp. He trailed a finger from her cheekbone to her jaw, then laid it over her lips. Probably to silence her, though she could hardly speak with his hand warm against her face.

"You'd be wasting your life." The breath from his whispered words brushed her face. "And you'd hate marriage to him."

She knew as much, but how did he? What enabled him

to discern such a thing after spending only five minutes' time with David?

His other hand came up to caress her cheek, and he inched forward until his face obliterated everything else from her vision. Her gaze dipped to his mouth. The slightest movement from either of them, and their lips would touch.

What would it feel like, being kissed by a cowboy? David's kisses had been smooth and seductive, but something told her kissing Luke Hayes would be in no way similar.

She should pull away. Shift back. Slap him. Move to the bench on the opposite side of the carriage. Anything to distract her from those lips.

But she didn't.

Instead, she leaned forward, propelled by some inward desire she didn't understand, part curiosity, part defiance, part longing.

Their lips brushed, and a wave of warmth started where their mouths met and traveled to her toes. She closed her eyes against the tender contact, the way time suspended as her lips rubbed briefly against his. Then she sighed and pulled back.

"Not yet," he whispered, taking her shoulders and covering her mouth with his own.

The man was controlled strength, no pretense or secrets. His lips were firm but not hard, demanding but not reckless. His muscled arms wrapped around her, drawing her closer. His unyielding lips kissed her slowly at first, his mouth whispering a silent message as it lingered against hers. *Trust me.*

Kissing Miss Wells was like unwrapping a present. Slowly drawing off the ribbon, then the wrapping. Taking the lid off the box, and digging through the tissue.

She had so many layers—the proper lady, the dignified teacher, the steely politician's daughter, the soft woman. He peeled them back until her heart shimmered like diamonds in his hands.

He knew the moment he had gained her trust. Her muscles relaxed, her breathing grew deeper and her hands became restless as they slipped from his neck to his shoulders.

And what was he doing? Kissing Miss Wells in a carriage, while she hadn't even a chaperone? She was a city woman who lived thousands of miles from his ranch. A politician's daughter who faced bigger decisions than kissing him. A teacher who did unfathomable good for her students and didn't need him getting in the way of her dreams or hurting her reputation.

He leaned back, abruptly breaking the kiss. But she clung to his shirt, her eyes closed, her face upturned, her breathing erratic. Then her eyelids flickered open, and he stared into pure, dreamy hazel.

He should have never ended that kiss.

He should have never started it.

A splotch of red stained her cheeks and spread until it covered her face and neck. She put a hand to her cheek. "Luke, I—"

"You don't kiss me like that and then try apologizing," he growled, more frustrated with himself over what he'd started than whatever she called him.

He hadn't thought it possible for her face to grow redder, but it did. She fixed her eyes on some teeny speck on the floor and wrapped her arms around herself in a half-hearted hug. "This… I… We can't do this. It will lead to trouble." Her eyes shone large and luminous in the lamplight; her lips full and swollen from his kiss.

He should take her in his arms and repeat the kiss. Only

this time, he wouldn't stop to worry about where she lived or who her parents were or what she did for a living. This time he'd kiss her and hold her like a man who planned to be in Valley Falls for the next fifty years. Because right about now, he wanted to be that man for her.

But he couldn't.

He didn't have time to get involved with Elizabeth, and even if he did muddle into a relationship, what happened when he returned to Wyoming? He couldn't take her with him. Where would she teach? The Teton Valley already had a teacher for its tiny schoolhouse.

And why was he thinking about taking her West? A man didn't up and pick a bride after one kiss.

Did he?

He swallowed. No. Definitely not.

"I, um…" Some of the flush had left Elizabeth's face, and her skin took on that irresistibly creamy hue again as she pushed words through her stammering mouth. "That is… I want you to know, that…I—I…don't really kiss…" Her finger traced an imaginary pattern on her lap. "Well, you remember what I told you? About how much I enjoy teaching? And the board of directors feels very strongly about its teachers behaving with the utmost propriety. So, you see, um…I can't really…"

"You won't kiss me again, but you'll consider marrying a scoundrel like David DeVander." The realization twisted something deep inside him. Maybe he was a tad crazy to get so moonstruck over one kiss. But the thought of her going to DeVander, kissing the snake the way she'd just kissed him, ignited fire in his blood.

"If you could please just keep from telling anyone about this, this…indiscretion. I didn't mean to kiss you, and it won't happen again."

"That's two indiscretions in the past hour I'm supposed to keep secret."

"Indeed. I'll be more careful in my future encounters with you."

"Tell you what. I'll keep your secrets, if you refuse to marry DeVander."

Her eyes flew up to his. "You can't make such a demand. My relationship with David is hardly your business."

"I'm making it my business."

Her spine straightened, inch by inch, revealing the steel hidden beneath her veneer of softness. "And why is that? Are you prepared to give my family the money they need to keep their house? Or maybe you'll make me an offer like David's. Marriage in exchange for helping my family?"

"Would you consider it?"

He'd gone daft. Crazier than a senile old man. What made him say that? Sure, Elizabeth was being smart with him, but he didn't want a citified wife in the first place, and certainly didn't plan to get one by making a business deal.

"I used to think I knew what I wanted, could reach my dreams." She stared blindly at the far wall. "But I don't think I can do anything anymore—except for marry the man Mother's picked out."

And now she was thinking her life worthless. She'd had a hard enough night already, and here he was being harsh on her all over again. He reached over and took her hand. "You've reached your dreams, and you're a good teacher. Do you realize that? Every one of your students is better for having sat in your classes, for having known you as a person."

"Most of my girls would rather run screaming from the room than study advanced algebra."

He grinned. "I doubt that, Lizzie. Really."

"Don't call me Lizzie."

"Beth, then."

If a look could shoot poisoned arrows, he'd be dead several times over.

"Say you won't marry DeVander, and I'll call you Elizabeth."

"You can't talk me out of marriage by threatening to call or not call me some name."

He scratched his forehead beneath his hat brim. "It makes me furious to see you all but forced into marriage."

"Why?"

Because marriage should be more than a business arrangement. Because Elizabeth loved teaching and should pursue that rather than chain herself to a snake like DeVander. Because Pa and Grandpa had spent forty years of their lives not speaking to each other over this very issue.

"Because I don't cotton to browbeating people into marriage." And for some reason he didn't understand, he'd forfeit his entire inheritance to prevent the smart little teacher beside him from falling into that trap.

Elizabeth pressed her palm against the cold bedroom window and stared out over the street. Luke's carriage had disappeared around the corner moments earlier, but still, she couldn't pull her gaze from the path it had followed.

She rubbed her eyes, trying to dispel the image of him inside the conveyance from her mind. Or the image of him squaring off with David. Or the one of him sending the reporter scampering away after the banquet. She could alternate between the images at will, but try as she might, she couldn't fully shake those clear blue eyes from her memory.

Or his words. *What does God want for your life?*

To teach, of course. The answer was so obvious to him that she hadn't the slightest notion why he'd bothered to ask. But then, why was the answer obvious to him, and not Mother or Father or Jackson? Why did a rancher from Wyoming understand her better than the people who'd known her since birth?

He'd sat in the carriage and held her, calm despite the storm raging inside her, open and straightforward despite her family's deceit.

And she loved him for it.

Oh, goodness. She *loved* him.

No. She couldn't. Perhaps she'd grown fond of him, and perhaps she counted him a friend. But she didn't love him, certainly not. David had hurt her too badly to love again.

She let the curtains fall, shutting out the world beyond her own little room. She didn't want to love a man, especially not a man who'd come to take his sister away and sell off Jonah's life work.

She moved from the window and sank down onto her bed. She wouldn't let herself love Luke Hayes. Perhaps he played the attentive gentleman—or rancher—when she was about. But hadn't David? Maybe he kissed her as though she meant something. But hadn't David? Perhaps he would even say he loved her. But she couldn't be sure he'd love her forever, couldn't say with certainty he'd still love her five years from now.

And so she wouldn't love him. It was a simple decision, really, to close off one's heart. She'd done it once before. She could do it again.

Chapter Fourteen

"Proposed? What do you mean Jackson proposed?" Luke shot to his feet as his words reverberated throughout his grandfather's office.

Samantha cringed but stood her ground in front of the gargantuan desk, the sapphire on her finger sparkling far too brightly.

"I said the two of you could go horseback riding… with a *chaperone*." He blew out a breath, long and hard. Control, he needed to find a bit of it, before he launched himself over the desk and went on a warpath to find a certain accountant and wrap his hands around the miscreant's throat. "I never said anything about agreeing to an engagement. The scoundrel didn't even ask me if he could marry you."

"He's waiting outside the door to do so now, if you'd stop shouting."

"I'm…not…shouting." It was more like hollering, really. "What's the point of him asking *after* he's put a ring on your finger?"

"There's no point of him asking you at all. You're not my father, and Jackson wrote to Pa nearly a week ago."

Sam's face had turned a ghostly shade of white, and her words came quietly, without hint of defiance or menace.

Luke scratched the back of his neck and paced behind the desk. He should have strangled the boy nearly a week ago. Right around the time he found the scamp kissing his sister's face off.

"Besides, Grandpa was good friends with the Wellses and would have given his approval in a heartbeat. Asking Pa is just formality. He has no reason to refuse."

"Grandpa and Pa didn't speak. If anything, Pa's likely to say no to Jackson simply because Grandpa liked him." Luke planted his hands on the desk and leaned forward. "And do you really think Pa's not going to ask my thoughts, just give you blind permission to marry some man he's never met?"

She gasped and took a step back from the desk, moisture shimmering in her eyes. "You wouldn't deny me the man I love out of spite."

He sighed. "Not out of spite, Sam. Out of concern. I don't trust him." And not only that, but getting Sam back home was going to be a heap harder now that she had a ring on her finger.

"How can you say such a thing? Jackson's wonderful." She blinked back the moisture in her eyes, but it did little good as a tear crested anyway. "You'd see that for yourself, if only you'd give him a chance."

"Don't cry." Here he was calling Jackson a scoundrel, but wasn't he the bigger scoundrel of the two of them? Seemed he made his sister cry every time they talked. He walked around the desk and offered his kerchief, then wrapped his arm around her shoulders. "You need to go home for a bit, Sam. Not stay here and marry. We can try to work something out with Jackson, and I'll meet with him. But that still doesn't change your needing to go home."

And it still didn't change his thoughts about not trusting the younger man.

Why didn't he trust Jackson? Because of the ten thousand dollars Sam would inherit upon marrying? If she didn't have an inheritance, would he feel differently about Jackson? Maybe he was being unfair. They'd begun courting before Grandpa had fallen ill—before Sam had become an heiress. And even if the man's parents were in financial trouble, that didn't mean Jackson was. The boy made a good salary at the accounting office, after all.

"I've told you before." Sam buried her face against his shirt as the tears fell. "I don't want to go home, not now, when I've so many things to do out here."

A hard knock sounded at the door.

"Hold on—"

"Come in," Sam sniffled.

The door swung open, and Jackson slid in. His eyes slanted immediately toward Sam, and he moved to her with the speed and agility of a wolf chasing its prey. "Samantha, love, what's wrong?"

Luke scowled but pulled his arm from his sister, who immediately threw herself against Jackson.

"Come now, our engagement is cause for celebration, not tears." Jackson spoke against her temple.

Luke took a step back from the entwined couple. Was he a monster? Some terrible ogre for not simply agreeing to the wedding his sister clearly wanted? Yet he could hardly agree when Sam needed to return home to Ma—and he wondered if the marriage would hurt Sam eventually.

"Two days," Luke croaked. "Give me two days to think

about the proposal. And, Jackson, I need to speak with you when you're done attending Sam."

What was he going to do? Luke settled his shoulder against the glittering gold doorjamb of his grandfather's bedroom, a room he hadn't yet entered since arriving in Valley Falls, and rubbed the back of his neck.

Coming to Valley Falls was supposed to be simple. He'd had two goals in mind: sell off Grandpa's estate and take Sam back home. What had happened to his plans? It seemed the longer he stayed here, the more confused he became. He was supposed to hate this town, this house, the staff, the insurance and accounting company. But he didn't.

Oh, sure, he'd been slow warming up to it all; but after a week of staring at numbers and looking over his grandfather's businesses, the companies didn't seem so intimidating. He wasn't a fan of the gilt trim and pristine decorations tacked up all over the house, but the structure itself was rather pleasant, with its sprawling design and wide window-filled rooms and kind staff.

But even more than the house, his work here mattered. Ranchers were a dime a dozen west of the Mississippi and though he'd employed a handful of people, his ranch only affected the dozen men that worked for him.

As head of Great Northern Accounting and Insurance, he had hundreds of employees depending on him, and that wasn't even considering the staff he employed here at the house, or all the good Grandpa's charitable endeavors had wrought.

Time was when he'd not been able to imagine himself living anywhere but on his ranch. But now, after a mere week in Valley Falls, he saw himself here, too. Waking up every morning to those shadowed Catskill Mountains and managing the legacy his grandfather had left.

He stared into his grandpa's room, fully lit in all its gaudy, golden splendor. Did the man regret the choices he'd made? The one that had forced his son away? He appeared to have changed at some point in his life. To hear Pa speak, Grandpa was a controlling, greedy self-made man. But a greedy man wouldn't give half his profits to charity or one of his houses to a schoolteacher.

Luke ran his eyes over the walnut-and-white-silk headboard, the gargantuan bed covered in snowy white, the elaborate nightstand and dresser. Who was this man, his grandfather?

He took a step into the room, then another and another, until he reached the dresser. The sun cast its fading rays through the windows as he opened the top drawer and began to sort.

Three hours later, chaotic piles littered the room. Clothes to be donated over here, things to be discarded over there, items to be saved beside it. Sam had already gone through the closet, leaving the heaps of clothing and other items on the far side of the room, and he was making an even bigger mess.

Luke opened the top drawer of the nightstand and pulled out a Bible. Flipping through, he trailed his thumbs over the worn, note-marked pages. He stopped at a passage in Psalms where it seemed every verse had been notated, then turned a few more pages. The Bible seemed to fall open to the first chapter of Proverbs on its own. And there, at the beginning of the book on wisdom, lay an envelope with the name Luke Hayes scrawled across it.

He ran his finger over the sprawling letters. Was it truly for him? Sure it carried his name, but a letter of any importance wouldn't be tucked into an obscure corner of

Grandpa's room, would it? Still, he slipped a finger beneath the seal and opened it. Inside lay a single piece of stationary and a smaller envelope with Pa's name.

My Grandson,

If you hold this letter, that means you have arrived in Valley Falls, likely as my heir, and are busy seeing to the business matters which I left you. It brings me joy knowing the son of my son is in my house caring for my legacy, and it brings me pain knowing I died without ever laying eyes on you.

Be wise, Luke. I leave you a life's work, some of it built upon ambition and greed, some of it built upon love and hard work. Do not make the mistakes I did during my early and middle years. Do not sacrifice family for ambition or love for greed. I pray when you one day reach my age and sit penning letters to your children and grandchildren, you'll look back on your own life with no regrets.

Keep the Bible, keep the house, keep anything of mine you wish. Use it wisely, and please give the enclosed letter to your father.

Sincerely
Jonah P. Hayes

Luke stared at the large, uneven handwriting until the words blurred. *Don't sacrifice family for ambition or love for greed.* The man would know. He'd made mistakes for most of his life and evidently only set about correcting them at the end.

But Luke was already on a better track than Grandpa. He sought to sell the things Grandpa left, so he could return home and reunite his family before Ma's death. Yep, he would place his family before ambition by selling the house and everything else.

And what about Cynthia and Everett? Are you forcing them to go back, as well? Sam's words rippled through his mind. But surely he wasn't supposed to take them back to Wyoming. He wasn't even obligated to see them. Cynthia had married into the family and held no blood relation.

But Everett…Everett was his twin's blood. Blake's legacy and heir.

A sickening sensation fisted in his gut. He was shutting out family—not so much for his own ambition, and not just because of his anger and grief, but to forget his own failures. And he would regret it one day. Confound it, he regretted it even now, the hard words he'd spoken to Cynthia over Blake's body, the way he'd sent her packing before she saw her husband buried.

And he was being just as controlling with Sam, in pressing her to make amends, to go back and see Ma, to be a part of the family once again. She was seventeen and standing on the edge of womanhood, yet he pushed her to settle things in his way and his time, not leaving any part of the decision up to her.

Luke sunk his head in his hands. Truly he was as bad as Grandpa. He was making all the same mistakes, just in different ways. Forcing those he loved to do something, regardless of his motives, was controlling and ruthless. And he wouldn't do it anymore.

He'd find out where Cynthia lived—somewhere near Philadelphia, if he recalled—and ask her to forgive him, see how she wanted to settle things. Maybe the woman wished to move back West. Maybe she wanted her son, *Blake's son,* raised somewhere else. Maybe she longed to be a part of the Hayes family again. He would leave the decision up to her but she'd have his support no matter what she chose.

As for Sam, he had to tell her about Ma. He'd promised Ma that he'd keep quiet, but he never would have made that promise had he known how much Sam loved her life here. Sam was grown enough to wear some man's ring on her finger, and if she was grown enough for that, she was grown enough to make her own decisions about Ma. He wouldn't be like Grandpa one day, looking back from the end of his life and wishing he'd been more honest with Sam, regretting that he hadn't let her make her own choices.

He only hoped it wasn't too late for Samantha and Ma. As for Cynthia…he'd find out where he stood when he got to Philadelphia.

"Luke?" A soft voice echoed from the doorway. Sam stood there, dressed for bed in a white lacy nightgown.

She glanced around the cluttered room. "You're going through Grandpa's things? Now? I can help some more. I don't mind. I just didn't want to sort through this stuff instead of attending school."

"I'm sorry, Sam."

She blinked. "For what?"

Everything, it seemed. "For trying to force you back West."

Her eyes turned wide as a boy's who'd just been given his first rifle.

"Come sit." He patted the floor beside him.

She came, trusting and innocent, and tucked herself up against his side.

He slowly rubbed circles on her back. "I never should have tried forcing you to go home."

"*This* is my home."

He held up a hand, stopping the argument before it

started afresh. "Forcing you *West*. It's your choice to make, not mine. And…" He fingered Grandpa's letter, its edges crisp beneath his touch. "I was afraid if I left things up to you, you'd choose the wrong thing."

Her eyes shot tiny sparks. "So you still think it's wrong for me to stay here?"

"Yes. No. I…" He growled and scratched behind his ear. "I have my reasons for wanting you to go back. The main one being Ma…"

His words jammed together in his throat, so many of them aching for release. But how to get them out without ruining things again?

"I know she misses me. You've told me before. And I miss her, too, but I'm not going to leave for Wyoming in the middle of the school year. Maybe later, sometime over the summer, I can come see her. I want her to meet Jackson, after all, and—"

"Summer will be too late, if you want to see her alive." The words fell from his tongue, hard and shattering and unavoidable. "She's dying, Sam. She's got consumption."

Sam grew still, her chest barely rising enough to give her breath. Her face drained of color, starting at the top of her forehead and slowly blanching until her skin shone white as snow. She reached a hand out and gripped his forearm, and her fingers trembled as they dug into his shirtsleeve. "No, she can't be dying. I don't believe it."

He placed his hand over her cold fingers. "I should have told you sooner. Ma wanted me to keep it secret, wanted you to stay out here and continue your life without worrying about her. But I look at you, and though I expected to find the girl I dropped off at the train station three years ago, you've changed in the time you've been here. You're grown up now, thinking about marriage, planning your future. You've got a right to know about Ma, a right to make your own decision about whether you see her before she dies.

"I was wrong for keeping it secret." He swiped a stray strand of hair away from her face. "I won't try forcing you to do things my way anymore. The decision's yours, but I'm telling you, your ma's dying, and if you want to see her, you've got to go soon."

"How long?" Moisture pooled in her eyes, and she didn't look at him but stared vacantly at a spot on the wall above his shoulder. "With something like consumption, a doctor can tell how long, can't he?"

"Maybe, sometimes. But Ma seems set on hiding how sick she is from the doc. Seems set on hiding it from everyone, really. The doc said she'll last through next summer, but she gets a little sicker every day, and she won't…" The aching sadness fisted in his chest again. One would think he'd grow used to saying the words aloud, but they caught in his throat every time.

"I want to go." Tears coursed down Sam's cheeks. "Now. As soon as I can. I can come back to school later, can't I? Come and finish up?"

"Whatever you want." He wrapped an arm around her shoulders and pushed her face into his chest, her body trembling against his. "Forgive me for not telling you sooner?"

With her face still buried in his shirt, she nodded.

He stroked his hands through her falling gold tresses in soothing, comforting motions. Or so he hoped. Because truly, one could do so very little to soothe when the pain inside ran as deep as life itself. "You'll need to decide about Jackson, as well. I won't stand in the way of you and him—"

"He can wait." She pulled back and met his gaze, determination etching her voice despite its slight wobble. "I need to see Ma. She's more important right now, wouldn't you say? And there's no need to rush on setting a wedding date, not with Ma so ill."

Sam twisted the sapphire ring, then slid it off her hand. "Maybe you should keep this for me until we sort things out. Do you think Jackson will wait for me to get back?"

Luke closed the ring in his grip and pulled Sam in for another hug. "The man would be daft not to."

"Thank you for meeting with me, Elizabeth."

Elizabeth smiled at Miss Bowen and took a chair across from where the headmistress sat behind the wide desk in her office. But rather than offer her usual prim smile or begin the conversation, the older woman looked down at her hands and fidgeted with a stack of papers.

Elizabeth swallowed. This couldn't be good.

"It's the academy, isn't it?" she blurted out. "The school board decided to close us down despite the money Mr. Hayes has donated and that favorable article in the paper."

Miss Bowen's gray eyes shot up to hers, and the lines of her painfully straight suit almost seemed to slump with resignation. "No, Elizabeth, it's not the academy we need to discuss but Mr. Hayes himself."

"Mr. Hayes?" The sandwich she'd eaten several hours ago for lunch threatened to come up.

"It's been brought to my attention that you and Mr. Hayes traveled back from Albany Saturday night in his carriage. Alone."

She tried not to cringe. "I...um..."

"Do you deny it?"

She stared at her feet, at the swirling golden vines and leaves on the rug. "No, it's true. I hadn't planned to be unchaperoned with him. It simply..." A vision of David standing on the steps making his marriage offer seeped into her mind. "It seemed the best choice at the time. My family and I were facing some…difficulties, and Mr. Hayes offered me a ride home."

"I'm glad to know it was an exception." Though nothing about the severe lines on Miss Bowen's face looked glad. "After all, you've been here over two years, and I've never received any complaints about your conduct until this morning."

Elizabeth fisted her hands in her skirt. A complaint, and David was the only one to see her leave with Luke.

"But you are aware of Hayes's policy regarding teachers courting?" Miss Bowen's tight-laced voice echoed loudly against office's sparse walls. "A chaperone is to be present at all times."

"Yes. A chaperone." Elizabeth licked her lips, as though she could still feel the firm pressure of Luke's mouth against hers, the way the stubble on his jaw brushed her chin.

Which was why a chaperone was needed—to prevent situations like that. Her cheeks burned, and she glanced away from the headmistress. "M-Mr. Hayes was only being gentlemanly. Being from Wyoming, he's not exactly aware of society's rules about chaperones and propriety and such. But I assure you, he didn't have any ill intentions." Except for the kiss. That exquisite, wonderful kiss. One which would likely remain unparalleled for the rest of her life.

At least she'd have something to give her sweet memories when she was eighty.

"You do remember the Code of Conduct you signed when first agreed to teach at Hayes?"

"Yes, ma'am." The document had been fifteen pages of painstakingly small rules. True, she couldn't recall every minute detail, but the chaperone one had probably been in there. "What's to be done, then? Do you need to inform the board?"

"I should. Our procedures ask that the board be notified in these types of situations." Miss Bowen sighed and repositioned her glasses on her nose. "Though your mother's illness did bring about some extenuating and unforeseen circumstances. I trust she has recovered?"

The moisture leeched from her throat. "Yes, quite."

"Well, then, since nothing inappropriate happened between you and Mr. Hayes…"

Her heart pounded. Nothing inappropriate? She'd hardly call that kiss "nothing inappropriate," but then Miss Bowen wasn't asking for confirmation so much as assuming the best.

"…And in light of all Mr. Hayes has done to keep the school open, I will refrain from informing the board this once. We can hardly have such a story leaking out and casting Mr. Hayes and the school in a bad light."

Elizabeth forced a smile. Luke wouldn't be the one seen in a bad light nearly so much as her, but if Luke's help with the school would get her out of this situation, then she'd hardly complain.

"So, Elizabeth, please make certain that you're not alone with Mr. Hayes again."

"Thank you for understanding. I'll be more careful from now on." And she refused to think about why that depressed her.

"I won't make another exception like—"

A knock sounded on the office door, and the secretary entered.

"Yes, Sarah?" Miss Bowen asked.

But Sarah didn't look at the headmistress. "Elizabeth… er, Miss Wells. There's a reporter here to see you."

"A reporter? From the *Morning Times?*" But she already knew the answer. Who else could the reporter be other than Mr. Reginald Higsley? And the man was likely seething since Luke had gotten that retraction printed in the paper. The reporter had probably come to find more lies to print.

What if he'd dug up an embarrassing piece of information from her past?

Or worse, what if he'd learned about David's recent "proposal"?

The air around her turned thick, and her hands began to tremble.

"Miss Wells?" Sarah held the door open. "He's waiting in the outer office."

Her feet weighed heavily as she followed Sarah through the door, but Mr. Higsley wasn't in the office. The man leaning over the desk and scrawling on a pad of paper was undoubtedly a reporter, but with his short stature and thick middle, he certainly wasn't the man she'd met at the banquet. He busied himself with the other secretary, Elaine, battering her with all manner of questions about the admissions process to Hayes. Poor Elaine could hardly answer one inquiry before he fired another.

"Those reporters are spectacles to behold, aren't they?"

Elizabeth gasped and turned toward the rusty voice. Luke lounged against the wall near Miss Bowen's door. As always, he wore those dusty cowboy boots, a leather vest and a kerchief around his neck, and his hands held a wide-brimmed hat. She smiled, her heart tightening as she took a step toward him.

And stopped. What was she doing? She couldn't go to him. Not after that lecture in Miss Bowen's office. Not after her decision to avoid him.

Though making that decision in her dark bedroom was

a lot easier than holding to it here, when Luke Hayes stood three feet from her.

That familiar half smile curved his lips, and he dipped his head toward her, his eyes lingering on her skirt. "You look lovely this afternoon, Miss Wells."

She glanced down, and sure enough, chalk smeared the fabric just below her waist.

Once, just once, she wanted to see Luke teach advanced algebra without getting chalk on himself. "Did you need something?"

"Certainly."

His gaze landed on her lips for a moment, so brief anyone watching wouldn't have noticed, but she flushed nonetheless.

He cleared his throat and pushed off the wall. "I wanted to bring the reporter—Mr. Thompson—by. Figured after school would be a good time for the two of you to meet formal-like."

"*You* brought him? Why?"

"He needs to settle some things with you."

She'd seen reporters settle things enough to know she wanted nothing to do with it. "If you'll excuse me, I have an appointment with one of my students." She turned and started for the door.

Luke reached forward and caught her elbow, the simple touch searing through her sleeve to her skin. "Oh, no you don't. You're not turning yellow-belly over some little meeting with a reporter."

Perhaps meeting with a reporter seemed insignificant to Luke, but she hardly shared his opinion. "It's been a long day, and I have a commitment tonight. I need to go."

He glanced up at the reporter, still inundating the secretaries with questions. "He needs to talk to you."

"I tried talking to a reporter last week. It didn't turn out well, if you remember."

"Did you know my grandfather owned a rather significant amount of stock in the Albany *Morning Times?*"

She stared at him, her brain sluggish to follow the direction his words were taking. "I don't see what Jonah's stock... Oh." She bit the inside of her cheek. "You own it now."

"I do. And the man before you isn't simply 'a reporter.' Mr. Thompson is the editor and chief of the paper, and he especially wished to speak with you."

"Then why's he interviewing Sarah and Elaine?"

Luke took her hand, settled it in the crook of his arm, and patted. "Because he's writing an article on how Hayes accepts scholarship students from poorer families."

"Oh." And what could she say to that? The fervent interest the editor showed in Sarah and Elaine didn't speak of a man who hated female education, regardless of what the editor had allowed to be printed in the paper before.

"Thompson." Luke interrupted the other man mid-question.

The older man turned. "Ah, Mr. Hayes and..." He stilled when he spotted her, then came forward. "You must be Miss Wells. Please accept my apologies." The editor took her hand, his eyes shining with sincerity. "I'm terribly sorry for the trouble those articles caused you and the school. We printed what Higsley wrote without doing adequate research on the topic, and we never should have allowed such things in our paper. Do forgive us."

"Thank you." She took her hand from Mr. Thompson's and stepped back. "Your apology means much to both me and the academy."

"Indeed. We plan to remedy the situation," he went on. "We've a series of articles planned on the benefits of female education. They will appear weekly on the front page over the next month. And we'd like permission to reprint a portion of that original editorial you wrote to be used in next Wednesday's edition."

A series of articles on the *benefits* of educating women? That's what she'd been intending when she first wrote that editorial. Plus, he wanted to take the original piece she'd written and use it in a positive manner. She let out a breath she hadn't realized she'd been holding. "That would be lovely."

"Yes. We expect the series to be rather popular, and I must say, we're excited to print it."

Just then Miss Bowen's door opened, and Mr. Thompson's gaze moved to the headmistress.

"Ah, Miss Bowen." He glanced back to her and Luke. "If you will excuse me?"

He stepped around them and nearly ran for Miss Bowen. "Might I have five minutes of your time? I'm very curious about the process Hayes Academy uses when determining…"

The editor's voice faded as Luke took her elbow and guided her into the hallway.

"Thank you for bringing the editor by, Luke. You didn't have to speak up for the school in such a public manner, and you surely don't have to keep me this informed."

But in some ways, she wasn't surprised. He'd made his decision to stand by the school, and now he was unashamedly sticking to it. He wouldn't worry about what people said or thought, either. He was so strong, so unruffled by society's opinions. It was why she loved him.

And why she had to keep away from him. "Please excuse me, though. I shouldn't be here right now."

He frowned as a group of students brushed past, their

girlish chatter filling the hallway. "What's wrong with the hallway?"

"The hallway isn't the problem."

His eyes narrowed.

She sighed. Best to just tell him and be done with it. "You are."

"Exactly how am I a problem?"

She could hardly look at his face without memories of the kiss flooding back—memories of a kiss she couldn't let happen again. And she was being ridiculous! She needed to start behaving like a proper spinster, not some smitten schoolgirl. "Miss Bowen knows about the carriage ride Saturday."

"What exactly does she know?" His voice smoldered.

"Th-that you and I rode back to Valley Falls unchaperoned. She's agreed not to tell the board this once, but if they find out anyway and determine I acted improperly, I could lose my job."

"Not while I'm here." Luke's jaw hardened into a determined line.

A trio of students emerged from a classroom down the hall, and she took a step back, putting more space between her and Luke. "Please, we have to be careful. You can't be alone with me again or touch me." *Or kiss me.*

He crossed his arms over that impossibly broad chest, and his eyes glinted with untamed anger. "DeVander did this."

"How it happened hardly matters. But you'll need to call me Miss Wells in public, and you can't…can't…"

"Can't what? Talk to you? Show you any attention?" He leaned so close his breath tickled the top of her head. "Kiss you?"

She shook her head furiously. He definitely couldn't do that again, not ever. "We have to be careful, that's all."

"Fine." And with that sharp word, he turned and disappeared back into the office, leaving the hallway beside her empty.

Elizabeth bit her bottom lip and stared at the suddenly vacant space. She drew in a deep breath and let it out in one giant rush. He'd brought the editor and chief of the paper to meet her and had finagled a way to get favorable articles printed about the school. How was she supposed to resist a man who did that?

She'd known she needed to be careful around him, but would carefulness be enough? What if, despite her efforts to keep her distance, despite Miss Bowen knowing about the carriage ride and Luke's leaving in another month, she couldn't keep from loving him?

Chapter Fifteen

Elizabeth sucked in a breath and leaned her head on the town hall's back door. She should have been indoors ten minutes ago, but couldn't quite manage to step inside the building. She knew what awaited her. People. Probably about three hundred of them—teachers and school board members come to hear her father and David speak on education. The speeches, of course, were an unofficial start to the campaign both David and Father would run through the coming year until the elections next fall. And who better to begin the event than her, a schoolteacher?

She rubbed her arms. Oh, why had she agreed to give this speech? She didn't know if she could look at Father or David after last Saturday, let alone stand on a platform and publicly beseech fellow educators to vote for them.

She glanced down at the paper crinkled in her hand, the wording for her speech scrawled in elaborate cursive across the page. She'd read it a hundred times and still had no idea what the paper said. The words just seemed to slip through her head without sticking.

And here she was, being a terrible daughter again. Truly she was the most hopeless daughter ever to grace the earth. Giving a speech was the least she could do to help her family, especially since she refused to marry David. She should be happy to aid them, not hiding outside the building and praying for the earth to open up and swallow her. But still, getting up on that stage and convincing people to support Father and David in the next election felt wrong somehow, fraudulent.

She closed her eyes as the cold autumn air stung her face. What had Luke said about Jonathan honoring God above his father in the Bible? Was there a way she could honor her family *and* God by giving this speech, even if she didn't respect her Father or David? It didn't seem possible.

With a sigh, she pulled open the back door and stepped inside.

"Elizabeth, there you are," her father bellowed. "Come, they've already started. Where did you disappear to?"

"I was…"

But he didn't wait for an answer, just grabbed her wrist and tugged her down the hall and toward the steps to the platform.

"…feeling a little sick," she mumbled.

"We haven't time for that. See?" He gestured up the steps, hidden by a thick curtain, to where a man in a tuxedo stood introducing the speakers. "Here, give me your cape." He yanked it off her shoulders until she stood in the faded green velvet she'd worn for the occasion. "And what are you doing with that paper?" He tore the page from her hand, scowling when she didn't let go and it ripped in two. "You've been giving memorized speeches since you were ten. You're not taking a paper up there with you."

Applause drowned out his words as he snatched the rest of the speech from her still-clenched fist and shoved her up the steps. The host stood at center stage, his smile wide and welcoming. Then, before she could even take a breath, the speaker left, and she stood alone on the platform with several hundred people seated before her.

She swallowed and stepped forward. Her hands were slicked with sweat, and her heart pounded in her ears. "I, um…" What had her paper said? "I came to speak to you about education this evening."

Of course she had. The entire event was about education. She'd hardly been asked to speak on derivatives or integration.

Her stomach tightened and lurched. She couldn't do this. Couldn't stand up here and recite platitudes to make her father and David look good.

"Education is…" She licked her lips and stared out into the audience. Mother and Jackson sat in the front row, both scowling, as she imagined Father and David were doing on the side of the stage. She forced her gaze past them to the other people filling the hall. Some she knew, like the teachers and board members from Hayes and its affiliate institutions. Some she recognized as teachers she'd met at similar events in the past, but many unfamiliar faces stared back at her, as well. All waited, thinking she had something important to say, something of value.

But what *could* she say? That her own education had saved her after she'd escaped from what would have been a terrible marriage? That if teachers truly wanted to educate students, they would endeavor to open up possibilities rather than stifle the country's future generations in societal expectations? No, she could hardly say such things, even if truth dripped from her statements.

And then she spotted them, clustered into the back right corner. Not a group of teachers from Hayes wearing polite smiles and dignified clothing, but a group of students. Samantha and MaryAnne and Meredith and Helen, surrounded by several others she couldn't make out, all beaming as though the sun rose and set on her.

Behind them stood Luke, leaning against the back wall, legs crossed and shoulders relaxed, in much the same way he probably leaned against a fence post on his ranch. He'd brought her students. She'd not mentioned more than two words about her speech to him, but evidently he'd known of it—and cared enough to come.

A bud of warmth unfurled somewhere deep inside, spreading heat to her icy fingers and a smile to her face. And with that smile came her answer. She didn't need to stand there and cite platitudes so people would support Father and David, she needed to convince people that education was significant, because students were people, with longings and desires and dreams, and their futures were important.

"Education is important." Her full voice rang with confidence over the fidgeting crowd. "Not so much because it teaches Shakespeare, quadratic equations and the War of 1812, but because it teaches students to dream."

"Your speech was wonderful."

Elizabeth stiffened at the masculine voice behind her. She stood on the side of the platform, peering out from the edge of the curtain and into the chaos beyond.

"Your speech was delightful, as well." She spoke without turning to face David, and glanced at her father, standing only a few feet from the stage, nearly swallowed by a horde of well-wishers and supporters. "The crowd really took to it. I'm surprised you're not out there greeting people, though."

Something large and brown flashed in the far corner of the room. Luke and his cowboy hat? She'd likely imagined it. Even if he hadn't rushed himself and the girls outside by now, she had no way of getting to him without being engulfed and waylaid by all the people.

"Looking for someone?"

"Pardon? Oh, um…no. Not really." She waved her hand toward the crowd. "I'm simply watching. You really should be out there, though. Wasn't your speaking engagement intended to give you opportunity to meet constituents and procure votes?"

"As always, you have an excellent understanding of politics and publicity. But the audience tonight would have slept through my speech had they not been so captivated by yours. I think when I came onto the platform, everyone was holding their breaths and hoping you would reappear for an encore."

"Don't be ridiculous."

He moved behind her, so close the heat of his chest radiated into her back. She shivered and huddled nearer the curtain.

"Now who is it you're watching for?" David peered over her shoulder, not giving her room to shift without touching him. "The Hayes heir?"

She bristled. Luke Hayes was the last thing she wanted to discuss with David. "You've gone from ridiculous to insane. Now please let me by. You're standing far closer than is proper."

He took a half step to the side, just enough so she could brush past. But rather than stay at the curtain, he followed her down the hallway. "And where are you going now?"

"It's none of your business."

"On the contrary. It's very much my business, if you're going to be my wife."

"David, I'm not…" She rubbed her temples, already beginning to throb, and lowered her voice. "I'm not going to marry you. Didn't I make that clear the other evening?"

His face remained firm and unyielding, as though chiseled in marble. "Step in here so we can talk." He opened a door to a meeting room and held it for her.

She halted on the threshold and looked about. It was hardly appropriate for her to be alone in a room with him…but then she hardly wanted someone overhearing their conversation, either. And David simply had to get this fool notion of marrying her out of his head. So she stepped inside, letting him close the door behind her.

"There's nothing to talk about. I don't love you, and if I don't love you, I can't possibly spend the rest of my life with you. I'd be miserable, and I'd make you miserable, as well. I appreciate your offer and…" Shame crept into her face, and she swallowed. How did she even discuss the situation without feeling like an expensive brothel girl? "…your willingness to help my parents financially, but I simply can't agree. Now if you'll please open the door. It's highly inappropriate to be in here together."

"Not any more inappropriate than you riding home with Hayes the other night."

"You shouldn't have told the headmistress."

"Who says I told and not your mother?"

She stilled at that. Could Mother have done such a thing? Surely not. Mother might not approve of her daughter teaching, but she wouldn't try to get her fired, not when the scandal would have negative implications for the rest of the family.

David came toward her, slowly, as though he had no reason to hurry, since he already had her cornered. "Your unwillingness to give my offer due consideration surprises me. What could cause you to spurn me so quickly, I wonder? Feelings for someone else? That cowboy, perhaps?"

Not a cowboy. A *rancher*.

"The only thing between me and Mr. Hayes is friendship." Or so she hoped, because if Luke loved her, too… but no. She wasn't going to love him back.

"Elizabeth."

David tapped her chin up. She met his eyes for a mere instant, and then his lips covered hers, hot and invasive and humiliating.

No. She attempted to say the word, to push him away. But his arms wrapped around her, pressing her tight against him. She clamped her lips together and tensed every muscle in her body. She might not be strong enough to fight him off, but he wouldn't get any satisfaction from holding her. Then his hands snaked up into her hair. She planted her hands against his chest and shoved, but it was too late. Her hair tumbled down in one giant mass, her hat landing on the floor at her feet.

"David!"

And the door opened.

Chapter Sixteen

"Hope I'm not interrupting," the intruder drawled lazily.

David released his hold on her, and Elizabeth sunk her head in her hands. She didn't need to see who stood in the doorway, the rusted twang of his voice gave him away.

"Fix your hair, Miss Wells."

Miss Wells. Such formal words, and this from the man whose eyes had emanated love and concern in the school hallway that afternoon, who had held her in his arms and let her tears dampen his suit two nights ago. What must he think of her? Kissing him the other night, speaking privately with him today, and found in another man's embrace this evening?

"Miss Wells." Luke spoke her name so firmly her head shot up. "The girls are waiting behind the building. They wanted to thank you for your speech. So unless you fancy parading around with your hair tangled and hanging every which way, I'd suggest you put it back up."

She flew into action, kneeling on the floor to retrieve her hat and pins, shoving her snarled tresses up beneath the too-small creation, and squishing it into place. She jabbed pins randomly through her locks. Now if only the arrangement would hold for the ride back to Valley Falls.

"And you," Luke said. She didn't need to look up to know he pointed a finger at David. "I trust she's given you an answer about your marriage proposal."

"Yes, as a matter of fact." David's smooth politician's voice filled the room. "We've decided—"

"Good. Don't come near her again."

Don't come near *her?* Luke was protecting her? After finding her in David's arms? She stood slowly and glanced at him, but he'd trained eyes so fiercely on David he didn't notice. Somehow he knew she'd been forced, knew she hadn't wanted David's kiss. Maybe her struggle had been obvious when he opened the door, even more obvious than her fallen mass of hair.

"This is the room we were in, isn't it?" A woman's words floated in from the hallway.

"Yes, I must have left it just in here." Mother, *her mother,* answered.

All moisture leeched from her mouth, and her hands grew icy even as they started to sweat. What was Mother doing back here?

"It'll only take a moment to retrieve it." Mother appeared in the doorway with Mr. Taviston and his wife.

Elizabeth's body turned cold, but she could only stare at the trio. Mr. Taviston's eyes locked instantly on her, then ran slowly down her body in that uncomfortably familiar manner.

"Oh, dear, sorry to bother you," Mrs. Taviston exclaimed, oblivious to the look in her husband's eyes and the tension radiating between Luke and David. "We'll only be a moment."

"I do hope we're not interrupting." Mother came farther into the room, her shrewd eyes surveying everything. "Elizabeth, I didn't expect to see you back here. I just needed to get my hat. I left it before the rally, silly me.

But what are you doing in this room, and with two gentlemen, no less?"

"No," she whispered, more to herself than anything. Beside her, David shifted subtly closer, and she began to shake. Mother and David couldn't have set her up. They wouldn't do such a thing. Mother was family, after all. And if David wanted to marry her, he had to care somewhat for her reputation.

But if Mr. and Mrs. Taviston had opened the door to find her in David's arms with her hair undone, she'd have lost her job and found herself in the middle of a scandal. A scandal that would have only stopped if she married David.

"Elizabeth." Mother inched closer, plucked a stray hairpin—from where, Elizabeth didn't know—and held it up, her eyebrows raised.

Heat rushed to her face, so forcefully she'd surely turned the color of a turnip. And all with the head of the school board still watching her.

"I hope you know how this looks, you being alone with two gentlemen." Mother sniffed.

"Miss Wells was just leaving." Luke's words, hard and controlled, permeated the room. "Some of her students came tonight and are waiting to speak with her outside. I believe Miss Wells was concluding a brief conversation with Mr. DeVander. Likely something to do with a business offer she's turned down." Luke nodded at her and extended his arm. "Now, Miss Wells, might I escort you to your students?"

She stared at his offered elbow. Two steps and she'd be at his side. But still standing next to David, with her knees trembling and her stomach tying itself in knots, she may as well have been on the opposite side of the Hudson River.

And then he was there, beside her and placing her hand

on his arm, the hard muscles beneath his sleeve radiating strength and confidence. "Just hold your head up and leave," he whispered against her ear. "We'll settle the rest later."

So she sucked in a breath, straightened her back and went with him.

He loved her.

Luke sat in the train, one seat behind the students surrounding Elizabeth, and stared at the back of her auburn tresses and fancy hat. She laughed when her students said something funny, nodded as they asked questions and thanked each of them for going to hear her speak. He didn't need to see her face to imagine the way her eyes lit when she smiled or sparkled with understanding as she answered questions.

Yep, he loved the woman, all right. And if he had any doubts before, tonight had shot them down. She'd had every excuse not to show up at the town hall and give that speech for her father and DeVander. But what did she do? She didn't run. Didn't make excuses. Didn't gracefully bow out. Nope, she fulfilled the promise she'd made and stood composed before three hundred people. And she hadn't lied. She hadn't convinced them to vote for her father or DeVander; she'd convinced them to vote for the children. It would be interesting to know how many of the people present tonight would vote for the opposing candidates a year from now.

Wells and DeVander had followed Elizabeth's speech by throwing out platitudes, empty thanks and trite sayings about education in New York State. Elizabeth had captivated the crowd's heart and probably still held it.

And her family had thanked her by setting her up. He clenched his jaw. If he hadn't brought a group of students tonight and headed off to find her, she'd have been caught alone in that room while DeVander forced her to kiss him.

He'd nearly plowed his fist into DeVander's stomach when he'd opened the door to find Elizabeth struggling in the rat's arms, would have broken DeVander's nose had he not heard the voices in the hall. Even then, he hadn't realized who the voices belonged to, or what Elizabeth's mother and DeVander had done.

He'd figured it out a second before Elizabeth. Then she'd given him that stricken look, and he'd wanted to wrap his hands around DeVander's throat. How dare he treat Elizabeth that way? How dare *anyone* treat her that way?

Luke blew out a breath. *I love you. I'll protect you.* The words had nearly poured out of his mouth when Elizabeth had looked at him with all that hurt shimmering in her eyes. But with four others crammed into the little room, it was hardly the time to start spouting his devotion.

He shifted and smiled as a tendril of hair slipped from the back of Elizabeth's hat and down her neck. Several locks had already fallen from their hastily crammed positions. She'd probably have to put her hair back up before she got off the train in a few minutes.

And he'd enjoy watching.

Yep, he loved the woman. He'd have to tell her. Maybe even tonight after the girls left. When a man decided he loved a woman, that wasn't something to put off.

But say he told her how he felt, what happened then? He would return to the Teton Valley in another month or so, and where would that leave her? He swiped a hand over his mouth. Hang it all. He'd known getting too involved would cause a mess from the first moment he'd laid eyes on her.

But knowing hadn't stopped it from happening.

When the train finally ground to a halt in Valley Falls, he herded the girls into the waiting carriages. The students, content to ride in two carriages on the way to the train station, all swarmed into Elizabeth's conveyance now, leaving Luke alone on the ride to the academy. But as soon as the girls headed inside, he ushered them up the stairs to their rooms.

And he was alone with Elizabeth.

At last.

"Let me walk you home." He extended his arm.

She looked away. "Not tonight, Luke. Perhaps you could just lend me use of your second carriage."

"I could, if we didn't need to talk."

She shook her head and took a step back from him. "We can't. Walking outside after dark is just as inappropriate as being in a carriage alone with you. Or in a room. Or even standing in this hallway. Please…" Her voice quivered. "Just let me go home."

"Look at me, Elizabeth." He stepped closer, peering into her pain-clouded eyes, and touched a hand to her cold cheek. "I can't let you go home like this. What will you do? Climb into bed and lie awake stewing until dawn? You can't hide from what your mother and DeVander tried to do. You need to talk about it." He knew. He'd have been a lot better off if someone he loved had forced him to face his problems after Blake died.

"I'm not hiding. Needing time to think and sort through my feelings isn't hiding."

"Then sort through them with me."

She seemed undefeatable standing there, her back stiff and chin high even with half her hair falling about her shoulders. But sadness haunted her eyes. Sure, she was strong, could handle almost anything she faced—at least on the outside. Inside, the woman seemed ready to shatter.

"Is there something you're not telling me?" He brought his hand down to cradle her neck. "Did DeVander hurt you when he had you alone?"

Her eyes turned flat. "I'm fine."

But she didn't seem fine, and she was shutting him out, much like Samantha had when he'd first arrived in Valley Falls. "Just tell me what to do, and I'll do it." He reached out and tucked a strand of hair behind her ear.

She jerked back as though he'd slapped her. "No. Don't touch me. Don't ask me to talk, and don't look at me that way. Just leave me alone."

"I only want to help. What your mother's trying to do... Elizabeth, you can't handle it on your own. Think. What if I wouldn't have come looking for you earlier tonight? You could have found yourself engaged to DeVander come morning."

She took another step back, shaking her head as tears pooled in her eyes. "I can't do this. I don't want this."

"You can't do what? Talk to me? Let me support you?"

"Be alone with you like this."

Confound it! Were all women this impossible? Her mouth said she didn't want his help, but her eyes begged for it. He'd have had her home by now, half the incident with DeVander and her mother talked out, if she would stop backing away from him and simply walk toward him. "Why can't you be alone with me? Because of what Miss Bowen said to you?"

"Because I—I..." Her gaze drifted to his lips, then back to his eyes.

"You want to kiss me." He closed the space between them.

"No."

He leaned down until mere inches separated his mouth

from hers. "You do. Why else would your eyes get sleepy and your breath catch when I'm this close?"

She pushed at his chest, her hands as firm and unyielding as iron bars. "You're wrong. I don't want anything to do with you."

"Hang it all, Elizabeth. Stop pushing me away and talk to me for a minute. I want to walk you home tonight. I want to see you tomorrow and the next day and the next. I want to court you. I'm in love with you."

Elizabeth wrapped her arms around herself, a sob catching in her throat. Luke still stood too near, his body radiating heat and strength and confidence, issuing that subtle message that he'd carried with him since the first moment she'd seen him: *Trust me. I'm safe. I'll protect you.*

But she couldn't latch on to him. Not now.

I'm in love with you. She'd heard those words from a man before. How many times had David told her that he loved her? Held her in his arms? Stolen a kiss from her? And then strode from her parents' house straight to the mistress he kept?

She stepped farther back from Luke, even though doing so trapped her against the wall. "No, it doesn't matter if you're in love with me."

Perhaps she loved him. But that would remain a secret. There would be no declaration of her feelings, no public courtship, nothing but the silent ache of her heart when he walked into a room.

He didn't approach her again but stood back, his arms crossed and hip cocked, watching her far too closely. "You're terrified of me."

Not of him. Of love. He claimed to love her now, and

probably did, at least a little. But how long until Luke lost interest the way David had?

"What have I done to scare you? Is it because I'm going back to Wyoming? Because I wasn't raised to be a fancy eastern gentleman? We can work through those things, Elizabeth. I don't have all the answers tonight, but give me half a chance to dig some up."

"It's not where you live or how you were raised. It's got nothing to do with you." Indeed. She'd never met a more wonderful, trustworthy man.

But was he trustworthy enough to love her ten years from now and not just today?

Was any man?

Marriage lasted until death, and Luke hadn't even known her two weeks. "I told you before, I don't want to get married."

"Every woman wants to get married."

She shook her head. "Not me."

"What's this about? Teaching? Are you so afraid I'll make you give up teaching that you won't let me walk you home or take you to dinner? Good grief, Elizabeth, I haven't proposed. I'm just asking for a chance."

If only the reason was that simple. If only she could easily claim she didn't want to give up her students for a family. But as much as she loved the girls who walked into her mathematics classes every day, they only made up half the problem. "Luke, please. Just let me go home."

He rubbed the back of his neck. "Fine. I'll send for the carriage, but at least let me take you to dinner tomorrow night."

She nearly groaned. "No. It isn't wise."

"Samantha can come. We'll invite along a gaggle of her friends, and I'll pay for the lot of them. Call it a school outing, if you want."

Oh, how unfair. Her students had been so sweet tonight, nearly making her forget the disaster with David, and now Luke offered an opportunity for her and the girls to have some special time together. She simply had to trust him.

She looked into his eyes, that deep, honest blue that seemed to promise the world, and had to ask. "Do you... do you have a mistress?"

He went deadly still, his face turning pale, as though his veins had been slit and every drop of blood drained from it. She expected blustering rage and a haphazard denial like David had displayed when she'd accused him all those years ago.

But Luke barely seemed able to breathe. "A mistress? You think I have a mistress?"

She stared at the floor. "I...I have to know."

He came close, moving slowly, the way one would if trying to catch a butterfly. And indeed, she probably would have flown from the building had he moved any faster. But he soon stood in front of her, pinning her against the wall while she stared at the buttons on his coat.

"No." Softness permeated his rusty voice. "And I never plan to, either, if that's what this is about."

She drew her gaze slowly up his buttons, to his strong neck and firm jaw and chiseled cheeks, before finally staring into those trustworthy blue eyes. "I...I believe you."

The words twisted something inside her. Perhaps they freed her, or maybe they further chained her. Either way, they hurt, and she just wanted to go home, make a cup of tea, curl up on her bed.

And cry until the sun came up.

"My butler told me why you called off your engagement to DeVander." His breath brushed her face, warm and sweet and with the barest scent of mint mixed in.

"I've known since the night I first asked about why you weren't married."

She ducked her head. At least she hadn't needed to voice her shame, to admit aloud she hadn't been woman enough to keep her last fiancé. "So you understand why I can't let you court me. I can't take a suitor, Luke. Any possibility of me marrying ceased the night I ended my engagement to David. If I opened up myself that way again and got hurt, I'd shrivel up and die inside."

He didn't back away but stayed close, so close she only need raise a hand to touch him, so close the subtle heat emanating from his body warmed her skin. What she wouldn't give to rest her head in the crook of his shoulder as she had that night in the carriage. To draw from the strength and steadfastness of Luke Hayes.

"Lizzie." He pressed his palm, warm and callused, against her cheek. "Do you have feelings for me? Tell me you don't. Just say it, and I'll back away."

She pressed her eyes shut. She should say she felt nothing. Then he'd let her go, and life would be easier for both of them.

But she couldn't lie, not to a man as honest as him.

"You're leaving." They were the only words that came out. "Whatever you feel for me, whatever I feel for you, it doesn't mean anything. It can't, unless you stay here and manage your inheritance. I won't leave my students."

"I'd never ask it." He smoothed a strand of hair off her forehead. "But I'm not requesting your hand tonight. I'm asking you to dinner. I'm asking you to be my friend. I'm asking for a chance to earn your trust. Please, Lizzie. Have dinner with me tomorrow evening, and let's see how things go."

She swallowed. Trust and marriage loomed ominously

before her but giving him a chance? She gave her students a chance every day when they walked into her classroom. How could she do any less for the man she loved?

Chapter Seventeen

The Philadelphia Society for Children buildings sat drooping and dirty on a half-forgotten street in Philadelphia. An occasional person or carriage passed by the aging brownstone, but no one bothered to even glance its way. Perhaps because it stood farther back from the road than most establishments, perhaps because it held nothing interesting or unique enough to draw one's attention.

Luke didn't care so much whether the orphanage sat in the middle of Philadelphia's business district or on a forgotten twenty acres in the country. He only cared about one thing: seeing Cynthia Hayes.

His hands slicked with sweat and his pulse quickened as he waited for her in a cramped, stuffy parlor. Would she be willing to see him? She might have the worker who had shown him in come back and send him away without even laying eyes on her.

And he'd deserve it.

He'd treated her no better after Blake's death.

Luke plopped down in a faded chair and attempted to still his antsy legs. At least he was trying to make things right. A person couldn't blame him for that.

Something swished gently near the door, and he looked up.

She stood there, framed in the peeling blue-trimmed doorway, with no clomp of footsteps or creaking floorboards to introduce her. Then his eyes landed on the boy beside her, gripping his mother's hand with a white-knuckled fist, and the breath left his lungs.

Clear blue eyes peeked out from beneath a mop of floppy blond hair. He looked like Blake. Exactly, completely, entirely. From the way he awkwardly held his shoulders—too big for the rest of his little body—to the curiousness in his eyes, to the half smile curving one side of his mouth.

Luke swallowed. If the boy looked like Blake, then the boy looked like him, too. An ache started somewhere deep inside his chest, and he wasn't quite sure what to do with it.

Cynthia hadn't changed, save for a few extra lines around her eyes and mouth. Her flaming hair was tucked up into a haphazard bun, and a serviceable black dress with a white apron draped her figure. But otherwise, she looked much the same.

The image of her kneeling over Blake's lifeless body flashed like fire through his mind, and the pain, old and bruised, came flooding back. *Get out!* his mind screamed. And his mouth nearly formed the words.

But he wouldn't do that again. He couldn't blame Cynthia for what had happened to his brother any more than he could blame himself. Rafe McCabe had fired the gun that had killed Blake, and the man had swung from a tree for his crime. The matter should have been settled the day Rafe was hanged, but instead of letting go, Luke had clung to his pain with the same bitterness and vengeance Pa harbored toward Grandpa.

"I'm sorry," he blurted out as he stood. "For what I said over Blake's body, for the way I sent you packing seven months pregnant."

She stood still, as though etched in granite with her rigid posture, tight muscles and white skin. Her throat worked back and forth, the only sign she hadn't turned to stone, then her eyes filled with moisture.

"I don't blame you." Her voice sounded like cracked glass, thin and frail and ready to shatter if he breathed wrong. "You were right. I may have been able to save Blake that day, but I'd…I'd…chosen to be ignorant about the ranch. I'd been there a year. I should have known how to ride a horse or hitch a wagon. I should have found rags to stop the bleeding, rather than stare at Blake and cry." She reached out to steady herself on the back of a chair. "Excuse me—I need to sit down for a moment."

He offered his hand to help her into the chair.

The gesture was basic, simple. Anyone would have done it. But rather than take his palm, she stared at it, the battle flashing in her eyes. Touch him or refuse? Accept his help or decline?

Then she looked into his face, the corners of her mouth tipping up into a soft smile before she placed her hand firmly in his.

And he knew. A weight, three years old and as strong as steel fetters, fell from his chest and cracked into a thousand unrecognizable pieces. Cynthia had forgiven him. God had forgiven him. And he was finally making amends for how he had handled Blake's death.

Elizabeth let herself into her brother's office, the building empty on this early Saturday evening. Jackson probably didn't even remember the key he'd given her over a year ago "in case of an emergency." And in truth, finding out about another wrong shipment of food wasn't an emergency per se. But how many wrong shipments and unpaid bills needed to pile up before they became an emergency? This was the fifth time since the beginning of the school year that something hadn't aligned with the payments recorded in the school's accounts. Yet she'd entered everything in her ledger and had spent the better half of the afternoon poring over it to find the discrepancy.

As usual, she found nothing.

So she would compare her books to Jackson's. She'd asked him about the finances again Monday at the political rally, and he'd been too busy to answer. Not that she could blame him, enamored as he was with Samantha. But the world still spun on its axis, regardless of whether Jackson had proposed, and tonight she was getting to the bottom of this. She'd find his ledger and take it to dinner at her parents. While Jackson and Samantha spent the evening huddled together in a corner of the drawing room whispering their goodbyes before Samantha left for Wyoming on Monday morning, she'd plop down at one of the tables and review the two books until she found the errors.

She sighed. In truth, she should have looked into the wrong food shipment earlier that week. It had arrived on Wednesday, but she'd gone out to dinner with Luke on Wednesday—and Tuesday and Thursday—and hadn't stopped by the kitchen until yesterday afternoon, after Luke had left for Philadelphia.

That man. She pressed a hand to her flaming cheek. He was too handsome and understanding by far, and the added layer of Western charm only sealed her demise. He drove all sensible thoughts from her head, had been doing so since first they met. She could hardly recall the Pythagorean theorem when he was around, let alone her name or any semblance of why she shouldn't be spending time with him.

She rubbed the heel of her palm over her heart. Falling in love with him felt wonderful—at least right now. He would still leave her one day, and her heart would likely break. But that didn't mean she couldn't love him today. Couldn't let herself dream of a future with a husband who loved her and children she could cherish while teaching an advanced mathematics class or two.

And goodness. Look at her. Here she was, standing in Jackson's office daydreaming instead of finding that ledger. She'd told Samantha, waiting in the carriage, that she wouldn't be more than a couple minutes, and she'd spent those minutes thinking of Luke.

She walked deeper inside the darkening office and rounded the desk to where her brother's ledgers rested on the shelf, everything organized alphabetically. Her eyes scanned the *G*s and *H*s, before landing on a leather binding clearly marked Hayes Academy. She pulled it down. Columns detailed the academy's regular expenditures, but the accounts were from last year, not this year. Jackson must have started a new ledger at the beginning of the school year.

She slipped the binder back into its slot. But the books on either side read Gomer's Millinery and Headings Mercantile, with no vacant space indicating another ledger for Hayes Academy. Standing on her toes, she brushed her fingers over the bindings on the highest shelf. Perhaps Jackson had simply labeled the ledger as Academy.

But no book labeled such sat in the *A*s. She frowned up at the too-high books. The spot where the Academy book would have stood held an unlabeled ledger. Maybe that was it.

She pulled it down, but the book wasn't for Hayes. The

pages held random labels, with columns of dates and items and money listed, then smaller monetary figures running along the far right. Greater Albany Hospital, Maynard's Bakery, Albany Ladies' Society, Headings Mercantile, St. Thomas Orphanage, and various other names had been scrawled across the tops of the pages. The businesses seemed to have no rhyme or reason for the order in which they appeared, or for the single page of accounts dedicated to each one.

Then she spied it. Hayes Academy for Girls printed neatly across one of the middle pages, and an open column of numbers beneath. Entries for foodstuffs and teaching supplies with larger amounts of money had been recorded in one column, and a second column of smaller amounts ran along the...

Coldness swept her body. She dropped the book, and it crashed to the floor in a flutter of pages. But she didn't need to glimpse the page again to make sense of the numbers. She knew those figures, had them circled in her own ledger. They weren't sums paid to suppliers. They were the *missing* sums. The money for the food, only two-thirds of which had arrived two weeks ago and again on Wednesday. The new slates ordered for the beginning of the school year that had come with a third of the slates missing. The note from the insurance company saying it hadn't received its full payment last month. The amount of bills for the school Jackson had claimed to pay pitted against the actual supplies and creditors' notes that had arrived at the school.

And Jackson had the difference recorded in his book. A book that didn't just include Hayes Academy, but hospitals and orphanages, small businesses and... She hunkered down on the floor beside the ledger and flipped through pages. The numbers blurred, but the names of the organizations branded her mind.

Jackson couldn't have. He wouldn't. He was her brother, after all. Surely he wasn't embezzling money from so many different places. Certainly he didn't have a bank account somewhere in the city where he had all these funds collected.

She found three pages for Maple Ridge College and Connor Academy for Boys. The columns on the left listed salaries, books and office supplies, among other things. On the right were the sums that must have been rerouted to a separate account. As if the girls' academy wasn't enough for him to steal from.

What was she going to do? She had to tell someone. Luke? No. He wouldn't be back until later this evening, and she couldn't wait that long. The police? But she couldn't just walk into a strange police station and accuse her brother of…of…

Oh, goodness, she couldn't even think of the full ramifications if he had indeed embezzled funds from all these establishments. So where did that leave her? She swallowed back the bile climbing into her throat. Dinner. She was still going to dinner, wasn't she? Her family expected her, and she needed to talk to Jackson.

Maybe the book she held was some mistake. Her brother probably had a sensible explanation for the entries that meant the situation wasn't as it appeared. Yes, of course Jackson had a logical reason for everything. Why not these accounts? She needed to see him before she did anything else.

"Elizabeth?"

She straightened and slammed the book shut.

Samantha stood in the doorway, concern engraved on her too-innocent face. "Are you all right? What's wrong?"

Samantha started toward her, but she held up her hand. "No. Don't come any closer."

"What's happened? You've been in here for half an hour. Any longer and we'll be late to your parents'."

She used the desk to pull herself up onto wobbly legs, then grabbed the ledger and clutched it to her chest. Jackson was this girl's fiancé, even if the wedding was temporarily delayed. If the ledger was accurate and her suspicions correct, what would happen to Samantha? She'd be betrayed by her fiancé at a young age, similar to what David had done eight years ago. Only Jackson's mistress was money rather than a woman. Either way, Samantha shouldn't have to witness the conversation she needed to have with Jackson.

"No. You're not going to my parents'."

Samantha's mouth fell open. "But Jackson… You said…"

"Things changed. You're going home." She cringed at the harshness ringing through her voice, even as she came around the desk. "You get back in that carriage and head straight to your brother's estate. Don't stop anywhere or for anything. Simply go home."

Samantha searched her face. "Is this because of what Luke said yesterday? How he didn't think we should go to dinner at your parents? That your ma might do something she shouldn't?"

If only the situation was that simple. If only she'd accepted Luke's advice and stayed home rather than claiming she couldn't ignore her family. "No. It's got nothing to do with my mother or Luke. It's something else entirely. Trust me. Please."

Samantha reached forward and offered her hand. "But what about you?"

"I'll be fine."

She only prayed her words were true.

Chapter Eighteen

Elizabeth's heart pounded as the footman opened the door to her parents' drawing room and she stepped inside. She'd spent countless hours in this room growing up, quietly doing needlework or taking refreshments while Mother and her friends gossiped about the latest goings-on. Yet she hardly recognized it now. The room seemed different somehow—darker, emptier, even though the furniture and window dressings and people inside were much the same.

Mother sat on the settee, and David and Father stood by the fire discussing politics in muted tones.

The familiar feeling of betrayal wrapped itself around her gut. Of course David would be here. She should have expected it. It was evidently too much to ask her parents to shun the man who had nearly forced her into marriage the other night, especially when that man had money and political connections. Well, they were about to find out how deep David's love for her and the rest of the family ran. Because if the ledger she held in her hand proved true, he'd run from the house and publically denounce any relationship with them before noon tomorrow.

Elizabeth stared at Jackson, sprawled comfortably in

his favorite armchair. Surely there must be some mistake. How could he sit there in his expensive suit and act as though everything was normal if he'd been stealing money from schools, hospitals and orphanages?

"Good evening, Elizabeth, how lovely to see you."

Elizabeth ignored David and headed straight for her brother. "Explain this. Tell me it's not what I think." She threw the book in his lap.

Jackson glanced down, a flicker of recognition racing across his face, then he shoved the ledger off his legs onto the floor.

A flurry of footsteps and voices rushed around her.

"Elizabeth, what are you doing?"

"Is this any way to behave before dinner?"

"I see you're as excited to see me as I am to see you, darling."

"Jackson, what's that book?"

"David, perhaps you better excuse our family for a few moments."

But despite the chaos, Elizabeth didn't pull her eyes away from her brother.

"I don't know what you're talking about." Jackson shrugged indolently, as though there was nothing wrong with the world. As though that book didn't shake the very core holding their family together. "I've never seen these accounts before in my life. Now where's my fiancée? She was supposed to come with you, wasn't she?"

Elizabeth picked up the ledger and drew in a breath—it burned like fire down her throat and into her lungs. "Never seen it? I got it from your office! The entries are written in your handwriting! Unless I'm misunderstanding this ledger—which I don't think I am—you've been embezzling money."

"Embezzling?" Mother squeaked. "Jackson's been embezzling?"

"That's quite enough, Elizabeth." Father's voice boomed from the doorway.

She turned and scanned the room to find David gone, Mother looking ready to faint on the settee, and Father glowering.

"He's been stealing money, Father. Look for yourself." She came toward him, holding the book out.

"Stop being such a ninny. I know what's in there. But bringing the matter up before dinner is hardly appropriate."

She stopped, standing halfway between her father and Jackson. "You...you know what's in it?" It made no sense. How could her father know unless...

"No," she whispered.

Father laughed, a polished chuckle he no doubt used when advocating one bill or another in the assembly. "Where do you think all that money is? In some account for your brother?"

She pressed her eyes shut and tried to block off her ears, tried to prevent her father's meaning from sinking through to her brain. Her father couldn't be embezzling, too. He was a politician, for goodness' sake. The slightest whiff of scandal would ruin his career.

But why else would Father admit to recognizing the ledger?

"How dare you." She clenched one hand around the book's binding and another in her skirt. If only she could fly at him, rage and beat and kick until she was spent. Or maybe she could simply close her eyes and disappear, be somewhere else entirely. With Luke having dinner. In her classroom teaching quadratic equations. In her parlor helping MaryAnne get ready for the play. Anywhere but standing in her parents' drawing room.

"What were you doing, keeping that ledger where someone could find it?" Father crossed his arms and glared at Jackson. "You're lucky only your sister noticed."

"Maybe you should ask Elizabeth why she was in my office," Jackson shot back.

"Will one of you please tell me what's going on?" Mother said from where she still slumped on the settee.

Elizabeth turned to her mother. "Jackson has been embezzling funds from the accounts he handles at his office." Admitting it aloud made everything somehow worse. She was no longer asking questions, but stating facts—rather irrefutable ones that would have disastrous consequences for her family. "I needed to look up something for Hayes Academy in his books, and I uncovered the embezzlement instead. Jackson didn't just take from Samantha's school, he stole from hospitals, orphanages, ladies' clubs and—"

"Enough." Father slashed his hand through the air. "We see you've familiarized yourself with the accounts. Now give the ledger to your brother."

She clutched the book to her chest. "Give it back? Have you gone daft? Do you realize how much money's been stolen?"

"Elizabeth. Do be respectful." Mother fanned herself. "Whatever you've discovered, it's no reason to call your father names."

"Respectful?" At a time like this? Her mother couldn't be serious. "Why should I be respectful, when Father's known what Jackson's been doing and hasn't stopped him?"

"It was my idea, not Jackson's." Father leaned his wide frame against the door and watched her with an amused smile, as though enjoying the show at a circus. "Your brother merely had access to the funds."

The air in the room turned so cold she could hardly breathe it without her lungs freezing in her chest. "What would possess you?"

But she didn't need to ask, not really. The dates told her when the embezzlement had started. Seven months ago, just after the panic.

"We need money to live on," Father said mildly. "And you're aware of exactly how much we lost last March."

"But you mortgaged the house. That gave you money. I know you've gone through most of the funds by now, but—"

"Don't be ridiculous." Father waved his hand dismissively. "I merely invented that story when you and your mother started asking questions about how we could maintain our household staff and so forth."

"You lied." Fury surged through her as the full implication of his actions sank in, and she turned back to her brother. "And you lied, too. What reason do you have for this? You make a fine salary and keep apartments, with no great household to maintain."

Jackson shrugged. "My trust fund went the same place yours did when our bank folded."

"You're criminals." She squeezed the ledger against herself until it was sure to leave a rectangular imprint on her clothing. "I…I have to turn you in."

Moisture, hot and traitorous, stung her eyes, but she blinked it away and stared at her father. "And you truly will lose your house when you have to repay everything you stole."

"You can't turn anyone in, Elizabeth." Mother propped herself up from where she'd been lying on the settee. "I know you're upset right now, dear, but you'd ruin the family name."

"What purpose is there in a family name when the men who carry that name have no integrity? I'm not the one ruining anything."

She whirled toward the door. She had to get away and decide what to do with the ledger. But Father stood in front of the door. He hadn't moved so much as an inch since he'd shown David out.

She stilled, as the realization hit her. He hadn't moved from the exit since David had left…because he was keeping her in. While Jackson paced in front of the fireplace, looking ready to pounce on her and rip the ledger from her hand at any moment.

"We can't let you go. Don't you understand?" Mother dragged herself to a standing position. Devastation haunted her eyes, and the wrinkles around her mouth and across her forehead seemed more pronounced than they had just minutes ago. "This is why you have to marry David. He can provide us with the funds we need to maintain everything, and your father and Jackson can stop what they've been doing. I'm sure they're already sorry, aren't you?"

Father harrumphed and Jackson kept his dark eyes pinned to her as he paced.

"See there?" Mother spoke as if they'd both agreed. "The embezzlement will stop, and David will take care of us until your father gets his investments and campaign funds rebuilt. But you can't turn them in. You'd destroy our family." Concern rang through Mother's voice, and her eyes pleaded for understanding. The woman loved her family; no one would argue that. And she'd stay loyal, even if her loyalty meant she harbored thieves or murderers. Family always came first with Mother, which was why she'd attempted to arrange the scandal on Monday night. What was a little scandal, a little dishonesty, a little wrongdoing, when the family stood to benefit?

Should she do as Mother said and honor her family? Elizabeth's stomach revolted at the thought. When God said to honor your father and mother, to obey your parents, did He intend a son or daughter to do so at the expense of others? At the expense of the law?

Jonathan had honored his father. He'd followed King Saul into battle and ended up dead. But he'd honored God before all others and had protected David's life in spite of his father's wishes. Which choice was right for her? Did she follow her family at the expense of right? Or did she do right at the expense of her family?

She closed her eyes and saw her students' bright, smiling faces as she gave her speech on education. Saw Miss Bowen rushing up to ask how much money was left in the academy's bank account, and Miss Atkins's hurt face after hearing she couldn't help with the play. Saw Luke, arms crossed and hip cocked, as he leaned against her classroom door frame and watched her conclude a lesson, Luke offering assurance after Mother demanded she marry David, Luke brushing the hair from her face and asking her to give him a chance.

Luke had said something to her in the carriage last week. Something about family and God and obedience. What had it been?

We ought to obey God rather than men.

She'd looked up the verse the next day. The Apostle Peter had said it. He and several others had been thrown into prison for preaching, and that night God opened the doors of their cells and released them. Rather than run from the city, they'd gone straight back to the temple and started preaching again. Then soldiers came and brought them before the high priest who had thrown them in prison the day before.

And what did Peter say? Not that he would obey the priest. Not that he would cease preaching and leave the city. But that he would obey God rather than men.

Peter suffered a beating, more prison time and eventual death to obey God. Jonathan never saw his best friend and eventually lost his life in trying to honor both God and his father. And she…she'd lose her family, whom she loved and had once respected, and whose approval she still sought.

She opened her eyes. Her family stared at her, every one of them waiting for an answer. Yes, she would lose them. But she'd be following God. And she'd be protecting her students and the children at St. Thomas Orphanage, the patients at the hospital and the small business owners listed in the ledger.

She met her mother's gaze. "You've made your own choices. Now you need to let me make mine. I have to obey God and act as the law demands. I'm sorry you'll be hurt by my actions, but you've been throwing Bible verses at me since I was a little girl. You should be the first to understand why I need to obey them."

Mother's mouth fell open, then closed halfway before it dropped a second time. "But…but…" Confusion flitted across her face. Perhaps she was considering what she'd just heard, or perhaps she was formulating yet another way to plead for her family. Elizabeth hardly knew one way or the other.

"You're being ridiculous, Ellen," Father snapped, still standing guard at the door. "Why are you even considering the tripe Elizabeth's spouting?"

She moved toward him, tucking the ledger close against her body. "Please move so I can pass."

"Certainly, right after you give me the ledger." Father extended his hand, still keeping his back against the wood of the door.

"I can't. You know I can't."

"You don't have a choice."

She swallowed and glanced about the room. One door out. Two windows facing the street, and numerous pieces of furniture. Without access to the door, she had no way to get free short of smashing through the front windows. But maybe if she stayed and talked a bit longer, she could draw Father away from the door. He had to be getting tired of standing by now. But she'd need some sort of distraction, perhaps something to do with Mother.

Jackson appeared at her side, big and tall, with fury radiating off his body in tightly coiled waves. "Father said to hand over the ledger."

She shrank back from him only to bump into Father. "Perhaps we should talk about this some more. We seem to be at quite an impasse."

"The time for talking is done." Jackson gripped the ledger and wrenched it away from her trembling fingers.

"No!" She grabbed for the pages, rushing after him as he moved to the center of the room. But she wasn't fast enough. The proof of Jackson's deceit stayed in his hands only a matter of seconds before he flung it into the fire.

"How could you?" She raced forward as the pages ignited and reached for the poker beside the blaze. If she could pull out the book and save a few pages, one or two examples might be enough to prove what her family had been doing.

But Jackson's arms wrapped around her, hard and unyielding as he dragged her backward. "No, you don't."

"Let me go. You've no right to manhandle me." She

tried to pry his hold from around her waist and kicked at his shins with her heels.

"You can go, all right," he whispered in her ear. "Just as soon as you've watched every last page of that wretched ledger burn."

She turned her face away from the fire's orange glow, but the heat of the blaze, ravenous as it devoured the papers, seared her skin. A tear slid down her face, then another. "You won't get away with this. There's other proof of what you've been doing. There has to be. See if I don't find it. See if I let you walk off with all that money."

He fisted a hand in her hair and yanked it to the right, her head turning until she'd no choice but to stare into the flames once again. "We kept our bank accounts under false names, and my office has the only records for most of those businesses. Even if you go through my office, how do you know which accounts I altered and which I left alone? You can try to prove what I stole, Elizabeth. But your only proof is in that fire."

Chapter Nineteen

Luke's back ached as he turned his rented horse down the Hayes estate's long drive. He'd spent all day with Cynthia and Everett, staying so long at the orphanage he'd rushed to catch the last train out of Philadelphia and then rented a horse in Albany since the train to Valley Falls wouldn't run again until morning.

The lights from Grandpa's house gleamed in the distance, though he'd no idea why more than one or two lights would be lit at this time of night. What he wouldn't give to be in bed right now, curled up under a heavy quilt on a comfortable feather mattress.

Time was when he wouldn't have minded bedding down under the stars with a rock for a pillow, but this place was making him soft. And strange as it was, he didn't mind coming back here, welcomed the sight almost as much as he did the view of his own ranch. Returning to the place Grandpa had built felt almost right.

So if the place felt right, if he wanted to be here, why was he trying to sell it or find a manager for Great Northern Accounting and Insurance?

Luke rubbed his bleary eyes. These thoughts were Elizabeth's fault, every last one of them. Her words had nig-

gled in his mind ever since he'd told her that he loved her.
*You're leaving. Whatever you feel for me, whatever I feel
for you, it doesn't mean anything. It can't, unless you stay
here and manage your inheritance.*

Besides the lawyer on his first night in Valley Falls,
no one else had mentioned him staying until Elizabeth.
Luke stared at the acres of trim grass, passing slowly by
under the dim moonlight. Acres that *he* owned. Maybe
he'd have been better off staying in Wyoming and never
coming East, telling the lawyer to sell everything and
send the profits West. His life would have been easier,
for sure and for certain.

But then he never would have seen the Philadelphia
orphanage or ensured Hayes Academy stayed open. He
never would have looked into the faces of the students and
orphans Grandpa had helped. Never would have realized
his sister was growing up or faced Cynthia. Never would
have met Elizabeth…

He shifted in his saddle. Returning to Wyoming with
Sam used to mean reuniting his family, but with matters
settled between him and Cynthia, and with Sam scheduled to leave on Monday for Wyoming, going back West
for good took on a whole other significance. It meant end-
ing his ties with all Grandpa had worked for and pretend-
ing the orphans in Philadelphia and the young women
at Hayes Academy required nothing from him. Ignoring
the needs of the staff at the estate and the hundreds of insurance agents, accountants and actuaries along the East
Coast that he employed.

Was it right to rush away from the things Grandpa
had left him, or was it some form of neglect? And was
Grandpa even the one who had given him this vast inheritance? Or had God done that?

The thought echoed inside him like a shout reverberating through a mountain pass. His heart thudded slowly, surely, and he knew. Here he'd been blaming Grandpa for his new heap of responsibilities, but God controlled the world, not Jonah Hayes.

God could have let Grandpa's savings and assets be lost in the panic, as had happened to the Wellses and countless others. God could have led Grandpa to disperse his assets and estate himself, donating everything to charities rather than a grandson he'd never met.

Luke swallowed as a new thought took shape. And God could have seen him shot rather than Blake on that sunny morning three years ago. Then Blake would have inherited everything.

Instead, God had given it all to him, Luke Hayes.

He couldn't leave it behind and head back to the Teton Valley. Not anymore.

He could run the businesses Grandpa had left him well enough. In fact, it almost seemed God had used his ranch to prepare him for taking over Grandpa's holdings. Sure he had a few things to learn, but numbers made sense to him, always had. And managing a business didn't differ too much from running a ranch—except the workers smelled better.

He'd still miss the wide-open prairie, with those giant Tetons looming to the east. But the ranch would be well taken care of under Pa, and like Sam, he could go back and visit. Besides, New York had its own appeal. Though not as grand as the Tetons, the Catskill Mountains loomed to the west, their blue-shadowed slopes visible from his bedroom and office. He could take day trips into the wilderness or spend a weekend camping here and there.

And besides, if he stayed in Valley Falls…

He slowed his horse in front of the house. A vision of a woman, dressed in green velvet and standing in the hallway of Hayes Academy, curled around the edges of his mind. She looked hesitant, unsure as she said she'd have dinner with him the following evening.

A smile crept across his lips as he stared up at the white three-story mansion. Such a grand house needed a beautiful woman to run it. A beautiful woman with a heart for teaching and a wagonload of reddish-brown hair. Now he only had to figure out how to ask her—and hope she said yes.

He gulped. A woman as fine as Elizabeth would have plenty of reasons not to want a country bumpkin like him.

Luke swung off his horse and took the steps two at a time. The butler opened the door before he'd even reached the top.

"Stevens, what are you doing awake? Do you realize how late it is?"

"Yes, sir, quarter of two."

Luke stepped inside and waved his hand at the fully lit chandelier. "Then why's the house lit up like there's some fancy dinner going on?"

A sob echoed from the direction of the drawing room, and he turned. He knew that sound, had heard it far too many times when he'd first arrived. "Samantha's still up?"

"Yes, sir. You have a visitor, and I'm afraid she delivered some rather distressing news."

Distressing news? Was something wrong with Ma? Had Sam received a telegram after he'd left yesterday afternoon? He strode toward the drawing room and opened the door, only to find Elizabeth sitting on that fancy white and gold couch. What was she doing here? And in the middle of the night to boot?

He whispered her name, running his eyes over her unkempt hair and pale face. Samantha sat hunched in her arms, sobs emanating with every breath.

Elizabeth raised her head and looked toward the door.

"What's wrong?" He came closer, and she hugged Sam tighter to herself. Redness lined her eyes while devastation haunted the hollows and planes of her porcelain face. His heart thumped against his ribs. "Is it Ma? Or Jackson? Was there an accident? Is someone…"

Dead?

Sam pulled back from Elizabeth, her hands clenched into angry fists. "Oh, I wish there were some accident. I wish it was all some mistake, or maybe that I'd never met the conniver at all."

Luke strode toward his sister, his own fingers clenching in response. "What'd he do? Tell me, and I'll make him pay."

Sam leaped into his arms and started crying all over again. "I should have listened to you. You were right from the very beginning. All he wanted was money."

"Hush now." Luke stroked her hair, but the soothing movements had little effect on her. "It's all right. We'll work everything out, just calm down."

She only cried harder.

He lifted his eyes to Elizabeth's. She'd backed away from him and Sam, and stood near the fire, her arms wrapped around herself in a lonely hug.

Confound it. He should be holding Elizabeth in his arms at this moment, kissing her and whispering promises about staying in Valley Falls. But with Sam sobbing in his arms and that silent sorrow etched across Elizabeth's face, this was hardly the time. "What happened?"

"I'm so sorry, Luke." Her whispered words barely reached him above Sam's shudders. "I didn't know. I promise I didn't."

"Didn't know what?"

She shook her head, as though trying to deny whatever she needed to say.

"Go on, now. You can tell me."

"I tried to go to the police, but they wouldn't believe me."

"The police?" His hands tightened on Sam's back. "Why would you need to go to the police? What did Jackson do?"

"He…" Elizabeth pressed her eyes shut and rubbed her temples. "I'm sorry. This is harder than I'd thought."

"Here, Sam, sit for a minute." He set his sister on the couch and gave her a pillow to clutch before moving to Elizabeth. Tears glistened in her eyes, tears she seemed determined not to shed.

"Tell me." He reached for her, but she took a step back.

"No. Don't touch me. Not right now. Not after what my family did."

Her family. Dread, icy and hard, sank its claws into his chest. Had they coerced her into becoming DeVander's wife? Had she already signed a marriage license?

But then Sam wouldn't be so upset at Jackson. The fear constricting his heart loosened just a bit. "Will one of you please tell me what's going on?"

"You need to do an audit on your Albany office." Elizabeth stared into the fire.

"What?"

Her chin trembled, and she raised it, calling on that inner strength that had mesmerized him from the first time he'd met her. "Jackson and my father…th-they've been…" She swallowed, the tight muscles in her throat working far too hard. "Embezzling. From you. Since the panic, they've been using your accounting and insurance offices to steal from you and the companies you service."

Every idea about what had happened, every thought

about what he'd do to Jackson Wells, every word he'd planned to comfort Elizabeth with, deserted him.

"What do you mean, embezzling?" He heard his voice speaking, knew his mouth had somehow formed the words, but the implications of what Elizabeth had said seemed as vague and hazy as a mountain fog.

"I mean that I went to Jackson's office before dinner tonight to find his ledger for Hayes Academy. Sometimes the supplies and materials arriving at the school haven't matched the amounts that were supposedly ordered, so I wanted to compare my books with Jackson's." Her breath quivered as she blew it out. "I—I didn't find the ledger for the academy, but I found another ledger instead. It was an accident. I wasn't supposed to discover it. I never knew anything about what they were doing before tonight."

"Oh, Lizzie." He reached for her hand, but she pulled it away.

"You believe me, then?" Shock flared in her eyes.

"Why wouldn't I?"

Two tears slid down her cheeks, silent compared to Sam's noisy gulps on the couch, but almost more wrenching. "I went to the police station before I came here. The police officer—he wouldn't believe me without the ledger. Said I had no business going through the accounting office at all, and maybe I could be prosecuted for looking at Jackson's books without permission."

"Elizabeth, that's ridiculous. They're my offices, and I promise no one's going to prosecute you."

She wiped furiously at the tears on her cheeks.

"Where's the ledger now?" He didn't think it possible for her face to lose more color, but her skin blanched yet again, and she stared at the blaze in the fireplace.

"Jackson threw it… Father wouldn't let me leave, and—"

"Jackson? Your father?" He gripped her shoulders and jerked her around until she faced him fully. "You went to see them?"

She stood rigid in his arms, the warmth she'd shown him over the past week buried under layers of rigid hurt. "I had to make sure. What if I'd misread things? Imagined something that wasn't really in the ledger? You weren't here, and I couldn't walk into a police station and accuse my family of stealing thousands of dollars without knowing for sure."

He pulled her against him, pressing her head to his chest and wrapping his arms around her waist.

She only stiffened more.

"There were other companies listed in the ledger besides Hayes Academy. Connor School for Boys and Maple Ridge College with their normal operating expenses and the hospital in Albany. St. Thomas Orphanage and…" She sank her head. "I don't remember what else. I'm sorry. I should have paid better attention."

"Stop apologizing. You've done nothing wrong."

"Don't say I shouldn't apologize." Her eyes turned fierce, and she shoved at his chest.

He didn't have to let go. He was stronger and could force her to stand in his embrace. But forcing people into his will had caused him enough trouble of late. So he released her, though every muscle in his body screamed to keep her close.

"My family was stealing from my students. And what's worse, they expected me to keep silent." Elizabeth fisted her hands in her already wrinkled skirt. "They actually thought I'd marry David and let him take care of matters, while Father and Jackson walked off with the money and promised not to steal again. If I don't apologize for what they did, who will?"

He raked his hand through his hair. She stood only two feet away, but she may as well be standing on the other side of a mountain. His arms ached for the feel of her, but she wouldn't come, not now. And he could hardly blame her. She'd been hurt, and even though he hadn't been the cause of it, he was tangled in the mess right good, as he owned the company her family had used to steal. "Then let me apologize, too. I'm sorry for what your father and brother did and for the pain it's putting you through."

She shook her head and took her cape from where she'd draped it over a chair, then moved to hug Sam before turning back to him, her face as desolate as the prairie after a blizzard. "Thank you, for being my friend, Luke, and for believing me when no one else would."

You're more than a friend. I love you. I want to marry you. Didn't she see that? Didn't she understand he would stand by her through whatever trouble her discovery unleashed?

But she disappeared through the door before he could open his mouth to tell her.

Chapter Twenty

The knock sounded at two thirty-six the following afternoon. Not that Elizabeth was watching the clock. Oh, no. She had plenty to do as she sat in the parlor, rocking in an old chair and staring out the window at the side yard. She could be packing her books and belongings, going to Jonah's lawyer and asking that her house be put up for sale, writing a farewell to her students, or any other of the numerous tasks that awaited her.

But every one of those took energy, and as she'd cried through the night until the first streaks of dawn tinged the sky, she didn't have any left.

News of the rumored embezzlement hadn't appeared in the paper yet, but no doubt speculation circled through town. Indeed, with Luke likely at his office doing an audit and his entire staff knowing where he was, things could hardly be kept secret. Miss Atkins and Miss Tourneau, friendly this morning, hadn't even looked at her after they'd returned from church.

Elizabeth wrapped her arms around herself and shivered. She'd expected as much. She'd grown up in Albany and knew how gossip worked. Regardless of whether her father and brother ended up on trial and were found guilty, society had already formed their opinions. So if she planned to keep teaching, she would have to leave the area. And she had no choice other than to continue teaching. She needed to earn a living, needed food to eat and clothes to wear and a roof over her head.

Maybe she should go West. Not somewhere as remote as the Teton Valley, but newspapers always ran advertisements for teachers wanted on the other side of the Mississippi.

The knock sounded again, and the floor above her creaked. She stared up at the parlor ceiling, but no footsteps pounded down the upstairs hallway. Evidently neither Miss Atkins nor Miss Tourneau seemed inclined to answer the door. It was just as well, the callers would be there for her anyway.

She rose slowly, each step a concentrated effort as she headed out of the room and pulled open the front door.

"Miss Wells." Mr. Taviston removed his hat and offered a slight dip of his head, his lips pulled down into a frown and his eye devoid of their usual lecherous glint. "Just the person I needed to speak with."

"Indeed." She forced her lips to curve into a smile. "Won't you come in?"

She stepped back from the door, took his coat and ushered him into the parlor. If she wanted to be polite, she would offer tea and sandwiches, but why go through the flat, empty gesture? Tea or not, he would fire her.

She sat on the settee. "Mr. Taviston, let me make this conversation as quick and painless as possible. You don't need to fire me. I resign."

Tears, hot and coarse, crept up the back of her throat. Whether she loved her job or not, she'd no business facing her students again after how her family had stolen from them.

"We appreciate that overture on your part, Miss Wells." Mr. Taviston kept his frown in place, as though his actions somehow pained him. "You've always been a sensible woman, and I'm sure you understand why we can't allow you to continue teaching at Hayes Academy."

"Yes." She felt hollow inside. Like an eggshell drained of its contents and a breath away from cracking. "With the trouble my family is in, keeping me on would look bad for the school."

"Your father, of course, is also being relieved of his position on the school board. Nearly all the board members were in agreement regarding the actions to be taken toward both you and him."

"Nearly? Striking the Wellses from any association with Hayes Academy wasn't a unanimous decision?"

She was daft to ask, but something inside her had to know if Mr. Taviston's words meant Luke had dissented.

The man's eyebrows furrowed together. "Well, several of the board members couldn't be reached, but it hardly matters as more than a majority were in compliance with the recommendations."

"I see." Had Luke been one of the members left uninformed? Or perhaps he had defended her, and Mr. Taviston refused to admit it for one reason or another.

And wasn't she a heartsick fool, hoping for anything other than the obvious. Her family had hurt Luke, and there would be consequences. Losing her job was one. Losing Luke was another. She sucked in a breath and prayed Mr. Taviston didn't notice the underlying tremble.

"You should also know," Mr. Taviston continued, "that we'll be looking closely into your actions at Hayes Academy. We would, of course, hate to discover that you'd been aware of your family's illegal activities earlier and had hidden it to protect them."

She jumped from her seat. "I would never, *never* jeopardize my students like that. I turned in my family as soon as I discovered what was happening. Do you know how that feels, Mr. Taviston? To have to choose between your family and your students? Your family and honoring God?"

The man stood. "No, Miss Wells. I can't say I do, or that my family would ever put me in a situation where I'd find out. But if you're innocent, I'm sure an adequate investigation will show—"

"Go." She pointed toward the door, her finger stiff. "I refuse to sit in the house I own and listen to you accuse me of some crime I never committed. Get out. Now."

Mr. Taviston's jaw fell, and he stared at her as though she'd lost her mind. And maybe she had, telling off a distinguished gentleman like him.

"Well then, I'll take my leave. But first, someone requested I give you this." He dug inside his pocket and then held out an envelope.

David. She recognized his script before she even took it. The letter likely retracted his offer to marry her and claimed he'd found another woman more suitable to be his wife just that morning. She smiled bitterly. Had she really considered his offer, however briefly, to help her family? She wasn't just some heartsick fool, she was the world's largest one.

She straightened her shoulders and met Mr. Taviston's gaze. So she didn't have much dignity left or any reputation to speak of, but she wouldn't let a man like David DeVander humiliate her without even being present. Tearing the envelope in thirds, she dropped it on the floor. "As I said, Mr. Taviston, good day."

"I've got another one, sir."

Luke looked down at the accountant, holding out an

open ledger and pile of receipts. Hushed voices and the shuffle of papers filled Jackson Wells's office as men went from one ledger to another comparing original receipts to the amounts Jackson had written in his ledgers.

"Looks to be about a thousand dollars since March." The man pointed to a number he'd circled at the top of the page. "Though we'll have to go over it again to be certain of the amount."

Luke rubbed his hand over his mouth. A thousand dollars from an orphanage. How could people steal from such a place? He waved a hand toward the table where a wire-thin police detective sat. "You know where to take it."

Chest puffed and shoulders high, the employee weaved his way through the throng of policemen and accountants that spilled from the office into the hallway as they searched for more evidence of falsified accounts.

The frenzy had started last night, when he'd ridden back to Albany, awoken Jackson's assistant from bed and sent the man to the office. Then he'd gone to the police station to drag an officer over to Great Northern Accounting and Insurance. The accountant had found money missing from two places before they'd arrived.

Luke moved to the side of Jackson's desk and stared at the ledger he'd left open. How much longer would the officers be here? Did they intend to break for the evening and then return come morning? Because as a man who hadn't slept last night, he was perilously close to sitting down in Jackson's armchair and dozing off.

And yet, despite the fatigue plaguing his eyes and the haze encompassing his mind, sleeping didn't seem right. Not with all these men rushing about his company in a work-induced frenzy, and not without knowing how Samantha and Elizabeth were coping with all that had happened.

Samantha was still slated to leave on the train in the morning, but maybe she'd want to postpone her trip. Sure, he'd never liked Jackson, but he could hardly blame her if she wanted the comfort of her friends and familiar places for another day or two after the stunt Jackson and his father had pulled. But even then Samantha's heartache looked miniscule compared to Elizabeth's.

Luke raked his hand through his hair. How was she? Still as upset as she had been last night? He should go to her, see how she was and if he could do anything to help. She probably hadn't slept last night, either. But hopefully one of her roommates had found a way to distract her from all the rumors floating around today—and made sure she ate some breakfast and lunch.

Hang it all, he should be with her now, taking her for a walk, seeing that she got a decent meal and promising that he still loved her despite what her family had done. Instead he was stuck here going over ledgers and listening to workers mutter about cheating politicians and arrogant office managers.

"Mr. Hayes?"

Luke turned toward the half-familiar voice and frowned at the older man in a suit and hat. What was his name? Witman? Wiltern? He'd met him the night of the banquet and then again when he'd gone to the school board to convince them the academy needed to stay open.

"Ah, Mr. Wisner, what brings you by this afternoon?" Luke extended his hand.

"It's Wilhem, son, not Wisner."

"Sorry. I remember all the faces from the school board but can only seem to recall half the names."

He chuckled, a calming, grandfatherly sound. "Doubt I'd be able to remember everyone's name either if I were in your position." He glanced around the overfilled office. "Quite the day you're having, eh?"

Luke shrugged even as a policeman bumped into an accountant, knocking him into the table where the detective sat and sending a tall stack of papers fluttering to the floor. "I didn't exactly envision myself in this mess yesterday. But you're not here to tally numbers. What can I do for you?"

"For me? Oh, nothing at all. I wanted to find out if there's anything the school board can do to help you straighten out this...er..."

"Tangle."

The man's black-and-gray speckled eyebrows rose. "Yes. That's probably an adequate description."

Luke inched a ledger closer to the older man. "Don't suppose you've a mind for ciphering?"

Wilhem shook his head. "Own a shipping company but leave the book work to others. Still if there's any way we can be of aid..." Despite the chaos of the room, a shattered silence lingered between them. "You'll be pleased to know that Thomas Wells has been relieved of his position on the school board."

Luke crossed his arms. "Probably goes part and parcel with embezzling over twenty-five thousand dollars and getting yourself locked up."

"Too true." Wilhem looked down at the tips of his shiny black shoes. "Elizabeth Wells has also been relieved of her teaching position."

The words sliced through him, cold and slick. He didn't think, didn't swallow, didn't even breathe. Just reached for the man and gripped his lapels. "What?"

Every head in the cramped room turned at his shout. Wilhem was probably just the messenger, sent to relay a decision others had made. But Luke's hands tightened on

Wilhem's coat regardless, and he pulled the man closer. "Why don't you explain precisely what 'relieved of her teaching position' means?"

"Well, ah…" Wilhem gulped. "Surely you understand. I like Elizabeth, I do, and I've known her since she was a little girl. But we can't keep her in our employ when everyone will soon know her family has been engaged in illegal activities."

Luke sucked in a deep breath and let it out. He could control himself. He didn't need to explode. And he wouldn't break Wilhem's nose because he didn't like something the man said.

He hoped.

"I still see no reason to take action against Miss Wells."

"Ponder the situation a moment, Hayes. What parents would want their daughters taught by a woman of questionable character?"

"Questionable?" He dragged Wilhem closer.

"Mr. Hayes, is there a problem? Perhaps I might be of help."

Luke flicked a glance at the skinny police detective, now standing beside him. "There's a problem, all right, but I doubt you can fix it." He released Wilhem. "Why don't you explain why Miss Wells's character is suddenly questionable?"

Their eyes met, Wilhem's gaze holding an uncomfortable sympathy. "You won't like it."

Luke just crossed his arms and glared.

Wilhem's shoulders slumped. "We're looking into whether she knew of the embezzlement earlier and covered the matter to protect her family."

How could they accuse Elizabeth of such a thing? She was wholesome and honest and determined. Didn't the school board understand that the mere mention of this suspicion would destroy her? "That's nonsense. She's been nothing but honorable in this whole mess and I won't let you take teaching away from her. She's sacrificed too much for the academy and those girls to be treated that way."

Pink tinged Wilhem's cheeks. "I attempted to say as much to Taviston, but he refused to listen."

"Then we'll change Taviston's mind together." Luke whirled and stalked from the room with Wilhem's hasty footsteps following behind. Maybe he couldn't prevent Elizabeth's family from abusing her and stealing. Maybe he couldn't prevent the papers from informing the whole of New York about what her family had done. But there was one thing he could do. And he'd use everything in his power to accomplish it.

Chapter Twenty-One

Two trunks and three crates. Elizabeth had to fit everything she needed inside them, and she had so many things sitting about her house, all little pieces of the home she'd worked to create. Packing her room had been a simple matter of folding her clothes into squares, stacking them in the trunks and cleaning out the few other items she wanted to take. But downstairs she faced the settee and chairs, the curtains, the dishes, the pictures on the walls. And the two open crates on the parlor floor had filled far too quickly.

The five-shelf bookcase loomed in front of her now, full of textbooks and works by mathematical geniuses. Which should she take? Newton's *Principia* or Descartes's discourse on geometry? Leibniz on calculus or Gauss on geometry? She had room for maybe five texts total.

She moved to the shelf and pulled down *An Introductory Calculus,* the textbook from her first calculus course. Opening the cover, she ran her fingers over the letters on the first page.

*Elizabeth, May you use this book and the knowledge
you have learned in these classes to do great things.
Professor Strohm.*

This one would have to go with her, even if she had little hope of teaching calculus wherever she settled.

She reached up and took Newton down, then opened that cover.

My Dear Elizabeth, When you returned from your first year of school and I saw how much you'd come to appreciate calculus, I decided you needed the work of the man who fathered the subject. Happy Birthday.
Jonah Hayes.

She pressed the books to her chest and closed her eyes. How did one choose? How did one pack a life into two trunks and three crates? Perhaps the past two days hadn't been kind to her, but she'd lived twenty-six years in up-state New York. She couldn't wipe all the memories of pleasant times from her mind and heart because her family had been deceitful.

A knock sounded on the door. She jolted, then glanced at the clock on the mantel. Miss Atkins and Miss Tourneau wouldn't be back from the academy for another four hours. Who could possibly be here?

The pounding sounded again.

She walked to the window and peered through the lacy curtains, then stopped. Luke Hayes stood on her porch, wearing that familiar cowboy hat yet again. She stepped to the side of the glass and pressed her back against the wall lest he decide to peer through the window and see her.

Perhaps she had the strength to leave, selling her house and starting her life anew. But she hadn't the strength to face him or her students again. The ties that bound her to Luke and the girls at Hayes Academy had snapped the night she'd found Jackson's ledger, and the words *I'm sorry* could hardly repair the damage done.

Elizabeth blinked back the moisture pooling in her eyes. Crying seemed to be the only thing she wanted to do of late. But her tears couldn't fix what happened or change what needed to be done any more than the words *I'm sorry* could.

Something creaked near the back of the house, and she stilled. Had Luke broken in through the kitchen door? She clutched the base of her throat. Certainly not. The house simply groaned sometimes, all houses—

Footsteps echoed in the hallway, then his familiar silhouette filled the parlor entrance. "Miss Wells." He tipped his head and removed his hat.

"W-what are you doing here?"

"Front door was locked, found the back open, though." He watched her, those clear blue eyes seeming to bore into her soul, and held out a lunch tin. "Just got back from delivering Sam to the train station. She still wanted to go home, was more eager than I could have ever imagined to get away from Jackson. So I figured I'd stop by on my way home and make sure you got something to eat. Doesn't look like you've had a good meal in about two days."

He wanted to share a meal? Where was his anger? His rage over what her family had done? He'd been quiet and supportive when last they'd spoken, but that had been before he'd done the audit and seen the extent of her family's fraud.

"I'm not hungry. Thank you."

He snorted. "Figured you'd say something like that. It's about lunchtime, though. You won't mind if I eat?" He came into the parlor and plopped down on the floor by her crates, then emptied the contents of the sack. Cold ham, cubed cheese, crackers and *grapes*. Her favorite.

He shoved a piece of meat into his mouth and chewed. "You ever tried my cook's brown sugar ham? It's the best meat this side of the Mississippi."

She shook her head and pressed herself harder against the wall. A foolish place to stand, but she could hardly resume her packing while he watched, and if she got any closer, he'd finagle some way to have her sitting beside him. And surely she had some good reason why she couldn't eat with him—she just couldn't remember it.

"The best meat west of the Mississippi would, of course, be fresh beef from the Double H ranch in Wyoming, but Valley Falls is a little far for that." He popped a cracker in his mouth and rested a hand over his knee. He looked handsome and at ease sprawled on her parlor floor, as though he belonged there. His shoulders so broad and commanding she could hardly look anywhere else, his jaw stubbly and unshaven and begging for her to run her hand across it.

She'd been so certain she couldn't trust him, couldn't trust any man after David had betrayed her. But in the end, her family had proven untrustworthy, not the man sitting before her.

Why hadn't she been able to look past her own fears a week ago and see the heart of the man that loved her? What she wouldn't give to have him look at her with the tenderness his eyes had held when they'd talked after the speech, to feel his arms around her as they'd been in the carriage after she'd first confronted David. She sagged against the wall and wrapped her own arms around her middle—a rather poor substitute for Luke's.

"Care for a grape?" He popped one in his mouth.

Yes. She nearly said it. But he couldn't know grapes were her favorite, could he? Or that she longed to launch herself into his arms and bury her face in his shoulder and cry until her heart stopped aching.

She needed to get out of this room before she made a fool of herself.

He swallowed another bite, and the perfect excuse hit her. "Tea. You need tea or water or milk. Something to drink. Let me get it."

She hurried toward the doorway, but his hand shot out and fisted in the front of her skirt as she passed.

"Sit." He tugged the fabric.

"Mr. Hayes. I appreciate that you're hungry and will happily get you something to drink, but then you really must be on your way. It's highly inappropriate for you to be here, in my house, without a chaperone."

"Probably is." He stuffed more food in his mouth, but didn't release her skirt. "It's also highly inappropriate for your brother to use his position at my company to embezzle over twenty-five thousand dollars' worth of funds from various accounts."

Twenty-five thousand dollars? She hadn't any idea the amount was so large. The paper that morning didn't list any figures, just said her brother and father were in jail, charged with embezzlement and without the funds needed to post bail.

As for Mother... Elizabeth blew out a breath. Mother knew where she lived and hadn't come. "I already told you I was sorry. What more do you want?"

"As I said Saturday night, I don't know why you're sorry. You didn't do anything wrong. In fact, you turned your family in when looking the other way would have made everything a heap easier for you." He dropped his hand from her skirt. "But if your heart's set on getting me a drink, get on with it. I could stand to whet my whistle— I've got a while to talk yet."

"I don't understand why you're here at all. What's left for us to say to each other? My family stole, and the school board had me fired. Not that I feel like I could ever look my students in the eye again, but you and the others didn't have to get rid of me in such a manner. I'd already decided to leave anyway. I couldn't stay here while everyone gawked and whispered behind my back."

He sprang to his feet. "I didn't vote to fire you. I didn't even know what those idiots had done until a couple hours after Taviston paid you a visit." He reached into his pocket and pulled out an envelope. "Here, see if this changes things."

She stared at it dully, the crisp, straight lines too similar to yesterday's letter from David.

"Do you need me to open it?" He pulled a knife from his belt and slid it along the top fold, then held out the missive.

She scanned the contents. "This…this can't be right. It says the school board is reinstating me."

"It's right."

"You got me my job back? Why?"

"Because you did right even though it meant turning your family in, and the people you've spent the past two years working for should support you."

She shook her head. "I don't—"

"Hush. I've more to tell you, now that you've started talking to me again. On the way back from Philadelphia, I decided something—or rather, God showed it to me. I'm not going back West. I'm staying in Valley Falls to run the businesses Grandpa left me."

"Y-you're not leaving?" She could hardly breathe, let alone think, as she waited for his reply.

"No. And what's more…" He took her hand and held

it between them, her fingers dangling over his. "I still love you."

"Oh, Luke." He couldn't feel that way, not after everything that had happened. But his eyes didn't lie, and the deep blue of them shone with patience and support and love. All things she'd never had from her family. All things she'd never realized she wanted until Luke walked into her life. "I love you, too. I didn't want to fall in love with you, but it happened anyway, without me even realizing it."

A smile tilted the corners of his mouth. "Don't make it sound like a crime, Lizzie. People have been falling in love since Adam and Eve." He pulled a box from his pocket and opened it. An emerald ring gleamed dark and rich against the blue fabric. "Marry me. Spend your life with me."

Her throat shriveled into a gritty mass of sand. How easily she could accept the life he offered. How wonderful to be his wife and wake up beside him every morning, to go back to teaching and surround herself with students. She'd have a life she'd only dreamed of.

Yes. The word rested on her tongue, ready to tip over, fall out and cement her future to his.

But she couldn't.

She must have taken too long to respond, because he gripped her shoulders and pulled her so close her petticoats squashed against her legs. "You're going to tell me no. I can see it in your eyes."

She looked away.

"It's because of what happened with that cheat, DeVander, isn't it? You still don't think you can trust a husband." He trailed a finger down the line of her jaw and back up again. "I can't promise never to hurt you or disappoint you, Elizabeth. But I can promise to always be faithful. Before God and you, I promise. And if it takes another week or month or year for you to believe that, then that's how long I'll wait for you."

"Luke, stop."

But he didn't. He stroked a strand of hair behind her ear and leaned closer. "I love you for who you are, and I'm never going to take that love away and give it to another woman."

"You've been so patient with me. Too patient, really. I don't deserve you."

"Then why are you about to cry?"

She straightened her shoulders. "I'm not."

"Liar."

She shifted away and clasped her hands together. "Have you forgotten about my family? Surely you saw the paper this morning. The embezzlement scandal is huge, and it just appeared today. We haven't yet seen how voters are going to respond when they find out the politician they've elected for the past twenty years stole twenty-five thousand dollars. Or how the companies Jackson took from are going to react when everyone learns of his deceit. Why, you might lose half your accounting clients. More than half.

"And now you want to stay here and take your grandfather's place. Which is fine. It's what you should have done all along. But nobody will accept a thief's daughter as your wife. You can't…" *Marry me.*

The words stuck in her throat, but she pressed on, speaking the truth, the only logical answer despite her heart's screaming otherwise. "You're going to be a respected member of society, even with that wretched cowboy hat you like to wear, and me…I have to leave."

"Look at me." He grabbed her upper arms and waited for her eyes to meet his. His jaw had gone hard, his eyes glinting with determination. "I love *you*. I want to marry *you.* And as for what everybody else thinks about your family and the embezzlement—" he bent and kissed her forehead "—I don't care."

If only she could see the world through Luke's eyes. Black-and-white, right and wrong, and forget anybody who didn't agree. But society wouldn't hold with Luke's ideas about marriage. "You don't understand. A marriage can't work between us, not now. Maybe…" She drew in a breath. "Maybe in a few years, after the scandal settles and things calm, if you still feel the same about me, you can write to me and…"

He ran his hand back to cup the base of her neck and tilt her face toward his. "Maybe I want to marry you now," he whispered, his breath hot against her skin. Then he lowered his lips to meet hers. His mouth tasted of warmth and comfort, understanding and forgiveness.

Her knees weakened and her body went limp for the briefest of moments. Then she stiffened. Nothing good could come of kissing him. Not when she had to turn down his proposal. Not when she had to leave. But Luke Hayes had never been easily put off. He wrapped his arms around her back and pulled her closer, his lips gently lingering on hers, then broke to trail kisses down her jaw.

"I love you, Elizabeth," he whispered as his mouth trailed up to her ear.

"I love you, too. But we can't marry. You have to understand."

"Nothing to understand. We can marry without the heap o' troubles you're yammering about, and I'll prove it to you." His lips, still soft and warm, left her suddenly. Then he clasped her hand in his and pulled her toward the hall.

"Prove it? You can't prove something like that. And where are we going? I need to finish packing."

He dragged her out of the parlor and toward the front door. "There's another matter you have to settle first."

"Another matter? The house will be up for sale by the end of the week. My things are nearly packed. I answered several advertisements for teachers this morning. What's left to—?"

"Your students."

She dug her heels into the tiled floor. "I can't face them again, not after how I missed the signs of the embezzlement."

"Look at me, Elizabeth." He took her by the shoulders, rubbing her knotted muscles. "You have to see your students. Sure, you feel like you let them down. But you can't hide away in your house forever. Nor can you leave without fixing things. I know that better than anyone.

"There was a man once, a criminal who stole from the ranch." He sucked in a breath, as though telling the story robbed him of air. "After my twin caught and fired him, he returned and shot my brother, who died from the wound.

"I went a little crazy after his death. Holed myself up, let Pa send Sam out East where she'd be safe, and blamed myself over and over again for what happened. I got bitter at my sister-in-law, who I faulted for not stopping my brother's bleeding, even though the wound likely would have killed him anyway. And I shut out everyone else. In short, I wasted three years of my life blaming myself and those closest to me for something none of us could control.

"I love you too much to let you do the same." Pain etched his face and glittered in his eyes, but he gave her shoulders another squeeze. "Your family was wrong, yes. But you protected your students once you realized everything. You did right by them, and you need to go back and face them."

He was right, as always. Before God, she had nothing

to be ashamed of. She'd honored her Creator above men. Of course, society didn't judge people by God's standards. No. The socialites at church would rip her apart, and the teachers at Hayes probably gossiped even now.

Still, she owed her students one last visit, didn't she? Then she could start anew somewhere else, rather than hide.

"Let's go." Luke held out his hand.

She looked down at his hand, the same hand she'd covered in chalk dust the second time they'd met. The same hand that had wiped her tears after David had proposed, had anchored her hair behind her ears too many times to count and had cupped her cheek when he'd kissed her. And she put her palm in his.

Elizabeth had never before considered how ominous Hayes Academy for Girls could appear, with its redbrick jutting three stories and its plain windows staring down at those coming up the walk.

Like a prison without the fence.

Luke held open the door and waited. "No one's going to attack you for coming inside."

If only she could be so sure. "The first time I looked at this building, all I saw were dreams, both mine in possibly teaching here one day and the students' for the expanded opportunities they would have after graduating from such a place." She stood just outside the threshold and peered in at the austere white walls. "I never thought…that is…" She rubbed her damp palms together. "I never really noticed before how intimidating it looks."

He grabbed her hand and pulled her through the doorway. "Stop stalling."

The door closed behind them, sealing her inside. She

nearly pulled her hand from his and dashed back into the sunlight.

"I thought the same thing the first time I saw the building. Dull and void of life." He led her forward, so quickly she hadn't time to think of another way to slow him down. "A little teacher with rich mahogany hair changed my mind, though."

"Don't be ridiculous."

"I'm not."

She paused in front of the office and drew in a deep breath. She'd have to face Miss Bowen before seeing her students. What would the headmistress say? Then again, maybe Miss Bowen would kick her out, and she wouldn't have to worry about looking into her students' eyes.

"Stop slowing down." Luke yanked her past the office.

"But Miss Bowen. Shouldn't we—?"

"Nope. This way."

"The only thing down here is the dining hall...." Her voice trailed off as he pushed open the double doors.

Students crammed into the room, milling about and sitting at tables, eating and talking as an organized sort of chaos filled the room.

She tugged at her hand, but he still didn't release it. "Luke, I don't want to be here, not like this."

He hunkered down, placing his mouth beside her ear. "It'll be fine."

"No." She jerked harder on her hand, but the stubborn man had a grip like iron.

Then MaryAnne, who had been busily eating, looked toward the door and shot from her chair. "Miss Wells! You're back!"

The rest of the room fell silent, every eye turning to her. Her face heated, and her throat went achingly dry. She turned to go. Luke could continue to hold her hand or release her, but either way, she was plowing through those doors and heading straight back to her private little home.

"Miss Wells, wait!" MaryAnne approached her, as did Meredith and Elaine.

"Mr. Hayes said you would stop by today." Elaine ducked her head shyly to the side, stray wisps of brown hair tickling her cheek. "So we made these for you."

She thrust out her hand, a crisp, white envelope caught between her thumb and fingers. Another letter. Elizabeth's hands trembled too much to even reach out and take it.

Mr. Hayes stroked a palm down her back, then up again, the gesture warm and comforting, but still, she couldn't stop the shaking that plagued her limbs.

"Why don't you read it for her, Elaine?" Mr. Hayes's deep voice settled over the entire room.

Elaine dipped her soft eyelashes down, pink staining both her cheeks as she struggled to get the envelope open and unfold the letter. "Dear Miss Wells…" Her voice carried its usual softness, but the dining hall had fallen so quiet that the words likely reached the farthest corners.

"Growing up, every girl has teachers—not just one, but multiple teachers of different ages and backgrounds who endeavor to impart everything we need to know about womanhood. From this group of myriad women, every so often a teacher comes along who makes a difference in her students' lives.

"She cares about her students and what she teaches. You can see it in the way her eyes light as she lectures, and the way she agrees to meet students after school for tutoring. You can tell by the smile on her face when she answers questions and gives encouragement, not just about her subject, but life in general. Like the way you said you'd help me apply to Wellesley College for next year, and the way you've tutored Samantha Hayes with all that calculus.

"Please know that you've been that teacher for me and for my friends. My only complaint is that you teach mathematics instead of composition. Don't you know composition is a much more interesting subject?

"Thank you so much for all the effort you put into teaching us."

Elizabeth pressed her eyes shut, unable to meet Elaine's gaze. The students were thanking her? After what her family had done? She should be thanking them for letting her teach for the past two years, not the other way around.

Another voice rang out; MaryAnne's strong, clear cadence easily recognizable despite Elizabeth's closed eyes. Reading her own letter, the girl mentioned advanced algebra and having fun and not wanting her teacher to leave.

Then another voice started and another and another. Mr. Hayes kept one hand on her shoulder and his other on her back, stroking gently as the girls read, gripping tightly whenever tears threatened her. And read the girls did, letter after letter. Twelve of them, until every student in her advanced algebra class, save Samantha, had gotten her say.

Then someone near the doors started to clap. Her eyes flew toward the entrance, and there stood Miss Bowen. She must have entered the dining hall as the letters were being read, but instead of a dour frown crossing her lips, the headmistresses smiled, her eyes shining and even moist.

Someone else started clapping, Dottie McGivern, at the back of the room, a huge smile pasted on her face. Then a student in the middle of the dining hall stood and clapped, and another and another, until the entire room was standing and clapping and making so much noise, she nearly had to cover her ears.

She'd spent the past eight years studying and then teaching, trying to earn her family's approval in spite of her decision to attend college and teach. Trying to make her parents proud by doing something other than marrying a cheating scoundrel.

She'd never gained that approval.

But maybe, just maybe, she'd been searching for her family in the wrong place. Her family had betrayed her and destroyed itself, but God had given her these students and her fellow teachers. A different family that loved her despite her shortcomings and supported her when no one else did.

Her eyes moved to Luke standing beside her, so close the warmth from his strong body radiated into her, and her fingers rubbed the spot where her engagement ring would fit. God had given her that honest rancher, as well.

"You're thinking about me," the half-rusted voice whispered in her ear.

She raised her eyebrows. "You believe you've acquired the ability to read my thoughts now?"

"Not hardly, but when a woman looks at a man a certain way, all soft and moonstrucklike, he can tell what's going on inside that pretty head of hers."

"Do tell, then. I'm most anxious to hear what I'm thinking."

He glanced down at the finger she toyed with. "That you're ready to put my ring there."

All teasing fled as she looked at the finger and nodded.

He slipped his hand into his pocket and pulled out the gold circle set with an emerald. "You know, it's terribly unfair of you to accept my proposal here." He slid the cool metal onto her finger and bent low so his lips brushed her ear. "I can hardly kiss you with a hundred students looking on. Wouldn't be proper, I'm told."

"Luke Hayes, whispering such a thing in my ear is

hardly proper, either." Their eyes met and held, still and peaceful despite the chaos of the dining hall.

"You're getting married!" a student squealed, likely MaryAnne, as the noise overtook the sound of the fading clapping.

MaryAnne flung herself forward, and Elizabeth nearly stumbled as the girl's slender body plowed into hers. Before she could right herself, Luke stepped back, and Elaine hugged her from behind, Meredith slammed into her side, and Katherine encircled the three of them. Then the whole room descended into a torrent of squeals and giggles and hugs.

Elizabeth pushed to her toes and tried to find Luke through the melee. He stood watching the scuffle, his arms crossed, his hip and shoulder propped against the wall. His eyelid slid down into a wink, and her face heated anew. Then when someone bumped her from behind, she smiled. Not a forced curve of the lips, but the kind of smile that started deep inside and spread until warmth and joy coursed through every inch of her body.

With her students surrounding her and her eyes locked on the man she loved, she could hardly do otherwise.

Epilogue

Teton Valley, Wyoming
August 1894

"This is it?"

"This is it." Luke kept his eyes riveted on Elizabeth, his wife of seven months, as she looked around the deserted cabin where Blake and Cynthia had once lived, a building he hadn't stepped foot in since Blake's death.

"I'm glad we're staying in the ranch house."

He crossed his arms and leaned a shoulder against the wall. "Why's that? You don't like the layer of dust coating everything?"

"It feels eerie, unsettling." She eyed the sagging mattress against the far wall. "And look at that bed. It's only big enough for one person. Cynthia and Blake couldn't have slept in it."

He grinned slowly and ran his eyes over the small mound on his wife's ever-growing stomach. "That wasn't the bed they shared. Some of the ranch hands have used this place a time or two, so we moved a couple old mattresses out here. But we could both fit on it."

She shook her head. "We definitely could *not*. And I

can prove it. That bed looks to be about 6 feet by 3 feet, giving it a surface area of 18 square feet. You're about 6.2 feet tall and perhaps 2.5 feet wide through your shoulders. So let's say you take up 15.5 square feet. I'm approximately 5.3 feet tall with a width of—"

She squeaked as he swooped her up in his arms and deposited her on the bed, then fell beside her, squashing her against the wall. "See, we fit."

"Not comfortably," she growled. "Which is what I was about to point out before you interrupted me."

"Oh, it's very comfortable for me." He looped a hand around her back and drew her nearer. "But then, I like being close to my wife. Tell me." He ran his hand over the swell of her stomach. "How do you figure this extra lump here into your equation? That's not exactly a straight line."

"I was using averages, but calculus would give you the exact area." She elbowed him in the chest. Heaven only knew whether it was intentional with the way they lay squished beside each other. "Calculus is the study of curves, after all. But to determine the area of my belly, we could probably just take the equation for an ellipse and divide it by…"

He pressed his mouth to hers before she started spouting off a jumble of letters and numbers and symbols that would make about as much sense as starting a brush fire during a rainstorm. He meant to keep the kiss quick, a little silencing of her mouth. But her lips were too warm and her body too soft. He inched closer, using the hand not trapped between them to cup her cheek and slide down her neck…

"Luke? Elizabeth?"

He jolted upright at the sound of his sister's call, scrambled off the bed and headed to the open door. Sam and Pa each sat on a horse and watched the cabin.

"I wondered if you'd bring Elizabeth here…for your picnic." Pa's eyes twinkled.

Confound it. The man knew exactly what he'd been about in the cabin. At least Sam seemed ignorant.

"Pa and I were out riding and thought we'd stop by." Sam edged her horse closer. "Do you need us to carry anything back?"

Luke glanced at the spread blanket and empty plates beside the cabin. "Sure. It'd save me the hassle of taking things myself." He stepped down and headed toward the blanket. "You look like you're enjoying that ride on Dumplin' a little too much, Sam."

She patted her horse's neck. "I hadn't realized how much I missed it."

"Told you."

Indeed, she loved this place as much as he did—she'd just forgotten it for a while. She still planned to make it to college in another year or so, and he'd no doubt she would. But for now, she contented herself helping Pa around the ranch and filling the spot Ma had vacated when she'd passed last January.

Pa wasn't exactly happy about Luke's living out East, but the older man was coping. Of course, signing the deed to the ranch over to Pa hadn't hurt his convincing.

Reaching the blanket, Luke tossed the leftover food into the picnic basket and hefted it up to Pa, then threw the blanket across Sam's lap and gave Dumplin' a pat on the rump. "Now the two of you get on out of here and let me go back to courtin' my wife."

Sam turned Dumplin' around. "Courtin'? You're supposed to get all of that in before you marry."

Pa chuckled, low and soft. "The things you've yet to learn about life, girl."

"You sound like Elizabeth." Sam scowled and kicked her horse into a trot.

"Well now, Elizabeth's a pretty smart woman," Pa called, sending Luke a wink as he trotted away. "I'd listen to her."

The twosome were mere specks in a sea of prairie grass before Luke headed back toward the cabin. Though they'd likely as not decide to turn around, come back and ask him another question.

Annoying family. What was so good about having them all together anyway? He'd hardly gotten a second alone with his wife in the two weeks they'd been staying at the ranch. Almost made a man want to move into his brother's deserted cabin.

Luke stepped back inside the ramshackle building and paused. Elizabeth lay where he'd left her, curled on her side. Dusty sunlight filtered in from the window above, hitting her hands, belly and knees while casting the rest of her sleeping form into shadows. He moved closer and stroked a strand of hair back from her face. She slept so peacefully, as though she belonged on the lumpy straw rather than their soft feather bed.

And in a way, maybe she did. Not because the dusty cabin suited her or because she deserved the discomfort and aches she'd surely wake with, but because she filled the spot inside him that had lain empty for so long. He had his old family back, a sister-in-law and nephew who wrote him every week, and a new family starting. He had employees who depended on him and commitments to charities. He had God's forgiveness and a fresh hope brimming inside him. Indeed, for the first time since his brother's death, he was full enough to burst.

And being full felt good.

* * * * *

Dear Readers,

Wow! Does it feel good to get my second complete novel from my computer into your hands.

When I first started Luke and Elizabeth's story, I never envisioned all the twists and turns and nefarious schemes that would end up in the final version. From cruel former fiancés to meddling mothers to scheming brothers, this novel took on a life of its own. I was thrilled with the way Luke and Elizabeth changed and grew alongside the story. They constantly rose to meet new challenges and came through shining like gold tempered by fire. As an author, I'm a little sad to see them go, but I'm also busy working on more stories for you to read, so parting with Luke and Elizabeth then isn't too painful.

Family played an important part in the writing of *The Wyoming Heir*. Oftentimes in novels, the main characters have healthy, ideal families, loving parents and kind siblings. Unfortunately families in real life usually look a lot less perfect, and so with this story, I endeavored to examine "family" and everything that concept entails. Rules, social mores and expectations all play into the fabric that makes a family into…well, a family. I hope Luke's and Elizabeth's fictional struggles with their families gives you some personal hope and encouragement, and perhaps even sheds some light on what it means to be part of a "family."

Historically speaking, the Panic of 1893 started the worst depression the country saw before the Great Depression of the 1930s. Overextension and poor financing of the railroad industry coupled with the government driving up silver prices and a full-fledged gold run were the main causes of the panic, and many eastern families such as Elizabeth's lost their fortunes. Unfortunately the financial struggles that the Wells family and Hayes Academy for Girls face in *The Wyoming Heir* were very real, and probably not all that different from some of the current financial troubles plaguing the United States today.

Thank you so much for taking time to read my second novel, *The Wyoming Heir.* I hope you enjoyed it, and if you're interested in reading more of my stories, my debut novel, *Sanctuary for a Lady,* has been out for over a year, and its sequel, *The Soldier's Secrets,* will release in April 2014.

Like many other writers, I love hearing from readers. To contact me, or stay up-to-date on my newest stories, you can visit my website www.naomirawlings.com. Or you can write to me at PO Box 134, Ontonagon, MI 49953.

Blessings,
Naomi Rawlings

Questions for Discussion

1. At the beginning of *The Wyoming Heir,* Luke makes a serious promise to his mother. Have you ever made a life-altering promise? If so, what was it? And did you keep that promise at all costs or later decide it was more ethical not to honor that promise?

2. As the novel progresses and it becomes more difficult for Luke to keep his promise, how does he respond? Do you think he makes the right choices? Why or why not?

3. When we first meet Elizabeth Wells, we learn that education is very important to her. How do other characters feel about the way Elizabeth regards women's education?

4. How do you personally feel about women's education? Are women today better off because they have more educational opportunities than women of Elizabeth's day? What current advancements do you think need to be made in this area?

5. Elizabeth's father is a politician and not always honest. Do you think it would be difficult to be involved in politics and maintain honesty? Why or why not?

6. Elizabeth's mother loves telling Elizabeth that she needs to honor her parents. Does Elizabeth do a good job of honoring her parents in *The Wyoming Heir?* How so?

7. Do you think honoring someone means you have to blindly obey that person no matter what? Why or why not?

8. Who does Luke tell Elizabeth she needs to honor? What example from the Bible does Luke use? Are there other examples from the Bible that bolster his claims?

9. When Luke arrives in Valley Falls, he discovers his sister has changed in ways he never expected. Does Luke think these changes are good at first? How does his opinion of these changes evolve throughout the novel?

10. Have you ever known a person to change drastically like Samantha did? Did you find it hard to accept those changes? What things did you do so that you could better accept the other person?

11. From the very beginning of the story, Luke likes to control things. Is his desire to control everything around him good or bad? What problems does it cause throughout the story? Are you more apt to try to control things or to "go with the flow"? Has this been a good or a bad thing in your life?

12. Because of what happened with her previous fiancé, Elizabeth has a hard time trusting Luke. Has an event from your past ever hindered you from trusting people before? How does Elizabeth overcome her fear of trusting men? What have you done to overcome some of your past fears?

13. At the end of *The Wyoming Heir,* Elizabeth makes a very hard choice. What were some of the consequences of her choice? Was her choice right or wrong?

COMING NEXT MONTH FROM
Love Inspired® Historical

Available February 4, 2014

HEARTLAND COURTSHIP
Wilderness Brides
Lyn Cote

Former soldier Brennan Merriday will help Rachel Woosley with her homestead—but only until he has enough money to leave town. Can Rachel convince him that he has a home—and family—in the heartland?

THE MARSHAL'S READY-MADE FAMILY
Sherri Shackelford

Discovering he's the sole guardian of his orphaned niece has thrown Marshal Garrett Cain's world out of balance. Luckily feisty JoBeth McCoy has the perfect solution: marriage.

HEARTS REKINDLED
Patty Smith Hall

Army air corps informant Merrilee Davenport will do anything to ensure her daughter's safety—even spy on her former husband. When a crisis forces them to work together, will secrets drive them apart again?

HER ROMAN PROTECTOR
Milinda Jay

To rescue her baby, noblewoman Annia will search the treacherous back alleys of Rome. A fierce Roman legionary holds the key, but she must trust him with her life—and her heart.

LOOK FOR THESE AND OTHER LOVE INSPIRED BOOKS WHEREVER BOOKS ARE SOLD, INCLUDING MOST BOOKSTORES, SUPERMARKETS, DISCOUNT STORES AND DRUGSTORES.

LIHCNM0114